# FIRE

# FIRE

## THE CREED LEGACY
### BOOK ONE

## J.L. BERG

**Fire**
Paperback Edition
Copyright © 2025 by J.L. Berg

Love N. Books Press
An Imprint of Wolfpack Publishing
1707 E. Diana Street
Tampa, FL 33610

www.lovenbookspress.com

Edited by My Brother's Editor

Paperback ISBN 979-8-89567-185-6
Ebook ISBN 979-8-89567-184-9
LCCN 2025946312

*For every woman who's ever said "I'm sorry" for burning too bright. You are, and have always been, fire.*

# NOTE FROM AUTHOR

While extensive care and research went into creating *Fire*, please be aware that some medical details might be slightly inaccurate due to the timing and readability of certain story elements.

Also, because of the sensitive nature of some scenes, I believe it is my responsibility as an author to inform my readers of any content that might be potentially triggering.

- Panic Attacks (brief)
- Detailed medical talk & treatment
- Chronic illness
- Divorce
- Emotional abuse
- Depression

# FIRE

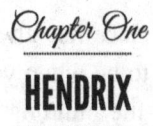

## Chapter One

# HENDRIX

"Do you want me to beg?" I ask the man staring at me from across the desk. "'Cause I will. I'll get down on my knees right here in the middle of this office and fucking beg."

He scrubs a hand down his face and exhales tiredly. "Jesus."

"Come on. I never ask for anything." His bushy, silvery brow rises in amusement, like, *are you fucking kidding me,* and I quickly amend my statement. "I mean, I never ask for anything *anymore.* Grown-up, remember?"

"Hendrix." The way he says my name is sort of like the long sigh you let out when you finally reach the end of a particular grueling work week. It's the same exact pitch and tone I would hear all those years ago when he caught me stealing candy from the pantry before dinner. Or erasing my chores off the whiteboard, only to put them under my little brother's name instead.

"Why?" I demand. "Give me one good reason." I lean forward in the plush leather chair, the familiar smell both comforting and annoying. I've been in this office more times than I can count.

Pretty sure my feet couldn't touch the ground the first time I sat in this chair.

Growing up, this place has always felt like a second home. It kind of has to be when your last name is plastered on the front of the building. But I'm not that kid who used to scribble naughty words on the conference room whiteboard anymore. I'm an adult—one who could sit across from Lance Creed as an equal.

Or, at least, I thought I could.

The man in front of me sighs and runs a hand through his salt-and-pepper hair. His beard is freshly trimmed, and he wears one of his prized vintage concert tees—the ones he collected decades ago while traveling the globe to make a name for himself.

"It'll look bad," he argues.

I glance around the spacious office. Awards, accolades, and photos of famous musicians adorn every inch—musicians who owe their fame to the man in front of me. My father, Lance Creed, owner of the Creed Agency.

The myth. The legend. *The Crusher of Dreams.*

My eyes focus on one face, particularly on his wall of fame, and I grin.

"Didn't seem to matter with Zander." I raise an eyebrow in challenge.

His gaze narrows as it lands on the same photo of him and Zander at the VMAs. My dad's arm is stretched over Zander as he clutches that little moon man in his hand. "That was different. He wasn't family when I signed—"

I smile as he realizes his mistake. I cross my arms over my broad chest. Those familiar blue eyes, almost identical to mine, seem to soften, making him resemble more the man who raised me than the man I work for.

"Come on, Dad. I know that's not what this is about. You've offered to sign me more than once, and you never gave a shit that I was your son." And I know he's probably thinking the same thing as me. If I had taken him up on his offer, maybe I wouldn't have fucked up so royally that I'd need to grovel in my father's office like a child.

At least he's kind enough not to mention it.

He frowns. "I did, but you never wanted my help. So why now? What's changed?"

I shift uncomfortably in my chair, unwilling to reveal the real reason. So I shrug and stick with the obvious. "It's the opportunity of a lifetime, Dad. How often does a band like this need a hired gun?"

"*This* band?" He scoffs. "A lot, apparently."

I chuckle. "Okay, yeah. Manic at Midnight may be a bit of a mess, but they've never needed a bass guitarist. This is my chance. This gig was made for me."

He stares at me for a moment. Then another, until he finally says, "Look, Hendrix, I'm gonna be honest with you."

"That's all I'm asking."

The look he gives me indicates that he doesn't believe me for a second, yet he carries on regardless.

"Manic is a total shitshow." He levels me with a weary glance. "Has been for a while. I thought they were back on track after that whole thing with Mitch…"

My foot starts bobbing in annoyance. "I don't need a recap, Dad. They lost their lead guitarist. Then they signed Zander. My best friend became famous. I was there, remember?"

It isn't exactly something you forget. Your best friend,

roommate, and honorary brother is out there living his best life as a session guitarist, hopping from one gig to the next until one day, he gets *the* gig.

Manic to Midnight, one of the biggest bands on the planet, needed a lead guitarist to fill in for their tour after a major scandal forced them to kick one of their original bandmates to the curb. Suddenly, he goes from a hired gun to a full-fledged member in a matter of months. Now, his name and face are plastered fucking everywhere.

That was two years ago, and since then, he's traveled the globe, performed in front of millions, and oh, married the love of his life and had a beautiful baby girl. I'm fucking ecstatic for the guy, but in that same span of time, all I've accomplished is some mediocre session work in the studio. Oh, and my all-important job as my father's assistant. Can't forget that.

To say I'm a little jealous is an understatement.

I'm dying to get my chance in the spotlight, but I'm stubborn. I've refused to let my dad sign me as a client, which is stupid for many reasons. The biggest one is that he's a fucking legend in the music world, and being on his roster could do insane things for my career. Instead, I've stubbornly turned down his help and advice, and instead, I work for him, helping other musicians make it big.

Doesn't make sense to me either.

"Right, well…" He leans back in his chair, looking more tired than usual. Dark circles frame his eyes. The man owns three businesses, is a devoted husband, and has raised five *mostly* successful adults. If this is getting to him, I know it has to be significant. "After Zander joined, they seemed solid."

*Yeah, until recently.*

"But then the pressure got to Evans, and after they finished recording the new album, he abruptly asked for some time off." I let out a frustrated breath and try not to sound annoyed, but the guy is stalling. "Dad, I know all this. That's why I'm in your office, begging for his damn job."

"It's not that simple." His gaze meets mine.

I blow out a breath, ready to argue or plead. Either option works for me, as long as I leave here with his word that he'll try to get me this gig. He's got a direct line to the band's agent and manager. He can make it happen. "It *is* that simple. I'm a bass guitarist," I remind him before amending my answer. "I'm a damn good bass player."

"You are, and I know you're more than qualified for the job."

"So what's the problem? And don't feed me the whole nepotism bullshit, because we all know if you vouched for me, the band wouldn't think twice."

I have four siblings, and almost all of us work for him in some capacity, from my oldest brother, who practically runs things around here, to my sister, who pours drinks at the bar. My dad has never given a shit about what people think regarding his kids.

"That's because I'm not an idiot. Only a fool would brag about their kid, only to get them placed in a job they're not qualified for. The five of you may have the benefit of certain privileges others may not, but it doesn't mean I'm not gonna let you shake through life because of it. That shit just looks bad. But regardless, it's not me who has the final say."

"Who is it then?" *And why am I wasting time here?*

"Asher."

I grin. Asher Knight is the lead singer of Manic to Midnight. He's Scottish, single, and has been named the sexiest man alive more times than I can count.

"Asher loves me," I inform my dream-crushing father. "Ever since I showed up to one of Zander's concerts wearing an official Knight Rider shirt and asked him to sign my chest."

He rolls his eyes.

"What?" I scoff as light streams in from the floor-to-ceiling windows behind him, making the silver in his hair stand out even more. "He was more than happy to sign it, and it made a great gift for Mercury. She tried not to, but she squealed like a little girl when I gave it to her."

"That's because she *is* a little girl."

I shake my head at that, enjoying my father's agitation just a bit too much. "She might be the baby of the family, but she's far from little anymore."

My dad grumbles and mutters under his breath as he fiddles with a pen on his desk. Mercury, the youngest of the Creed kids, just graduated from college and moved into her first apartment right after she started working at the family-owned recording studio. Dad is not handling the change well.

My mom refers to it as empty nest syndrome and has encouraged all of us to distract him with an engagement or even another grandchild.

I *think* she was joking, but I can't be sure.

At any rate, she already has one grandkid from my oldest brother, Cash. No marriage or engagements as he is a single father. He shares custody with Taylor's mom, but that woman hasn't been welcome in our house for years.

"So basically, what you're saying is..." I lean back in

the old leather chair, feeling a glimmer of hope. "All I have to do is talk to Asher, and I've got the job?"

He chuckles. "Your confidence is astounding."

"Learned from the best," I say smugly, though his hesitation is making it waver.

"Unfortunately, there is someone else you also need to convince. And he's going to make you work for it."

"Who?"

My father just leans back in his chair and grins.

## Chapter Two

# HENDRIX

"Zander? Can you get the door?" a female voice shouts as I stand on the other side and wait. I've been here for baby showers, movie nights, and more. But no matter how many times I approach this crazy house with its hand-carved wooden door and giant potted plants, I can't help but think, *My best friend is one lucky motherfucker.*

It's not like I grew up wanting for...anything, really. With the management agency, the recording studio, and the family bar, our family did more than all right. But even my parents' Malibu beach house feels small compared to Zander's new digs.

This is the kind of house rock star money buys you.

"Why the fuck is he ringing the doorbell?" Zander shouts back at his wife, Elena. "He checked in at the gate. We already know he's here!" His deep voice grows louder with each word, and I can't help but grin at his annoyance.

What's the point of life if you can't irritate your famous best friend now and then?

"Hell, if I know. But I have a child attached to my tit, so if you wouldn't mind?"

And that's why I ring the doorbell.

I do not want to ever walk into that house and stumble upon Zander's wife with her tits out, no matter what they're attached to. Pretty sure he would rip out my damn eyeballs for that.

He is quite fond of his wife. And her tits.

Footsteps sound toward me, and then that heavy ass door is pulled open, and standing before me is Zander Green.

The rest of the world knows him by his stage name, Zander Tate. But to me, he'll always be that teenage kid who wandered into my family's bar looking for a job. Dressed in gray sweatpants and a T-shirt, his nearly black hair is long and tousled on top with shaved sides. He's gotten rid of the eyebrow ring since his daughter was born, but he's added a few more tattoos. His arms are covered, much like mine, including the Creed family name on both our forearms.

Zander might not be a Creed by blood, but he is a Creed, nonetheless.

"Don't move," I tell him, reaching into my pocket to grab my phone. "I can get at least a couple grand for a candid shot of you in sweatpants. Double if you take your shirt off."

A grin spreads across his face as he gives me a gentle shove. "Oh, fuck off."

After a quick bro hug, I follow him inside, keeping my eyes fixed straight ahead. Zander glances back and sees me, his eyes crinkling with amusement. "She's finishing up in the other room. Still terrified of breast-feeding, huh?"

"No," I lie, then relent with a sigh. "Fuck, maybe. But don't get offended. I'm scared of everything that's associated with tiny humans."

"Oh, I know," he replies, sliding his hands into his pockets. "The last time I tried to hand you Marisa, you jumped so high that I'm surprised you didn't set a world record."

"Ha ha," I deadpan.

"You want a beer?" he asks as we walk down the hallway, his bare feet slapping against the hardwood as we head toward the spacious kitchen, covered in creamy marble and warm wood tones. When he moved out of our modest one-story home in West Hollywood and bought this place for himself and Elena, I thought he was crazy.

At the time, they had only been dating for six months, most of which had been spent on tour in Europe, but he was resolute. My best friend, who had never been in a serious relationship before, was suddenly head over heels in love.

It took me longer to pick out the new sofa in my living room, and I'm still not sure I was completely in love with it. How did he know she was the one in such a short amount of time?

"Nah, I can't stick around long." He walks over to the fridge and grabs himself some fancy microbrew.

"Are you sure? Because Elena and I were thinking about ordering food. There's this Venezuelan place we found, and she won't stop talking about it. If she hadn't gone back on the pill right after our little snafu, I'd swear she was pregnant again."

"Little snafu?" I chuckle, taking a seat on one of the

stools at the island. "Is that what we're calling your daughter these days?"

"I mean, not to her face." Instead of a beer, he hands me a bottle of water, which I happily accept. "She was definitely a surprise—a *good surprise*," he emphasizes. "But if Elena ever needs to switch up her birth control again..."

"You're wrapping it up?"

"Like my life depends on it."

As if she heard her name, Elena appears in the kitchen entryway. Her silky brown hair is piled high in a messy bun, and she's rocking the hot mom look in tight black leggings and an oversized green sweater that hangs off her shoulder.

She wanders over to Zander, and they share a kiss that is far from appropriate. His hand grabs at her ass, and I'm pretty there's tongue involved.

Christ, no one needs to see that.

She giggles, pulling herself away from his reach, and gives me a lazy smile. "Still ringing the doorbell, huh?" Marisa straddles her hip, wearing one of those footsie pajama things. It's covered in tiny cartoon guitars, and she's clapping her hands together like it's the most entertaining shit on the planet. She seems completely oblivious to her parents' mini make-out session.

At least one of us is.

Marisa appears to be an equal blend of both of them. From Zander's mesmerizing green eyes to Elena's light-brown skin and dark hair, I have to admit that the kid is cute.

Scary as hell, but still cute.

"Between breastfeeding and you two making out

every few seconds, I never know what I'm gonna walk in on."

"That's fair." She passes Marisa to Zander, who has set his beer aside for some quality baby time.

Is a one-year-old still considered a baby? They still carry her everywhere, but she can technically walk, even though she resembles a drunken sailor half the time. So doesn't that make her a toddler instead?

Fuck if I know.

"So if you're not here to hang out," Zander says while bouncing his kid on his hip, making her laugh. "What brings you here? Not that I'm *overjoyed* to see you."

I roll my eyes at his phony enthusiasm because he knows exactly why I'm here. He just wants to hear me say it.

Fucking asshole.

He stares at me expectantly.

"Gonna make me beg too, huh? Is that what we've come to?" My voice is strained as I lay the guilt on extra thick. "Is this what our friendship has become, Zander? Me having to come to my best friend—"

"For fuck's sake." Now it's his turn to roll his eyes. "Please stop. You're a terrible actor. Seriously shitty. Did you even try to sound sincere?"

Elena laughs as she leans forward on the marble counter.

I let out a huff. "Okay, no more bullshit," I agree. "But you have to be honest with me. What's the holdup, Z? Why did my dad just tell me that the entire fate of the tour hinges on you? Are you trying to ruin my life?"

"See, I told you he'd be like this," Elena says as she turns to her husband.

"Like what?" My eyes ping-pong between them.

But I guess I should have known. He's always wanted the spotlight for himself."

I couldn't believe it when the record label execs called us in to announce that, moving forward, they would only be representing Edwin. Everything said after that is still somewhat of a blur, but there was a lot of bullshit about needing a new sound and pursuing a different direction.

All I knew was our dream—the one he and I had been working on since we met our freshman year at Stanford—was dead.

The rest of the guys and I were dumped by our agent less than a day later.

"I'm not going there to mend any fences, if that's what you're worried about," I tell Zander. "It's just seeing that invitation in my mail brought up a lot of old feelings. Resentment, regret, and a lot of anger. And I hate feeling this way."

"So you gonna go egg his house or something? 'Cause I could help."

I laugh. "No, but I was thinking about giving him a very special engagement gift."

"Oh yeah?"

"Well, rumor is, his tour might be canceled after his last album tanked, so I thought he might enjoy knowing all about ours. Assuming it's not delayed?"

He grins. "Nah, it's not delayed."

I throw a fist pump in the air. "Now that that's settled. Feel like signing a T-shirt for me?"

"That's savage." He grins. "I'll go get a pen."

## Chapter Three

# ZARA

Standing in a long silky robe that isn't mine, I stare into the spacious walk-in closet that also isn't mine and sigh.

I so do not have time for this.

Down the hall, there are about four thousand boxes in my new room that need to be sorted and unpacked. *You can't unpack them, remember? You have no dresser.*

I am thirty-one years old, and this morning, I had to borrow sheets from my baby sister because I no longer own any of my own. And yet, here I am, trying to find something to wear because *he* asked me to—the man responsible for my lack of sheets.

So, this is what my life has become, huh? Begging and borrowing? At least I haven't reached the stealing part of that phrase yet.

"Are you sure it's okay if I borrow something?" I holler over my shoulder and then wince, realizing Violet isn't in the kitchen like she was a moment ago.

No, she's right behind me.

Jesus, she's like a sexy little ninja.

"It's fine, Zara." My sister laughs, unfazed by the

number I probably just did on her eardrum. She gently pushes me aside and gives her closet a cursory once-over before choosing a tight red number that still has the tags on it.

My eyes widen at the price. I don't think I'll ever get over how expensive designer clothes can be. Pretty sure my first car cost less than that. "Are you crazy?"

"Relax," she says, placing the silky fabric in my arms. Then, she steps back and assesses my dark-brown curls and makeup. It must meet the standard because she gives an approving nod. "I got it from work."

"That's a damn nice work perk. All I get is the occasional seasonal cold and sore feet."

"Yeah, well, I tried to persuade you to join the dark side before you dashed off to med school, but you were all *I want to help people.* Blah, blah, blah..." She shrugs, then walks over and flops down on her bed. The whole room is very girly and decorated in muted tones of blush and cream. It looks like something out of a Parisian salon.

Speaking of Paris.

She's just returned from Paris Fashion Week, and she would be enjoying a bit of downtime if I hadn't crashed it by moving in.

Yeah, she has that kind of job. The jet-setting, designer wardrobe-wearing, model kind of job. And yes, before you ask, of course, she's beautiful. Like me, she takes after our mother's mostly Greek heritage, with her olive skin and long, mahogany brown hair. But unlike me, she inherited our father's athletic skills and height. She likes to say I got all his brains and love of science because I'm the doctor of the family, but she's just being modest. My sister is damn smart too.

"Try it on." She motions to the dress in my arms.

I do as I'm told and start slipping off the silk robe. "There is only one model in our family, Vi. Seriously, look at these hips!" I point to my curves to emphasize my point.

I never used to be insecure about my looks. In college, I was so focused on schoolwork and getting into med school, I barely gave it a second thought. It wasn't until I got married that I really started to scrutinize my body.

Now, I feel insecure about...well, everything, honestly.

Having a model-perfect sister has never been part of the issue, though. She's never made me feel less than adequate. In fact, she often tries to convince me of the exact opposite. Like now, for instance.

She just rolls her eyes. "I have hips too, and trust me, the camera loves them."

I slide my arms into the straps and walk over to her so she can zip me up.

"See?" She turns me to the side so I can see all those curves for myself. "You've got the beauty and"—she finishes the zipper and then playfully smacks my ass— "the brains. Total package, right?"

Although the dress is tighter and definitely sexier than I usually wear to any event with Tanner, it's still suitable for the occasion. The knee-length, ruched fabric helps boost my confidence a bit. The wide straps and deep neckline also make my cleavage look amazing.

"If that were true, I wouldn't be here, divorced and —" I start to say, but Violet interrupts.

"Nope." Her head shakes back and forth. "You're not allowed to say mean things to yourself in this dress. Says right here on the label."

I roll my eyes.

"Speaking of your asshole ex, why are we doing this? The dressing up and going out with him, I mean." She arches one perfectly sculpted eyebrow at me. "Usually, when you sign divorce papers and move into your sister's swanky ass apartment—you're welcome, by the way—you aren't required to attend functions with your husband anymore. That's what the *ex* in ex-husband is for."

"I know." I let out a frustrated sigh. "But he insisted. It's one of his buddies from college, and since his parents haven't made the official announcement yet—"

"So...he doesn't want to be the one who has to tell everyone, so he's making his mommy and daddy do it?"

I nod. "Well, his dad is a senator. I guess there has to be a statement."

"And they couldn't have done that in the last six months?" She rolls her eyes. "That family is a piece of work." I open my mouth to protest, but she holds up a finger. "Don't make excuses for the man, Zar. That's not your job anymore. You may have served him the divorce papers, but he deserved it after the shit he said."

***

*"Are you happy?" Tanner asks, and I come to a screeching halt in the middle of our kitchen. It's such a random, off-the-wall question for him that I find myself momentarily stunned.*

*Why is he asking?*

*It's been a long day for both of us. Maybe that's it?*

*There's a stomach bug making its way through the local schools, and with fall sports coming up, everyone's rushing to get physicals done by the end of the summer.*

I place the salad bowl down on the counter and turn toward where he's perched on a barstool, watching me.

"At this specific moment? Or in general?" I ask, trying to lighten the mood, but the way he's looking at me tells me he isn't amused.

"In general, Zara."

"Of course I'm happy." *Or I thought I was until about two minutes ago when you started this conversation. Now, I'm nervous, anxious, and kind of nauseous.* "Why?"

"I'm just..." He lets out a deep breath. "Bored."

"Bored?"

He nods, and I feel my stomach clench.

"I just thought it would be more interesting, you know?"

*It?* "You thought what would be more interesting?"

"The clinic." He waves his hand in a sweeping gesture. "Life. But it's just the same thing day after day. Running noses and sprained ankles." He lets out a heavy sigh. "I just keep thinking to myself, 'Is this really it? Is this how boring life is for regular people?'"

"Regular people?" I stare at him, stunned.

"You know what I mean," he snaps before his face goes slack again. "I don't know. Maybe I just need a vacation or something. Perhaps a week in St. Barts will help. I haven't visited the family house there in years."

*I don't miss how he seems to be planning a spontaneous tropical vacation for one.*

"Next week?" I gape at him. "What about the practice, Tanner? You have patients. You can't just cancel a week's worth of appointments to fly off to St. Barts."

*A flash of annoyance crosses his face. "Right. You're right."*

*And then he rises from the stool and stalks off, muttering under his breath about balls and chains and how he's never going to break free.*

*The next week, he flies to St. Barts and leaves me to run the clinic by myself.*

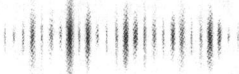

I take another glance at myself in the mirror. "Do I look okay? It's not too...revealing?"

My sister gets up off the bed and snorts. "You look hot, sis. And if you're worried he's gonna think it's too revealing, then it's perfect. Goes great with your nails too." My eyes instantly go to the French manicure I meticulously gave myself the night before. "Plus, I have a perfect pair of sky-high heels that'll really piss him off."

I turn to the side, and damn, my ass looks amazing. "Great. Can I borrow some earrings too?"

"Now you're talking!"

## Chapter Four

# ZARA

It takes me all of ten minutes after arriving at the engagement party to remember why Tanner and I never hung out in college, not that he even knew I existed.

Back then, he was—and still is—the son of a state senator who only ever hooked up with rich sorority girls and lived in a swanky house paid for by his parents with a few friends. There, they lived like royalty, like some real-life version of *Animal House*.

I, on the other hand, was the quintessential nerd who spent most of my four years at Stanford trying to maintain the grades necessary for my full-ride scholarship. Even though my family is considered middle-class, I knew my parents would never be able to take on four years of student loans on their modest teacher salaries.

Plus, I had the expense of med school to look forward to.

It wasn't until then that I met my future ex-husband.

"I love your dress," Edwin's fiancée—Lani? Lanor?— says, pulling me out of the mind fog I've fallen into thanks to Tanner and his boring ass friends. *Seriously, who cares about stock portfolios this much? And custom-made cufflinks? Who even are these people?*

"Oh, um...thank you," I reply, managing a polite smile as Tanner maintains his tight one. Definitely not a fan of the dress. When we were married, his mom always had to approve my wardrobe selection before a function. *We have an image to maintain, Zara.* "It's my sister's. She got it at a runway show or something."

"Oh?" Her eyes light up with genuine interest. "Is she a makeup artist or a stylist? I might have worked with her." With her slim figure, shampoo commercial-perfect hair, and boobs that seem to defy gravity, she definitely looks like she belongs on a runway.

"Leann is a model," Edwin gushes. *Leann! That's her name. So close.* I try not to roll my eyes at how blatant he is in his bragging about his fiancée. It would be one thing if it were just genuine pride, but this feels more like a kid showing off a new toy. *Hey guys, look what I scored!* Violet would never put up with that kind of shit.

"Zara's sister is a model, and she's fairly successful too. Violet Valentine," Tanner answers for me. It's a habit I used to overlook, but now? Well, now it kind of pisses me off. Also, my sister is *very* successful, and Tanner knows it. He just doesn't like admitting it.

Leann's eyes widen. "Vi Valentine is your sister?"

I nod, giving Tanner a sideways glance. *See?* "One and only."

"She's amazing. I've always wanted to—"

"Lee-lee, let's go refill our drinks and mingle a bit, okay?" Edwin says, interrupting her mid-sentence. Rude. She seems less offended than she should be, and it hits rather close to home.

Because, not too long ago, that used to be me.

Constantly being dragged around like a pretty little show pony. Being introduced as the wife of Dr. Tanner Price and nothing more.

She simply nods and smiles as Edwin wraps an arm around her waist and practically drags her away.

"Lee-lee?" Tanner snorts, taking a sip of his red wine, and I realize we're alone for the first time since he picked me up from Violet's.

I hate the casual way he tries to strike up a conversation with me.

Like the last six months meant nothing.

Like the words he said didn't hurt.

Like his life hasn't changed at all.

I don't take the bait.

An awkward silence fills the air as we stand in the corner of Edwin's spacious living room, people watching. Edwin, or Ed Eaton as he's known on stage, is a pretty good singer. Kind of a mix between Shawn Mendes and Niall Horan, but not nearly as hot. Maybe that's why he's prancing around with his fiancée as if she's some sort of show pony. If he paid any actual attention to her, he'd notice the way she winces when she walks. Shoes too tight? Ankle injury?

*Not my business...*

I start to fidget. Tanner looks over at me, the annoyance clear on his face as he looks down. "Don't pick at your nails. It's unbecoming."

*I know. You've only told me a hundred times. But please. One more time should break the habit.*

"I'm going to go find the restroom," I tell Tanner the moment I see one of his other douchey friends coming toward us.

I don't give him a chance to reply. If I have to be

present for one more bro hug with another guy he knows from college, I'll scream. Or stand there while one of them looks at me inappropriately and then says something like, "It's so weird that we all went to school and never knew each other."

The moment I step into the hallway, I let out an audible sigh of relief when I find myself alone. I should never have agreed to this. I hated going to events like this when we were married, and I like them even less now. And okay, my sister is right. A divorce means not having to do shit like this anymore, no matter what family you married into.

Deciding to carry through with this whole bathroom farce, I continue down the hall. At the very least, I can check my makeup. That will take a few minutes. Grabbing a drink will take a few more, and then only another couple of hours of mind-numbing conversation to go.

*Fuck my life.*

The massive hallway is a tribute to Edwin and his accomplishments. Awards, magazine covers, and photos with famous friends decorate the walls. I can't blame him for feeling proud. He's achieved a lot at his age, but that huge painting of himself? That seems a bit excessive, and it distracts me because while I'm looking at it, I don't notice the door opening to my left.

Or the man who is stepping out.

I crash right into him.

"Oh my god, are you okay?" I step back just in time to look up and...

His familiar blue eyes travel down and then back up again, pausing on my legs and the curve of my breasts. When he finally meets my gaze, I notice the recognition and the surprise.

"Cupid?"

There's only one person in the world who's ever called me that. The nickname brings back a flood of memories: the smell of library books and the sound of his deep, rich laugh.

The anger when he left without so much as a goodbye or a thank you.

*It's him.*

"Jimi," I reply, knowing he hates it when I call him that almost as much as I secretly love it when he calls me Cupid.

*"Your last name is Valentine? Like Cupid?" he asks.*

*"No, like the saint, you dumbass." I fight back a smile.*

*"Saint doesn't have quite the same ring to it." He leans back in his chair, crossing one foot casually over the other, and gives me an appraising look. I nervously push my glasses up under the weight of his stare. "Though you do look very...pure. I could help you with that, you know? As a thank you for tutoring me."*

*"You want to trade sexual favors for tutoring lessons?" I ask, my voice barely above a whisper, because I don't want to be overheard. And we're in the library.*

*He casually shrugs, confidence nearly oozing from him. "Seems like a good trade to me."*

*I lean forward, and even though I'm wearing only a T-shirt and cardigan, his eyes dart to the way the V-neck dips, revealing the slightest hint of cleavage. "Here's the thing, Jimi." I force a smile that exudes way more confidence than*

*I feel. "I may look sweet, but I'm far from innocent." I lean
back in my seat, and he nearly groans in his. "And the only
form of payment I accept is cash."*

*"Jimi?" he asks, his voice slightly hoarse.*

*I grin—a real one this time. "Tit for tat, Hendrix."*

"It's been a while."

He blatantly checks me out again. "Clearly."

"I guess I don't need to ask why you're here," I say,
taking a moment to return the favor and check him out.
Hendrix seems to be one of those guys who has only
gotten hotter with age. His sandy-brown hair straddles
that fine line between styled and wild. His beard,
however, is perfectly trimmed, allowing the sharpness of
his jawline to shine through. The black suit he's wearing
fits him like a damn glove, but the tiny wisps of ink that
peek out from his wrist and curve down his hand and
knuckles only add to the appeal. Even the silver rings
that adorn his fingers are hot, especially since he's
missing one on the all-important ring finger. "I'm
surprised you aren't marrying the guy."

"Funny," he deadpans. "But *Ed*..." He says his stage
name with a strange mix of contempt and...sadness?
"And I haven't been friends in years."

"Oh?" I raise a brow in surprise. When I met Hendrix
during my junior year—he was a year ahead of me—he
and Edwin were basically besties for life. They were
forming a band and determined to make it big. Obviously,
that didn't work out, since Edwin is a solo act. Neither

did their friendship, apparently. "So what are you doing here then? Checking out the catering?"

He grabs the back of his neck in a gesture that almost makes me think he feels embarrassed. Then, I realize where we are and glance over his shoulder at the door he just stepped out of.

Not the bathroom, but a bedroom. "Is that...were you just in their bedroom?"

"Depends," he answers.

"On?"

A woman's laughter echoes down the hall, and suddenly, his hand is grasping my wrist, and I'm being pulled through the open door into Ed Eaton's bedroom with my secret college crush.

This is not how I thought this evening would go.

## Chapter Five

# HENDRIX

Zara Valentine.

If there's one person I didn't expect to run into tonight, it's definitely her.

This is not her scene. Or at least, it wasn't. The Zara I knew wore cardigans two sizes too big and spent way too much time in the school library. That Zara was relentless and pushy and drove me fucking nuts for an entire semester.

*I cannot believe I just offered this girl sex for tutoring.*

*Who does that?*

*I also can't believe she didn't kick me out of the library for it. I definitely would have deserved it. I stare at her as she flips through my textbook, marking several chapters and then writing a few notes on a legal pad. A strand of hair slips out of her braid, and I have to stop myself from reaching out and tucking it behind her ear.*

*I do not need another reason for her to hate me.*

*And I really need this tutoring.*

*"Okay, here's what we're going to do, Jimi." She smirks, sliding over what appears to be a game plan for the first few weeks of the semester.*

*"Sticking with Jimi, huh?"*

*"Maybe I am. Worried you can't live up to your namesake?"*

*I bark out a laugh. "Oh, I know I can't. That man is a legend."*

*Her smirk turns into a full-blown smile, and the sight of it makes my heart rate double. "Bring back an A on your first quiz, and I'll reconsider."*

*"Deal. But you're stuck with Cupid either way."*

I not only scored an A on that first quiz, but managed to pull an A for the whole damn semester. Considering I bombed the class the first time around, it was a goddamn miracle.

*She* was a goddamn miracle.

And now, she is standing in Edwin's master bedroom with me.

I slam the door behind us.

"What the hell?" She looks up at me, her eyes wide.

"Sorry," I say. "Panicked. Didn't want to be caught near the scene of the crime." Of course, now I'd inadvertently put myself back *at* the scene of the crime.

With a witness.

This is so dumb. I should have just walked out like I planned. The moment I stepped up to the grand entrance of Edwin's mini-mansion, I knew this was a mistake. But I charged ahead anyway, and less than two steps into the entryway, I heard his stupid fucking laugh and panicked.

What was I thinking?

Was I really going to storm into his engagement party, filled with all of his fancy ass friends and family, and do what? Brag that I finally scored a temporary gig on a tour with my best friend's band?

He would laugh in my damn face.

So I turned around and bolted, but not before I made a quick detour back to my car and snuck back in here for a bit of revenge work.

After all, he's the one with a house so wide open that any asshole could waltz right in.

Tonight, I'm that asshole.

"Why—" Her words are cut off, and her eyes widen as she takes a wide look at the room.

"Yeah, that."

"Oh my god. What have you done?" Her voice is a mixture of awe and horror. Honestly, I get it. I feel the same way as I take it all in.

I may have gone a bit overboard. But I'm petty as fuck.

"Okay, so I might have discovered Edwin's fiancée is a bit of a Manic at Midnight fan," I tell her as I awkwardly shove my hands into my pockets.

"And so you decided to do...this?" She gestures toward the gaudy display of Manic memorabilia. "Where did you even get all this stuff?"

There's the T-shirt Zander signed. That's honestly

what started this whole shitshow. While he was digging through boxes in his cluttered office to find one, I started pulling out random swag he'd received—beer koozies, posters, hats—and had an awful idea.

A lot of women love the band. Well, they mostly love Asher. But still...

Just a few minutes on Instagram, and I had my answer. Miss Leann soon-to-be Eaton is a total *Manic Fanatic*.

Yup, that is indeed what the fans call themselves.

"My best friend is the lead guitarist," I tell her, pointing to the poster I haphazardly stuck on the wall. "And I did it to piss Edwin off." I shrug, still unsure why she's even at this party. Not that I'm complaining.

Her eyes drift over to the T-shirt of Z, sweaty and shirtless on the front—signed, of course. Just when I'm about to say something, though I'm not sure what, I hear a laugh. It starts out quiet, almost a snort, and then Zara Valentine is practically doubled over in that skin-tight dress, cracking the fuck up.

My shoulders sag in relief as she looks up at me in amusement. "Wow, you were not kidding. You really aren't friends anymore, are you?"

"Nope."

"So why are you here, then? Aside from the obvious?" She makes a sweeping gesture with her hand.

"A little payback, I guess. Are you going to tell on me?" It comes off as playful, just as I intended.

She smiles, and damn. Seeing her like this after all this time is somewhat jarring. After graduation, I always thought she'd be at some prestigious hospital, married to a super-smart neurosurgeon. I never expected to run into her at Edwin's outlandish place in Brentwood.

"Depends," she answers.

"On?"

She leans against the bedroom door, and I take the opportunity to let my gaze wander. Again. Zara has always been a stunner. Even in college, when she tried to hide behind bulky sweaters and quick comebacks, she was irresistible to me. It was irritating, to be honest, mostly because she seemed completely immune to my good looks and witty banter.

"Will you let me hide in here with you for a bit?"

Well, this just got a little more interesting. "Sure, but who are we hiding from?"

Her head drops back against the door with a soft thud as she lets out a deep exhale. "My husband."

My eyes dart to her left ring finger. The one I scoped out moments ago. Right before I checked out her tits. And her ass. Yep, still no ring. "Husband?" And then I realized where we were and who we were with. "Wait, who are you married to?"

She hesitates. Her lips press together before she finally replies, "Not important, actually."

"Not important?"

She shakes her head, her dark-brown hair brushing her bare shoulders. "Nope, because as of last week, he's actually my ex-husband. Still getting used to saying that."

I cock my head to the side and stare. "Is that how you ended up at this party with him then? 'Cause you forgot you divorced this mystery ex-husband?" Or is she still in love with him? An unexpected surge of jealousy hits me square in the chest.

Where the fuck did that come from?

"No, but he's not ready to admit it to his douchey friends. So he brought me to save face."

The relief I feel is...*unexpected*. I rub my chest, feeling a dull ache between my ribs. I used to have a thing for my hot tutor back in college, but that was ages ago. "I'm sorry. No wonder you were fleeing down the hall."

"I wasn't—" She starts to say, but then relents. "Okay, yeah. I definitely was."

My mouth curves into a smile. "They're literally the worst, aren't they? Edwin by himself was decent back then, but as a group?" I fake a shudder, causing her to laugh.

"They compared cufflinks. I stood there for twenty minutes while they inspected each other's heirloom cufflinks. Did you know Drew's family jeweler has crafted pieces for the royal family?"

"Wow, what a bunch of pretentious twats. No wonder you need me to rescue you."

"Hey, I didn't say anything about rescuing," she argues. "I just need a place to—"

"Disappear?"

"Yes."

"What if, instead of staying here and running the risk of getting caught, we just left?"

"Together?" The way she says the word makes me think of her and me and all the things we could do... *together*.

And now I'm half hard. Because once there was a time when all I thought of was the things that woman and I could do together.

Is tonight my second chance?

"Sure, unless you want to stay..."

"Nope."

I grin. "All right then, Cupid. Let's get out of here."

Tanner will be furious when he finds out I ditched him.

Especially if he found out who I left with.

Edwin isn't among Tanner's close friends. He's always looked down on people in the entertainment industry, even if they came from wealth like Edwin had.

*Hollywood is filled with nothing but cheap attention seekers.* His words, not mine.

I'm sure he would have a field day knowing I left with *the* Hendrix Creed. He was popular back in college, which I'm sure annoyed Tanner, and he was a musician from a well-known family in the industry.

I still remember the way he looked all those years ago, with that large guitar case strapped around his chest.

*"You gonna be famous one day, Hendrix Creed?"*

*"You better believe it, Cupid."*

I smile to myself as Hendrix pulls away from the curb. I see him stretching the fingers of his right hand. He rotates his wrist a few times, and I wonder if it's from pain.

I take my phone out of my purse before it gets

awkward, and I start suggesting the stretching exercises I gave my mom last month.

I tend to struggle with separating my work life from my personal life, and I have to remind myself that not everyone is a walking patient.

> **ME**
> You'll never guess what I just did.

> **VI**
> Told your ex to take a hike and then ditched his sorry ass?

> **ME**
> YES!

> **VI**
> Wait. Actually?

> **ME**
> Well, not the part about telling him to take a hike. But I totally ditched him. I snuck out of the party and left him there, Vi.

> **VI**
> YES! About fucking time. Wait, how? Did you call an Uber? Omg, please tell me you left with someone.

I bite my lip as I glance over at Hendrix. He tossed his jacket aside the moment we got in the car and rolled up his sleeves. Either I'm horny as hell or his forearms are so cut, they're downright pornographic. The way his muscles flex as he grips the steering wheel, and the tattoos inked across his skin...

I swallow hard.

ME

...

VI

ZARA HAZEL VALENTINE.

ME

I may have run into a guy I knew from college.

VI

And...

ME

And we're on our way to a bar.

VI

Okay, read these words very carefully.
Are you paying attention?

ME

😊

VI

Don't make me full-name you again...

ME

Yes, I'm listening.

VI

You're single now. Act like it.

Also, I won't be home tonight. Plan accordingly. 😊

I stare at the screen and blink.

Does she expect me to take him home to...?

My stomach flutters with nerves, or maybe it's anticipation? He made plenty of jokes about us hooking up in
college, but that's all they were. He never meant anything
by it.

Surely, this grown-up version of Hendrix isn't thinking that we could...

I think back to the way he blatantly checked me out in the hallway, how his eyes lingered on the curve of my hips, my bare legs, and my breasts.

Okay, so maybe it's crossed his mind. And he did leave the party with me.

"So what bar are we actually headed to?" I ask, realizing we never really discussed specifics. I was just so relieved to leave that party—and Tanner—that I basically leaped into his car. He could be taking me anywhere.

"Only the best bar on the West Coast."

"And that would be?"

"My family's bar. Obviously."

I raise my eyebrows. "You're taking me to your family's bar? Trying to show off, Jimi?"

He scoffs. "I thought we agreed you wouldn't call me that after I earned my first A?"

"You still call me Cupid."

A wicked smirk spreads across his face. "Told you I was sticking with it. And besides, you like it when I call you that."

I try to come up with a witty reply, but I come up blank. Because he's right. I do. I liked it back then, and I like it even more now.

He must notice because his grin widens. "And no, definitely not showing off. Just taking advantage of the family discount. Have you bought a drink in this town lately? It's ridiculous."

I laugh. *He's* ridiculous, and it's ridiculous that I find it charming. "I didn't know your family owned a bar. Doesn't your dad do something in the music industry?"

He nods. "My dad is a manager for several musicians,

which is the primary family business. There's also the recording studio, our newest venture, and then the bar in Malibu, which is sort of my parents' pride and joy. Besides me, of course."

"Of course." Cars zoom past the window as we drive down the 101 toward the coast. "So will your family be at the family bar?"

"My sister Presley might be bartending, but that's probably it. We don't hang out there twenty-four-seven like some weird family sitcom."

Well, that's a relief. Not that I'm sure they're lovely, but I'm not really up for meeting the whole family tonight. "Presley? Hendrix? I'm sensing a theme."

"Ah, yes. My dad really loves his music legends. And my mom? Well, she loves my dad enough to let him name all of us after them."

"All of you? How many are there?"

"Five."

"Five?" I almost gasp. "That's—"

"A lot? Yes, it is. And that doesn't even account for all the bonus siblings."

"What the hell is a bonus sibling?"

"You know, like a best friend or longtime employee that just sort of becomes part of the family. My parents have always been the more, the merrier type. Holidays are nuts in our house."

"That's really nice of them," I say, unsure of what else to add since I haven't really experienced the big family thing. My dad is an only child, and his parents passed away when I was young. My mom's family is actually quite large, but scattered, from the West Coast all the way to the Greek Isles and everywhere in between. As for friends, that was always more my sister's area of expertise.

"So tell me all their names."

"The bonus siblings? Well, there's Zan—"

"No." I chuckle. "Your regular siblings. The ones with the crazy names."

"Oh." He chuckles. "Well, there's the oldest, Cash, then there's me and Presley. After that is my brother Myles and my youngest sister, Mercury."

"Wait, Myles as in—" The other ones are easy to identify. But I try to think of a famous musician named Myles. "Miles Davis?"

He just shakes his head. "No, but I'm sure that's what people think when they hear his name. Myles was adopted, so he got off easy when it came to crazy names. My oldest brother, though, was almost named Halen, which he could not pull off—at all."

"They didn't consider naming you Bono or Prince. Oh, how about Zeppelin?"

"I could absolutely rock a name like Zeppelin," he says with a straight face.

"I don't think you could. Honestly, I'm not even sure you're cool enough to pull off Hendrix."

"What the fuck? You can't just shit talk a guy's name, Zara *Hazel* Valentine."

My eyes widen. "How—"

"Your phone screen is really bright." His grin is so damn smug. "So are you going to invite me over?"

*Oh my god.* My cheeks burn. "You know, reading someone else's text messages is considered a violation of privacy?"

"I gotta say, I really missed that sassy mouth. You're

always so quick with the comebacks, especially when you're embarrassed."

"I'm not embarrassed."

"No?"

"No."

"So you weren't thinking about inviting me over to your empty apartment tonight?" His voice is so smooth, I feel it all the way down to my toes. *And so many other places too.*

"Yes," I respond before quickly correcting myself. "No. Wait—" I'm so confused.

He laughs, enjoying my flustered state. "How about this?" he offers. "I'll give you a choice. I can either continue toward Malibu, and we can go to Creeds for a few drinks, and then I'll drop you off at your place and say good night. Or—"

"Or?" I swallow, waiting for him to finish.

"Or I can turn around and—"

"Yes." I don't even wait for him to finish. My sister told me not to overthink things tonight, so that's what I'm going to do. For once in my life, I'm going to be spontaneous and wild.

"Yes, what?" He sneaks a glance in my direction, and I shiver. "Be specific, Zara."

"Yes, I want you to turn around and take me back to my apartment. And then I want you to do all those dirty things you promised you'd do back in college."

The car practically swerves as he takes the next exit to get us back to LA.

No turning back now.

## Chapter Seven

# HENDRIX

*Thud, thud, thud.*

My skull is pounding.

*Thud, thud, thud.*

No, wait. That's not my head. That's the door. Or a door? Fuck, where am I? I crack an eyelid open and search my surroundings. Familiar dark gray walls. Vintage oak dresser. The boho rug I got on sale at Ikea.

Home. I am home. And alone.

But wasn't I...

The pounding stops, and it's replaced with the sound of the doorbell. Who the hell is that?

Before I have a chance to recount the events of the previous night, I throw on a pair of sweats and a T-shirt and jog down the hallway. I scrub a hand down my face as I try and fail to knock the residual brain fog from my mind. I'm not hungover, but fuck, I'm tired.

Walking through the living room, I flip the lock on the front door and am nearly clobbered the second I pull it open.

"What the hell?"

"Sorry, gotta pee," my sister hollers over her shoulder, a streak of honey-blonde hair, as she barrels down the hall.

"Is that why you were pounding on my door at—" I check my watch. "How is it already ten in the morning?"

"I don't know, dude," Presley shouts from the bathroom. "But you texted me last night to say you were stopping by the bar and never showed. So I came over to make sure you weren't dead."

"Thanks, I guess? But can we continue this conversation when you're not urinating?"

"You're such a fucking baby," she mutters with amusement before I hear the toilet flush and the faucet start. I make my way to the kitchen to start some much-needed coffee. As I begin to scoop coffee grounds into the machine, Presley reemerges from the bathroom and begins to rummage through my fridge like the mooching little sister she is.

"Don't you have food at your place?" I ask as soon as I see her pulling out eggs and a block of cheese.

"I mean, sure. But why waste it when I could just eat yours?"

She cracks two eggs into a bowl and then reaches for a third. I give her a dirty look as I watch her separate just the whites and add them to the bowl. "That was like five bucks of egg yolks you just tossed down the garbage disposal."

She rolls her eyes. "It was not, and it's not like you're hard up for cash, Hen."

"Oh, right. I forgot. Dad gave me a raise. I'm now getting six figures to fetch his coffee and answer the damn phone." She doesn't miss the sarcastic tone in my voice.

"It's not like I'm making bank managing the bar, and I swear half my income goes to rent. At least you don't have a house payment, thanks to Z."

Yeah, okay. She's got me there. Another perk of having a rock star best friend? Zander and I used to co-own this place, and when he moved out to marry Elena, he insisted on paying off not just his share but mine too. So here I am, in a modest three-bedroom house in the LA suburbs worth more than it has any right to be, and it's bought and paid for. In cash.

"I think you can spare a few eggs for your loving sister, whose only reason for showing up today was to make sure you were safe."

"Only reason?"

"Okay, the food may have been an added bonus. The Starbucks near my apartment was insane. I swear, half of LA County must have been there. And you know how I get without coffee in the morning."

"Well, if you're gonna eat all my food, at least make me some."

"Egg sandwiches okay?"

As long as I didn't have to make it. "Sure."

She continues to flit around my kitchen, and now that the coffee is brewing, I choose to get out of the way and take a seat on one of the stools at the island. She's dressed much like me—weekend casual—in a pair of dark-gray sweats and a hoodie. Her blonde hair is piled on her head in a messy bun, highlighting the tiny cluster of stars she has inked behind her ear.

"So what happened to you last night?" she asks over her shoulder as she flips the burner on and drops a few dollops of olive oil into a pan. "And I don't want details if it isn't PG."

I laugh because *same*. Presley is only two years younger than I am, and we've always been tight. Growing up, we shared everything: toys, friends, secrets. But right around high school, when our guy friends started to realize that Presley was an actual girl and Presley, in turn, did the same with our guy friends, was around the time we agreed maybe we don't share *everything* anymore.

Because there are some things you just don't want to know about siblings.

The details of their sexual exploits are at the top of that list. Honestly, that pretty much makes up the entirety of the list.

"I went to an engagement party last night and reconnected with a girl from college," I explain, leaving Edwin's name out of the explanation because I don't need that conversation this morning. "I, uh, was going to bring her by the bar, but—"

She raises a hand. "You hooked up instead. No need for further details."

I wasn't going to offer any, but that doesn't stop my mind from conjuring them. I swallow hard as every detail comes rushing back.

The awkward trip up to her apartment, where I started to second-guess myself. She literally just got divorced. The ink was barely dry.

A better man would turn around.

But this was Zara Valentine.

The one girl from college that I always wanted but could never have.

The one girl who always turned me down was now saying yes.

I would be an idiot to walk away, right?

So I followed her inside.

And the rest of the night was...

"So what the fuck are you doing home already, Romeo?"

My head snaps up to my sister, feeling almost startled by the interruption. "I, uh..." I choke on my words, but Pres thankfully doesn't seem to notice as she scoops the eggs out of the pan and plops them onto the toasted bagels. "I never sleep over. Gives the wrong impression, you know?"

But that isn't true. I've spent the night at a woman's house before. Not a lot, but occasionally, when it's late, or I'm too tired to get home. Last night, it wasn't late, and I definitely wasn't tired. Which is precisely why I didn't, because I knew that if I did, I would have spent the entire night wrapped up in Zara.

I would have fucked her until the sun came up and maybe even longer.

It was *that* good.

I think I have scratch marks down my back from her nails, and I know she's suffering from some serious beard burn between those silky thighs of hers.

She rolls her eyes. "You know, there's nothing wrong with sleeping with the same woman more than once," she says, a hint of amusement in her tone. "I know you act as if monogamy is some kind of contracted disease, but it's not."

"I've slept with the same woman more than once." I point out, but then drop it because having a casual hookup for a week isn't that different from a one-night stand. "Look, Pres. I know you're all about relationships now that you're happily in one. But it doesn't mean it's for everyone."

She walks over and puts a plate down in front of me,

with a bit more force than necessary, I might add. "This isn't about me and Jace. And how would you even know? Have you ever even tried? I mean, do you really want just to have meaningless sex for the rest of your life?"

"Clearly, you haven't had enough meaningless sex to know the value of the word." My eyes widen in horror. "God, why did those words just come out of my mouth? Gross. Anyway, moving on 'cause I don't ever want to know the answer to that."

She laughs as I stuff a bite of the sandwich in my mouth. It's good. Way better than anything I could whip up. She even poured me a cup of coffee and dumped in the proper amount of cream and sugar.

Damn, maybe she should stop over more often.

"It's not that I don't want a relationship," I begin. Her eyebrow arches, and I let out a sigh. "Okay, what I mean is I'm just not looking for one right now." My mind, for some reason, goes immediately to last night to the feel of Zara's slick, naked body writhing under mine.

*Fuuuck.*

I nearly choke on the coffee I'm drinking as my mind goes blank. What was I saying? Right, relationships. "It's just that where I am in my life, where I'm headed with the tour and everything, I just can't have any distractions. I need this tour to work out, Pres," I insist.

I need to prove to Edwin and every other fucker who doubted me.

I need to prove I'm worth something.

I need to...*succeed.*

"It will," she assures me. "Dad told me you were in his office yesterday, gunning for that gig. They'd be stupid not to sign you as Evans's replacement."

"Temporary replacement," I clarify, for her sake and

mine. I can't let myself get comfortable. "He's not leaving forever."

"Which means you have the tour to showcase your talent all over the country. It will get you noticed, and then bands will be falling all over themselves to sign you."

I appreciated her enthusiasm, and I really hope that's how it all pans out, but there are still so many hurdles left between here and there. And to get there, I need to be at the top of my game.

That means total focus.

Nonstop practicing and absolutely *no* distractions.

"I went over to Zander's yesterday, and I think I've got the gig. But, he wants a doctor on tour," I tell her after I guzzle down nearly half my mug of coffee.

"That's great, Hen. But why a doctor? For Marisa?"

I nod. "He's worried about her getting sick or hurt or witnessing her first orgy."

"What?" She nearly spits out her coffee.

I just shake my head. "Never mind." I wave my hand. "The point is, we need a doctor, and we need one fast. I might have made it sound like I could get him one, or at least Dad could."

Her eyes widen. "But the tour starts in just a couple of weeks. How are you possibly going to find someone willing to leave their job on such short notice? No one even remotely qualified would do that..." She holds her hand up to stop the argument I am about to throw her way. "Even for the opportunity to gallivant all over the country with rock stars. Nowhere reputable would hold a position for someone that long. Doctors are in short supply as it is."

I know all of this. It is exactly the same shit that has

been racing through my mind ever since I left Zander's yesterday.

But what the hell else am I supposed to do?

Zander is my best friend, and he wants to protect his family. I can't fault him for that.

"Well, it's either that or risk the potential fallout of having to delay the tour because, as rich as Zander is, I don't think any of them want to incur those costs. So which one is worse?"

She leans over the counter on the other side of the kitchen island, holding her coffee mug tightly in her hands. I can tell the gears in her head are turning. Finally, she says, "You could check with Cash tonight at family dinner."

"Why?"

"I think his best friend from college is a doctor. He might know someone."

"I hate asking Cash for favors."

She shrugs. "I don't see you coming up with any bright ideas. It's not like you happen to know of any doctors, do you?"

"Right, yeah." I scoff. Everyone I know is either a musician or...

A flash of dark hair and a pair of chocolate-brown eyes flashed through my mind, and suddenly, I'm struck with an idea. A really bad, but possibly good idea. "Actually, I just might know the perfect person."

*Chapter Eight*

# ZARA

If there were a guidebook to divorce, I'm pretty sure there would be a whole chapter dedicated to why you absolutely *should not* work with your ex.

We are barely a week into this, and I already want to kill him.

When I filed for divorce, I didn't ask for anything. We had a pretty straightforward prenup, but my lawyer said I could try to push back and get more. But I didn't want to. I didn't want any of it. Not the house nor the business. Not even that plush ivory chaise I loved so much. I was so devastated and so damn angry that the life I'd built with this man was just considered such a waste of time to him that I didn't want a single reminder when I walked away.

I just wanted to forget.

But, of course, Tanner's male pride wouldn't allow for that. I thought he'd be happy about the prospect of a divorce and the fact that I was being so agreeable and civil about the whole thing. But, once again, I found myself surprised and a bit taken aback when he chose to be offended instead.

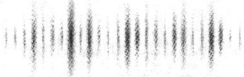

"*What else was I supposed to do, Tanner?*" *I shout as I pace back and forth across the living room. He had angrily tossed the manila envelope he was served in my face the moment I returned home from the gym.*

"*What do you mean, what were you supposed to do? Maybe not blindside me with a fucking divorce, Zara. That's a start.*"

*I scoff.* "*Blindside you? Are you serious? You made it clear you weren't happy. Has that changed?*"

"*Well, no, but—*"

"*But what, Tanner?*"

*He hesitates. Looks away.* "*This looks bad.*"

"*We aren't living in the nineteenth century, Tanner. People get divorced all the time.*" *But then he finally looks at me, and I understand the full meaning behind his words.* "*Oh, you mean this looks bad for* you? *Because your parents didn't get a chance to get ahead of this first. Because if it comes out that I filed the divorce papers—a 'regular person,' as you so eloquently put it—you'll be embarrassed.*"

*He doesn't deny it.*

"*You know what, Tanner? Tell people whatever you want,*" *I snap, picking up the papers once again. I hand them over.* "*Whatever makes you happy. After all, that's all that matters, right?*"

When his parents did find out, they entered what they called "damage control" mode.

For nearly six months, I reluctantly agreed to live under the same roof with my soon-to-be ex while they worked out the particulars of our divorce. I moved into a guest bedroom, and we only spoke when absolutely necessary, which was pretty much at work, leaving me in a constant state of limbo.

During those six months, I started to look back on my marriage, and I didn't like what I saw.

What I had always imagined as some grand fairytale was starting to look more like a grim nightmare, and I was ashamed I'd let myself fall for the illusion.

As the months dragged on, Tanner's admission that night in the kitchen started to feel more like a blessing and less like the tragedy I thought it was. I mean, I didn't even fight to save my marriage. That had to say something about my feelings toward the man I pledged myself to, right?

I'm not even sure what Tanner's high-priced lawyers spent so much time working out, seeing as his family had money, a prenup, and mine had none. Perhaps they were waiting for his father's approval rating to go up. Maybe they were digging into my past, looking for something scathing to pin on me.

After a while, I even began to wonder if they were secretly trying to find Tanner a new bride to lessen the blow of the divorce, but that announcement never came, and eventually, the paperwork was signed.

As expected, he got everything. When I was offered a small amount of spousal support, I declined. I never want to be tied to him or his family again.

I want to leave it all in the past.

I have a feeling, though, that it won't be that simple with the Price family.

It's Monday morning, and I'm in the small kitchenette that's stuffed in the back of our modern medical practice, trying to guzzle down a lukewarm cup of tea when Tanner strolls in. He gives me an appraising stare. We've agreed I can stay on as a physician as long as I want, with the understanding that I am no longer considered a partner.

Just a staff member.

That's right. My ex is now my boss too.

Oh, and as expected, he's pissed that I ditched him Saturday night. When I texted him late Saturday night after Hendrix left, I lied and told him I got a migraine and didn't want to interrupt him while he was bonding with his college bros.

The fact that he didn't respond was confirmation enough. You did not walk out on Tanner Price.

I almost considered telling him the truth, just to piss him off further. But this divorce thing is new, and I've got enough on my plate without having to deal with a jealous ex.

Besides, it's not like I'll ever see Hendrix again.

I didn't even get his number. Oh my god, I didn't get his number. Damn, why am I so upset about that? *Probably because it was only the best sex of my life.*

"Did you visit room four yet?" Tanner asks, eyeing me coolly.

No, I'm just chilling in here with my cup of tea while the mom and her sick baby wait for me. "Yup," I answer instead.

"And?"

I do not appreciate his tone. It reminds me of this attending physician I worked with during my residency who always acted like the female residents were simply there to annoy him.

"And...she was positive for strep."

"Did you check for the flu too?"

It takes every ounce of strength I possess not to roll my eyes. Or toss my drink in his stupid face. He does remember how I practically carried him through med school, right? "Of course."

He's about to say something else—something idiotic, no doubt—when one of our receptionists, Loren, knocks on the open door to announce herself. We both turn to see her sheepish smile spread. "Sorry to interrupt. Zara, you have a visitor."

My brow raises. "Who is it?"

Her pale skin turns fire-engine red. "I, uh, forgot to catch his name."

That's not like her. She's usually so organized, she puts Monica Gellar to shame. I watch her fiddle with her curly blonde hair, avoiding eye contact with a visibly annoyed Tanner.

"He's super tall. Tattooed. *Hot.*" The emphasis on the last word, if possible, makes her cheeks flush even redder.

*Shit.*

What was I saying about never seeing him again?

Tanner's head jerks to mine. "What the hell, Zara? Are you seeing someone already?"

"No," I deflect, knowing I need to get out of this kitchen. Fast. "Also, we've been separated for six months, Tanner. And, not that it's any of your business, but he's just a friend. Someone I know from college."

Just a friend. *Do friends fuck?*

I turn my attention back to Loren. "I'll meet him up front."

I'm about to make my exit until Tanner's third degree resumes. You would think he's jealous, but really, I think he's more concerned about appearances than anything. Can't have me moving on first. How would that look? And before the formal announcement? *Gasp!*

"From college? Who? And since when do you have visitors at the office?"

"Since today." I shrug, giving him an arduous expression. "I didn't know he was popping in, but it's not a big deal. It's—"

"Hendrix Creed?"

"What? How did you—" My gaze follows him, and *oh my god*, he's right there. Barely inches from where I'm standing at the entrance of the breakroom. Tall, tattooed, and dressed in faded jeans and a black tee. His last name is inked in bold, black script along his sculpted forearm.

I blush. I've licked that tattoo.

His eyes meet mine and then go to Tanner and widen ever so slightly before I see his expression harden.

Oh, right. I did omit that detail, didn't I?

"Hey, Tan. Good to see you." His words seem friendly, but his tone clearly isn't.

Tanner's jaw tics. If there's one thing he hates more

than anything, it's being called Tan. "I didn't realize you and my wife were friends."

Hendrix leans against the doorframe and folds one muscled forearm in front of the other. "Your *ex*-wife and I go way back." He pauses as if letting that information sink in, but offers no further explanation. On purpose, I'm sure. Then, his gaze shifts, and those striking blue eyes find mine. My stomach does this stupid fluttery thing. "Can we talk?" His gaze flicks back to Tanner for the briefest moment. "In private."

I see Tanner's knuckles turn white at his sides, and I fight a smile. "Follow me."

The second I close my office door behind us, we both try to speak at the same time. But before I can get out even the first syllable, I hear him say, "Tanner Price? You married *Tanner fucking Price*?"

I assumed Tanner and Hendrix knew each other in college because of their mutual friendship with Edwin, but I never mentioned to Tanner that I had tutored Hendrix. I think I knew what he'd say—what he'd think —and I wanted to keep those memories free from his opinion.

They were mine.

I wince as I make my way around the desk to sit down. "A decision I distinctly regret, if you remember our conversation the other night."

"At least it makes a little more sense why you were there."

I scoff. "He is the *only* reason I was there. And after Saturday, I can definitively say that will be my last appearance as Mrs. Price."

"You're not, though," he says, taking the chair opposite me. His eyes seem to linger on my breasts before I realize he's looking at the name embroidered on my white coat. "Mrs. Price? Because I found your practice by searching under Valentine. Didn't bother checking who your douchey doctor husband was, though. Was a bit in a hurry…"

My lips quirk. "Yeah, quite the sore subject in the Price family. That I didn't take his name," I reiterate. "But I knew how intertwined our careers would be, and I needed mine to be separate from theirs. In hindsight, it was a good choice. Saved me a shitload of paperwork."

The corners of his eyes crinkle in amusement. "So are you going to tell me how the hell you, a ball-busting academic, ended up married to a guy once known on campus for wooing his female TAs for better grades?"

"Wait. What?"

"You didn't know this?"

I shake my head. "I didn't really know him as an undergrad."

"Well, I did, unfortunately. He had this thing he would do with his female TAs. Sometimes it was flowers or a date. But what he really loved to do was give them a necklace. One with a—"

"T," I finish his sentence, feeling queasy all of a sudden as I remember those first few tutoring sessions.

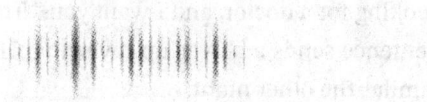

*Tanner flashes a grin as he leans over the arm of the chair in the study lab. "I got you something."*

*"What? Why?" I blurt out. Why do I feel so nervous*

*around this man? I've tutored dozens of people, and none of them has ever made me feel this...anxious.*

*Like, I have no idea what he will do from one second to the next.*

*I can't tell if it's a good thing or a bad thing.*

*"Because I wanted to." He simply shrugs and produces a tiny blue box from his pocket.*

*My eyes widen as I look up at him. "No," I find myself saying. "It's too much."*

*He laughs as if he finds this notion ridiculous. "It's not." And when he opens the lid and I see the tiny gold T staring back at me, I feel my insides melt. "And it would mean the world to me if you wore it."*

Was anything between us real?

Hendrix must sense the turmoil in my gaze because he suddenly shifts the conversation and blurts out, "I want to offer you a job."

Did he say...

"A job?" I give him a puzzling stare. "You do remember what I do for a living, right?"

"Yeah, I know. That's exactly why I'm here. I'm looking for a doctor, and I want you." The last part of that sentence sends a shiver up my spine. He said something similar the other night.

*God, I want you, Zara.*

"For what, exactly?" I clear my throat. Is it hot in here?

"To go on tour with me."

My eyes widen. "Like a concert tour."

He nods.

"The loud kind, right? Not the string quartet kind?"

"Yeah, definitely the loud kind." He smirks.

"For how long?"

"Five months."

"Five months!" I screech before adding, "Wait, with who?" *Please say Taylor Swift. Please say Taylor Swift.*

"Manic at Midnight."

Dammit. I figured he was going to say that. Their music is catchy, and that Scottish lead singer is hot as hell, but who wouldn't wish it were Taylor? She's iconic. Wait...

"You're in Manic at Midnight?"

"No."

I stare at him, confused. Finally, he answers. "I'm a hired gun for the tour." I double-blink, confused again. "I'm filling in for the bass guitarist, Evans. He's taking a leave of absence. Personal stuff, I guess."

So Hendrix would be there. Five whole months of...

This is insane. "I can't just up and leave." He looks at me with a raised brow, as if he's waiting for me to finish that sentence, and I'm trying. I really am, but I'm coming up empty because, in the last six months, my life has turned into a bit of a shitshow. "I can't leave...my sister."

"Your sister? The traveling model?"

Dammit. I forgot I mentioned her on Saturday. He licks his bottom lip, clearly trying to stifle his amusement.

"Yes. I just moved into that apartment with her," I ramble, as my face goes flush, remembering all the places those lips had been. I swallow. "It would be rude of me to just leave after she graciously allowed me to stay there. Plus, she gets...lonely."

Violet is the type of person who has a lover in every city. She is *never* lonely.

"Well, lucky for you, we don't leave for two weeks. So you'll have time to...settle in." He grins.

"You think two weeks is enough time to settle in?"

"Isn't it?"

I throw my hands up in frustration, annoyed by how chill and confident he's being. He acts as if I've already said yes, or at the very least, I'm about to. "You haven't even told me anything about the job. Why do you think I would even be interested?"

"Why wouldn't you? It's the opportunity of a lifetime."

"Um, because I already have a job and a practice," I state, throwing my hands up in a frustrated gesture. "Or didn't you see the sign when you came in?" *Had. I had my own practice. Man, when is that going to sink in?*

"Your practice is named after a tree," he replies dryly. "And you mentioned something about wanting to leave your practice the other night."

"I did?" Why can't I remember anything other than...I avert my gaze. "Right," I say quickly. "Well, I haven't exactly made up my mind."

"You said that too."

I blink back at him as a conversation from Saturday night before starts to come back to me. We were driving back to my place, and I was nervous. Really nervous. So I just started to talk, *and talk*.

I told him about my sister the model, and how amazing she was to let me stay with her. I told him how weird it was to live with her after all these years, especially since we were polar opposites.

I mostly skipped over my divorce because I didn't want to be the person who talked about their ex, but I did mention the practice and how much I loved my patients. I left out the part about how I was now my ex's employee and said I was thinking about moving on to something else.

Eventually.

After the morning I had with Tanner, though, I'm not sure I can hold out for "eventually."

"So what do you want to know?" he asks, raising an eyebrow at me.

I scoff. "Uh, everything?"

He grins. "I've got you invested now, don't I?"

I open my mouth to protest, but before I have a chance, he produces an envelope from...Actually, I don't know. Had he been holding that the whole time?

I look down at it. "What is this?" I ask.

"A job offer," he says in an amused tone.

"Wow, you're really serious about this, aren't you?" I stare down at the crisp white envelope in slight shock.

"You thought I was joking?"

I give him a half-shrug. "No, I just didn't expect you to be so...organized. Don't they have people who do this sort of thing?"

"Yup. That's me. I'm one of those people."

I stare at him, confused. I feel like that's all I've been doing since he got here. He points to the address at the top of the envelope.

*The Creed Agency.*

"I work for my dad," he explains, his expression tight, like admitting that cost him something. "As his assistant.

This offer comes with his blessing. Everything you need to know is in there."

"And your dad works for the band?"

"He represents a few of them, yeah," he answers. "But the band as a whole has their own manager, Ridge, who you'll meet on tour. My dad is just helping facilitate a few things."

"Like a doctor?"

"Yeah." He smiles. "Like a doctor."

"Why does the tour need a doctor, exactly?" I ask, watching as he leans back in his chair. He seems to swallow the whole room with his presence. I can't tell if it's his tall, muscular frame. Or just him. But either way, my office has never felt smaller. Or hotter. "It isn't typical, is it? To have a dedicated physician travel with the band?" I know it's not. Otherwise, I would have heard of it before now, especially living in a place like LA.

"No," he admits with a shrug. "Not usually. But Zander, the lead guitarist, made the request, and—"

"What a rock star wants, a rock star gets?"

That amused expression is back. "Something like that."

"Right, well what about..." I'm grasping at straws because, honestly, the idea is both tempting and terrifying. I don't want to stay here and work for Tanner or his family, but I don't exactly have any viable alternatives at the moment. Why couldn't that somewhere else be a tour with a group of rock stars and—"What about us?"

He cocks his head to the side. "Us?"

"We've slept together."

A slow grin spreads across his lips, and that grin ignites all kinds of feelings in my libido that I attempt to ignore. "I remember."

"Well." I swallow, trying to calm my racing heart. "Don't you think that's a bit of a conflict of, um... interest?"

He shrugs, acting far too nonchalant. I can't tell if it's an act or if he really is this casual about...casual sex. "It's not against the rules, if that's what you're worried about."

"I just don't want things to be awkward. I'm not..." I puff out a breath of air. "I'm not looking for anything serious."

His blue eyes stare into mine for a moment before he gives a firm nod. "Good, then we're both on the same page, because neither am I. This tour could do big things for my career, and I've got to stay focused."

"Right." I shift in my seat, my hands tightly clasped together. "Understandable."

"And I'm in peak physical health, so I doubt we'll even see that much of each other."

"All right."

"But just to be safe..." He holds up a finger. "Maybe we keep it to ourselves. The guys may look like stone-cold rock stars, but they gossip like a bunch of middle schoolers."

"You're assuming I'm even taking this ridiculous job?"

His eyes fix on me for a moment before he stands. I watch him rise to his full height, taking a moment to appreciate the way his jeans mold around his thick thighs and tight ass. "I know you, Zara," he says, which causes my heart to race for some reason. "And whether you realize it or not, you've already made up your mind." He steps toward the door, his hand closing over the handle. "See you soon, Cupid."

After growing up around the music business and working for my dad, I thought I understood what went into preparing for a tour of this magnitude. But when the time comes actually to prepare myself to go on one, I realize I have no fucking clue what I'm doing.

Like, how do you pack for several months? We'll have some downtime and breaks, but I'm not sure I'll come home for all of them.

And then there's my house...

What am I supposed to do about my plants? Will my car battery die if I just leave my car in my garage for a month or more? What if I accidentally leave cheese or something in my fridge? If I open it, will I have a full-on hazmat situation on my hands?

Okay, the last one is a bit of a stretch. But my car battery dying is a real thing, which is why I loan it to my sister, hoping it's still in one piece when I return. I also hire a landscaping service, put my mail on hold, and give Pres a key so she can keep tabs on everything. When it comes to packing, I just toss in everything I can think of and hope for the best. It's not like I won't be able to grab stuff along the way.

This band travels in absolute luxury.

Manic at Midnight used to do the whole tour bus thing before Zander joined, and then their fandom grew to the crazed lunatic status it is now. While many bands still enjoy the nostalgic feel of a bus and the convenience of not having to pack your shit up every other night, Manic's security team hates it.

Guarding a five-star hotel that's used to hosting high-profile clients is much easier than keeping track of multiple buses while overworked musicians fight over bunks, women, and fridge space.

Plus, let's face it, who wouldn't rather spend a night in a luxury hotel than be crammed in a tour bus with five other dudes?

Not me.

"Hey, big brother." Mercury's sing-song voice echoes behind me in our parents' kitchen. I'm rifling through the fridge, looking for a soda, and I peek my head out to look at her. She's got her long brown hair pulled back in a sleek ponytail. It's our last family dinner before Zander and I leave on tour.

"Hey, little sister." I parrot back at her in the same tone.

"You ready for tomorrow?"

I shrug, grabbing a Coke before shutting the door to face her. "Ready enough."

"You gonna give me your autograph before you leave?" She pops a hip against the marble countertop and gives a mischievous grin. Sometimes I forget just how grown-up she is. Dressed in designer jeans and a creamy white top, she looks more preppy than rock and roll, and it's hard to believe she just put in a ten-hour day at the recording studio with an up-and-coming goth band.

It feels like yesterday she was blowing up my phone, crying over her first middle school boyfriend.

"Will you sell it on eBay?" I ask, joining her at the kitchen island. I pop open the can and take a sip.

She folds her arms across her chest and scoffs. "I would, but I doubt it would go for much."

I press a hand to my chest. "Harsh, Merc. That's just harsh."

She simply shrugs, then swipes my Coke and takes a long drink. When she's done, she sets it down in front of her as if it had belonged to her all along. "If you want hype, go find Pres. She loves talking about music."

"And you don't?"

"I do," she agrees. "But it's different. She loves the emotional aspect of music. I love perfecting it."

"God, you're a nerd."

"A music nerd," she says, correcting me with a smile. "Which is how I know you're going to do great on this tour. You're a brilliant musician, Hen."

She beams up at me, and I am once again struck by how grown-up she's become. "Brilliant, but not famous?"

Her smile transforms into a wide grin. "You're a bass player. Let's not get ahead of ourselves." I snort a laugh, and she hooks her arm in mine. "Come on, rock star. Let's go find everyone else."

The *everyone else* she refers to is sitting in my parents' giant family room, which overlooks the Pacific. It's dark, and the sun has sunk below the horizon hours ago, but you can still hear the rhythmic crashing of waves outside.

That sound used to calm me and lull me to sleep at night.

Now, it's just pure nostalgia. Hearing it reminds me of home.

My mom is the first to notice us. Her silvery-brown curls are pulled into a loose knot, and she's dressed down in lounge pants and a long cardigan. "You found him," she says, not bothering to rise from her spot next to where she's wedged herself between my dad and the sectional.

"I just look in the most obvious location. The—"

At first, I think she's pausing for dramatic effect, but then I feel her body tense and turn to see what's got her so worked up.

Standing by the window next to Zander, looking slightly out of his element, is Asher Knight, the lead singer for Manic at Midnight.

My eyes dart back to my little sister, who stands perfectly still, staring at him. Completely starstruck.

Mercury is not typically the fangirl type. She once accompanied my father as his date to the Grammys and walked right up to the Artist of the Year to share her thoughts. She was half his height and barely in double digits, but that didn't stop her from informing him that his latest album was pitchy and pedantic.

I say usually, because there is one exception.

And that is Asher Knight.

It's usually something we love to tease her about relentlessly. But right now, I feel kind of bad, because this has got to be mortifying.

Even I'm a little embarrassed for her.

"Hey, man." I step forward, offering my hand, when it's clear that my little sister has entered a state of full paralysis at that point. "Good to see you."

"You too," he replies, taking my hand. "Lance has

been trying to get me over for dinner for a while. Glad I could finally make it, and we're thrilled you're joining us on tour."

"Me too. Although I wish it were under better circumstances," I say. He nods in agreement, his eyes briefly shifting to Merc before focusing back on me.

"It is what it is," he says, running a hand through his unruly dark hair. "We've all been working nonstop for what feels like forever. I'm glad Evans is taking some time for himself. He needs it."

Zander catches my gaze, and his eyes dart to Mercury as if to say, "What the fuck is wrong with her?" and "Do something before it gets weird."

I make a mental note to kick him later because why the hell doesn't he just do something?

"Uh, yeah. That's awesome. Hey, have you met my sister Mercury?" I blurt out, feeling like an asshat. *Good job, Hen. Put the focus on your statuesque little sister. That will make things better.*

Zander stares at me, the corner of his mouth twitching as if trying hard not to laugh at my slip-up. *Asshole.*

Mercury, suddenly cured of her temporary paralysis, turns her head to the side to stare at me with a look of horror and betrayal. *Sorry, sis.*

"No," Asher grins, clearly unaffected by my sister's discomfort and my sudden lack of social skills. "Can't say that I have had the pleasure. Nice to meet you."

Did I mention that Asher is Scottish? He comes from one of those snobby families that have fancy titles and castles. Pretty sure he's a lord or some shit, but he left all of it behind to become a musician. I've never really heard the whole story, but I don't think he keeps in touch with the mom and pops anymore.

You can still hear it in his voice, though. The hint of aristocracy. The impeccable manners. *The charm.*

Mercury swallows audibly and turns to face him.

"Mercury just graduated last May and is working at the recording studio." My dad beams. Mercury's cheeks flame red from embarrassment. "She's become quite the asset over there."

Ash's brow furrows. "Wait, did you work with Mason's Revenge?"

"Yeah, a couple of months ago." Mercury answers, which is a bit surprising. I was starting to wonder if she had forgotten how to speak. "Wait, you know the guys from Mason's Revenge?"

He grins. "Yeah, I met Mason a couple of years ago at a festival when he was in a different band." He shakes his head, amused. "They were terrible, but Mason is fucking brilliant. Didn't know it was you they were working with over at Creed's."

She manages a shrug, acting more like herself now. "I use my mom's maiden name when I'm at work. I want people to listen to me because I know what I'm doing and not because my name is on the door."

"Why can't it be both?"

"It can be," she agrees, and I find my eyes darting between the two of them, before turning and walking over to Zander. "It should be, but right now, I need to be sure."

"What the fuck is up with that?" Zander says under his breath, pointing to Asher and Mercury.

I shrug. "What do you mean?"

He stares at me for a beat and then just shakes his head, just as the doorbell rings and pizza arrives.

After the dozen or so pizzas were hauled in, the whole family pitched in by grabbing plates and napkins and then helped themselves to drinks.

Family dinners at the Creed house are never formal occasions.

Cash and Taylor arrived at some point during the mayhem, and the presence of a three-year-old only intensified the craziness.

"Are you glad Elena and Marisa stayed home?" I ask Zander as we dig into the pizza. I do my best to cram three slices onto my plate, while he sticks to two.

"Hell yes," he answers. "Usually, I'm all for the insanity this family brings, but with how on edge Elena has been over the past few days, it's the last thing she needs."

"She's on edge? About what? The tour?"

He nods, and we take a seat in the dining room. Mercury has apparently gotten over her fangirl freak-out, as she and Asher excitedly ramble on about bands they both know and various other things they have in common. Zander looks across the table and smirks.

Just then, my niece zooms into the room and plops down on Zander's lap. He doesn't miss a beat as he wraps an arm around her, continuing our conversation while Taylor steals one of his pieces of pizza.

"Yeah, she's really nervous. Having Dr. Valentine

there is a definite bonus, but there are just so many unknowns, you know? Toddlers are used to having a routine. Meals, naps, bath time, and bed, they all run on a schedule, and she's just not sure how to manage all that when we're constantly moving from one place to another."

"You'll adapt," a deep voice interjects, and I turn my head to see Cash leaning against the doorframe. He's still wearing his dark tailored suit and tie he wore to work. He may work for the family business, but he looks about as rock and roll as an accountant at a wine bar. "You both will. I swear, kids are like bloodhounds." Zander snorts. "They can sense fear and stress, so if you learn to roll with it, she will too. And if shit does hit the fan and something goes wrong, at least you have that hot doctor Hen found you."

"What the fu—" My big brother cuts me a look that can only be described as the dad stare. "F-f-fudge, man?" I manage to say, making Zander choke out a laugh. "And who told you she's hot?"

"No one. I saw her with my own two eyes."

"What? When?"

"She came in to meet Dad and sign papers last week, and I ran into her in the hallway and chatted." I grind my teeth together in annoyance because the thought of my brother laughing it up with Zara makes me want to punch something, and I have no idea why.

It's been nearly two weeks since the day I was in her office. Twelve days since I got a text from her with a single word: Okay.

*Okay?*

That's all you have to say to me? *Okay?* What the fuck.

Apparently, she had plenty to say to my brother, though.

I'm not entirely sure what I expected. A thank you, maybe? A teensy bit of enthusiasm or gratitude?

Actually, no. I don't give a shit about any of that.

What I really want to know is whether she's thought of me. Because I sure as hell have thought about her. After that day in her office, when we both agreed to keep that night to ourselves and remain friends or whatever, I think I somehow unintentionally cursed myself.

Because, as it turns out, *that night* is all I can think about.

"Hey, losers." Presley pushes past Cash and makes her way to an empty seat, carrying a plate of cheese pizza and a beer.

"So nice of you to join us." Cash's deadpan delivery is really putting the *big* in big brother tonight. "Where's your boyfriend?"

I don't know why he bothers asking. None of us likes the guy. They've been dating almost a year now, and a family dinner without Jace is something we all prefer. The last time he was here, he asked Zander who the hottest groupie he'd ever hooked up with on tour was. In front of his wife.

The guy is an asshole.

"Couldn't make it. And didn't you get here late too?" she says around a mouthful of pizza, completely unfazed by the rock star sitting next to her. He doesn't seem to notice her much either, offering a polite nod before returning to his conversation with Mercury.

Thank God for that. Not to say Asher wouldn't be a step up from Jace, but his life is insane. Just last month, someone broke into his house and tried to snap pics of him sleeping in bed. He can barely go out in public without being mobbed.

I wouldn't want that for my sister.

"I did," he replies. "But—"

She cuts him off, turns, and smiles sweetly at Zander and me. "What were you talking about? What'd I miss?"

Things have always been a bit frosty between Cash and Presley. It's not that they don't love each other. I wouldn't even go so far as to say they dislike each other.

Their personalities just...clash.

There is a reason Cash works on the business side of the company. He's incredibly practical and disciplined. Presley, on the other hand, is creative and spontaneous. And even though she's done some amazing things with the bar lately, my brother only seems to see her as an impulsive woman with no real goals.

"We were talking about the doctor who's going on tour with us," Zander says.

"Oh, right." Pres nods before pulling her hair to the side to keep it away from her food. "What's her name again?"

"Zara," Cash answers, clearly feeling left out of the conversation. "Zara Valentine." He turns his attention toward me. "She mentioned that the two of you went to school together?"

"Uh, yup," I manage to say while suddenly becoming transfixed by the greasy slice of pepperoni pizza on my plate.

"You didn't tell me that," Zander says. I can feel his eyes boring into me. "Why didn't you mention it?"

"I don't know." I shrug, trying to act nonchalant and failing miserably. I told Zara I thought keeping our night together a secret was a good idea. What I failed to mention, however, is my inability to keep an actual secret. Or lie. Two skills that are absolutely paramount when growing up in a house with four siblings.

Because of this, those four bastards liked to gang up on me a lot. Christmastime was a goddamn nightmare.

And don't even get me started on the time I had to sign an NDA when Zander signed with Manic. Minus the few days I spent visiting him in North Carolina, I think I locked myself in my house and pretended I was sick with the worst flu on the planet just to make it through those three weeks.

"Wait." Presley's eyes go wide. "Is she the one you hooked up with at that—"

I lunge for her, trying to cover her mouth with my hand, but it's too late. The entire room already heard her, and now I'm gonna have to kill my sister.

It's a shame, really.

I think she might be my favorite.

"You hooked up with the doctor?" I hear Zander say.

"No!" The word comes out in a rush. "Fuck. Maybe."

"Maybe?" Pres's brow furrows. "What does that even mean? Do I want to know what that means?"

"It means..." I let out a frustrated sigh, realizing that I now have the attention of everyone in the room. Even Mercury and Asher stop their intense conversation to listen to this. Great. "It means yes. Okay? But I didn't bring it up because it happened before the job offer was even in the picture and—"

"Oh my god, you like her!" Presley squeals excitedly.

"This is an HR nightmare," Cash grumbles. I ignore him, because if my brother knew the type of shit that happens on tour, his pencil-pushing heart would probably have a heart attack.

"No, I don't." I cut my sister a look that says I'll deal with her later and sigh. "It's not like that. It was just a one-time thing. We've agreed to keep it professional for the tour."

"So we just hired your one-night stand?" Zander stares at me, and I hear Asher chuckle. "Jesus."

"She's not—" I let out a groan and ran my hands through my hair. "Look, this is why I didn't say anything."

"Because it looks bad?" Cash offers.

"What looks bad?" My dad asks, sauntering in with a glass of wine.

"That Hen hooked up with the hot doctor."

"For fuck's sake," I mutter.

"Uncle Hen said a bad word," Taylor whispers into Zander's ear.

"You what?" my mom asks as she enters the room.

So much for keeping it a secret.

## Chapter Ten

# ZARA

ME

What the actual fuck was I thinking?

VI

Oh, good, you're right on time. You never disappoint, sis.

MOM

A little late, honestly. I thought we'd get the freak-out text first thing this morning. I had coffee ready.

I stare at my phone in disbelief. I expected this from my sister. But my mom? Aren't moms supposed to be the sensible ones? The prudish woman who clutches her pearls and tells me that taking a job where I jet-set all over the country with a bunch of hot as fuck rock stars is just about the worst idea ever.

Instead, when I set them both down and told them about this crazy job opportunity, *my mom*, a sassy feminist who teaches math at a community college and plays the harp *for fun*, practically jumped out of her seat and screamed, "Dooo it!"

Come to find out that the woman who raised me is a closet Manic fan and thinks Asher Knight is the hottest man on the planet—*except for your father, of course.* Gross. She now plans to live vicariously through me for the next five months and wants every single detail.

Life just keeps getting weirder and weirder, I swear.

ME

> Did you know that you don't go through security when you fly on a private jet? They just drive you right onto the tarmac?

VI

> Of course I knew that.

MOM

> Yup.

ME

> How did you both know that?

VI

> I had this boyfriend...never mind.

MOM

> I saw it on Netflix. What boyfriend?

VI

> He wasn't exactly a boyfriend. He was a...friend.

MOM

> A friend? What does that mean? I thought you were dating that nice makeup artist. Marta? She had the prettiest skin.

VI

We weren't dating. We were…This is why
I said never mind, Mom!

ME

Guys, I have actual problems going on.
Can we focus?

MOM

I'm never getting grandchildren.

VI

Not with that attitude…

ME

LADIES!

VI

Zara, chill. You're gonna be fine. Where
are you?

ME

In the fancy car. About to pull up to the
fancy plane. There is sparkling water in
here. And snacks.

VI

STEAL. THE. SNACKS!

MOM

Can you send me a pic of Asher when
you get there? I want to make it my
home screen.

ME

There will be no snack stealing and
absolutely no selfies. You are supposed
to be helping!

VI

We are? I don't recall offering those
services.

MOM

Party pooper.

ME

You both suck. I'm going now. Also, Mom, don't forget those hand stretches I told you about for your tendonitis.

VI

Yeah, go get on that private jet with all those rock stars. Poor Zara.

MOM

I will if you get me PICTURES!

I roll my eyes and try to steady my breath. The car rolls to a stop, and I look out the window.

*Holy shit.*

When I imagined a private plane, I immediately thought of something small, with a few plush seats and maybe a room in the back.

This plane is *not* small.

This plane looks like it could carry an entire NFL team. Wait, how many football players actually make a team? Twenty? Thirty? I have no idea. All I know is that when I step out of that sleek black SUV, my palms feel sweaty, and I definitely feel out of my league.

The Prices are wealthy, but this is a whole other level.

I start to reach for my bags as the driver hauls them out of the back, but he politely intervenes. "I've got it, ma'am. Unless there's something you wish to take with you onboard?"

"Just this," I say, patting the large strap of my medical bag currently slung over my shoulder. I doubt I'll need it on the plane, but as of today, this giant thing is my new best friend. I'll have a better setup when we're on site at concert venues, but this bag has everything I'll need in a pinch. "Do I just...?"

He gives me a warm smile, showing no trace of judgment or amusement at my obvious nervousness. "Yep, just head on up the stairs. The crew will get your ID and get you situated."

"Thanks," I say, wondering if I should tip him. But before I decide, I hear someone shout my name over my shoulder.

"Dr. Valentine!"

I turn, and I don't know why, but I feel immediate disappointment when the person walking up to me is unfamiliar and not...

*Yeah, okay. I know why.*

It's been two weeks since Hendrix walked out of my office.

It's been two weeks since he made it abundantly clear that if I took this job, he and I would be nothing more than acquaintances. And I should be relieved, right? I'm the one who just got out of a messy divorce and am definitely not ready to date.

Still, the brushoff he gave me hurts.

More than I like to admit.

"Hey." Mystery man offers his hand. He's tall, and I have to crane my neck up to look at him. His dark-brown eyes match his skin tone, and his smile is breathtaking. "I'm Ridge, the band's manager."

"Yes, we've chatted through email." I nod, shaking his hand. "Please call me Zara. It's nice to finally meet you, and thanks for all your help with the supplies. I know it was a lot in a short amount of time."

Ridge emailed me about a week ago, asking me to

make a list of medical equipment, supplies, and drugs that I would need.

I was thorough.

"That? That was nothing compared to some of the things I've had to procure." He chuckles, then hands a wad of cash to the driver before steering me away.

I try not to calculate how much that must have been.

We walk side by side as he asks about my drive over. We both commiserate about the LA traffic, and I realize that his voice has a slight British accent. Has he lived here so long that he's lost it, or does he purposely try to mask it?

*Interesting.*

When we reach the plane, he lets me go first. It's one of those times when I truly wish male chivalry were dead because I would love to have someone to hide behind right now.

But I did not endure a million years of school, a hellish divorce, and two weeks of pep talks to turn back now.

Let's do this.

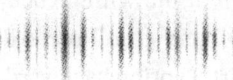

What's the first thing I do when I step onto the private plane filled with mega hot rock stars?

I trip.

And it's not the kind where you quickly catch yourself before anyone notices. No, this is the kind of fall that makes your arms flail and people gasp. It's the attention-grabbing, cheeks-heating kind of fall.

I take one step forward, and I don't know if it's the ridiculously plush carpet or if the gods themselves have chosen to smite me from the heavens. But suddenly, my shoe catches on something, and I'm falling face-first into —a chest?

"Nice entrance, Cupid."

I freeze because, of course, it's him. It couldn't be a random assistant or a flight attendant.

No, it has to be Hendrix fucking Creed.

I look up and inwardly sigh because, yep, he's just as hot as I remember.

His eyes are a soft denim blue with the tiniest flecks of gold near the irises. He looks as if he's had a haircut since I last saw him because he's rocking an edgy under-cut, and his honey brown locks are pushed back like someone just ran their fingers through them. His beard is neat and trimmed, and I try not to think of all the places I've felt it scrape across my skin.

I was sort of hoping I had built him up in my mind and that all those sexy tattoos and lean muscles were just a figment of my imagination.

He stares down at me with a cocky smirk, and that's when I realize my hand is still pressed between his pecs. Gripping his T-shirt. I spring backward.

"Sorry," I mutter. "I didn't mean to..." *Grope you? Fondle your man chest?*

"Who is this, then?" I hear someone say from behind Hendrix in a posh British accent. He turns and sighs at the giant beast of a man. His tawny brown skin is covered in intricate tattoos, and his thick, wavy brown hair is pulled up in a messy man bun at the crown of his head.

Is everyone in this band tall?

"This is Zara Valentine," Ridge answers. He managed

to make it onto the plane unscathed and stands next to me looking impeccable while I try to reclaim my dignity after nearly face-palming it moments ago. "She will be our on-site physician for the duration of the tour."

"We have our own doctor now? Brilliant!" Tall guy grins, offering his free hand. The other is wrapped around one of those giant energy drinks. "I'm Darius, the drummer. Hey, will you be supplying condoms?"

"Dar, what the fuck?" Ridge mutters.

"Jesus," Henrick groans.

"What?" Darius shrugs, looking completely unbothered. "It's a genuine question. I always run out. This one time, I brought back these gorgeous blonde triplets to my room, only to find out I used my last rubber the night before. I don't know about you, but I go through a lot of them when I'm in a ménage situation." He notices Ridge staring at him. "You've never had that problem?"

I can't help the tiny smirk that tugs at my lips. This guy seems to have no filter.

"No," Ridge answers flatly.

"Well, you'll be glad to know I come fully stocked with Band-Aids, over-the-counter meds, and yes, even condoms."

"Splendid. Well, if you ever need a visual aid to demonstrate proper placement—Ow! What the fuck?" Hendrix whacks him across the top of his head.

"Stop harassing her."

"I'm not harassing her. I'm just being friendly. And kind. That's what we do for newbies here."

"I'm new," Hendrix reminds him.

"No, you're not," Darius argues. "You and Z are so attached, I was starting to wonder if you were in some sort of throuple situation we didn't know about. And we'd be okay with that, just so you know. Love is love, right, Doc?"

"Um, yup." See? No filter.

"A throuple? Seriously? If you think Zander would let anyone touch his wife, even his best friend, you clearly don't know him well enough yet."

"Speaking of Elena," Ridge interrupts. I follow his gaze and see a woman with chestnut brown hair and a gorgeous smile. She's dressed comfortably in high-waisted leggings and a cropped hoodie, and I'm guessing the toddler wrapped around her is the reason I was hired. "I'm going to go introduce her to Zara."

"Lovely to meet you, Doc!"

"You too, Darius."

I don't say goodbye to Hendrix. He doesn't say anything to me either, but I feel his gaze on me as I walk away, like an electric current running up my spine.

Definitely not going to be awkward at all between us.

I can already tell Elena and I are going to be good friends.

When she turned around and exclaimed, "Oh, thank God. This group needs another female to liven it up a bit," I couldn't help but laugh.

She then proceeded to boot her husband out of his seat so I could sit across from her as the plane taxied out of the gate and left LAX for Miami. Elena explains that we start in Florida because it's "hot as balls," and it's better to get it out of the way in late spring rather than summer.

I can't argue with that logic.

Over the next five months, I'll visit sixteen states and fourteen countries.

In the last thirty years, with the exception of my honeymoon, I've barely left California.

"So...are you ready for this?" Elena asks about an hour into the flight. We've already gone through the basic get-to-know-you stuff. She's a lawyer turned suspense author who publishes under a super-secret pen name she doesn't share with anyone. She likes keeping that part of her life separate from this one.

She's originally from Texas, but her family moved to Virginia when she was in high school. She had a brother, but he died several years ago in a ferry accident off the coast of North Carolina. It's through her best friend, Marin, that she met Zander. Their husbands are brothers.

"If you're asking if I'm prepared to do my job, then yes. My medical bag is stocked, and I've got everything I need to set up a pretty sweet med station backstage," I answer, biting the corner of my lip as I look across the aisle where Marisa is sleeping soundly in her car seat, which is buckled to one of the plush leather seats. "But if you're asking about anything outside of that, then no. I have no idea what to expect, even if I'm ready for it."

"That's fair." She nods, leaning back against the seat, which looks like a damn recliner. Nothing on this plane seems like it belongs on a plane. No boxy carts that run over your feet or pull-out trays in this baby.

No, everything is hand-delivered, and it is all bougie as fuck.

Even my Diet Coke is served in a fancy glass with a lime wedge.

"I was really nervous in the beginning too, but I had

Zander to fall back on. I can't imagine what it must feel like to just be thrown into all this."

"Is it that bad?"

She shakes her head. "No. Manic is pretty tame. Or at least they are now. The scandal with Mitch mellowed them out, plus they're older now."

"Yeah, the thirties are brutal."

She laughs, but is quickly interrupted by Marisa, who makes it clear she is no longer asleep. Before long, Elena has her in her arms and is gently rocking next to her seat, but Marisa is not having it.

I notice her tugging at her ear.

"Do you have a bottle or a pacifier?" I ask.

"No, I'm still breastfeeding," she answers. "But she's starting to wean herself, I think. She's down to once or twice a day."

"Think she'll be up for it now?"

She shrugs. "Maybe. Why?"

"Her ears may be bothering her. It could be due to a change in pressure. Could be something more. Have you noticed her fussing with her ears?"

She shakes her head. "No, but she's had ear infections in the past."

"Well, let's see if she'll let you feed her, and if it's just the cabin pressure, it should help. In the future, we can have you do this when we take off and land, or if that's too much for her, we can look into getting her something to suck on during those times."

She's already taking her seat again and getting comfortable, lifting her shirt and starting to unclasp the top hook on her nursing bra.

Suddenly, a tall, tattooed man stands in front of her. "Whoa, what the fuck, Louie?"

*Who's Louie?*

"What do you mean, *what the fuck*?" God, she mimics her husband's deep voice perfectly. Chef's kiss.

"You can't just—" He struggles to finish his sentence as Elena looks up at him with an annoyed expression. "The guys are like right there."

"And?"

"And *those*"—he waves a hand toward her chest and drops his voice to a whisper—"are for my eyes only."

"Jesus Christ, Z," she mutters. "You are ridiculous. No one is gonna be looking at my tits when they're attached to our kid."

He turns to look at the rest of the band, Ridge, and the other random people I haven't met. Only a handful can hear what is happening, and it happens to be Hendrix, Darius, and Asher.

Hendrix holds up his hands, eyes firmly on the floor. "You know I'm scared of anything baby-related."

I snort out a laugh. Why does that not surprise me?

Asher has his head buried in a book. I haven't had much of a chance to check him out yet. We haven't even been properly introduced, but I take this moment to observe him.

Okay, not so much observe as blatantly check out.

There is a reason this man is on the covers of magazines on a regular basis. He is like Harry Styles hot. His floppy brown hair is pushed behind his ear, showing off some seriously chiseled cheekbones. And he's wearing glasses. That's like a nerdy girl's kryptonite.

He acts like he's in another world, buried in that book. He doesn't even bother to look up and just waves at Zander, as if he's shooing away a fly.

Darius, on the other hand, has his full attention and

tosses a hand in the air. "What if I told you my interests were purely academic?"

"Get the fuck out of here," Zander growls.

"Yes, sir." He jumps out of his seat and heads further down the aisle toward the bar, cackling like a lunatic the whole way.

Yes, a bar. This plane is ridiculous.

"You happy now?" Elena looks up at him. She sounds annoyed, but the grin she's struggling to hide suggests otherwise. "Can I feed our daughter now, or do you need to question Zara too?"

I hold up my hands in protest. "Not into girls, but even if I were, I'm a doctor. And a professional."

"Right." Zander nods. "Yeah. Of course."

He's still staring down at his wife, but his somewhat insane caveman expression has softened as he watches her go through the motions of unhooking her bra and nursing their child at her breast. She looks up at him once Marissa quiets, no doubt soothed by the feel of her mother's touch, and I find myself turning away.

The love they share is palpable, so painfully obvious in the way they look at each other. I can't help but wonder...

Did Tanner ever look at me like that? I'm not so sure.

Because I'm starting to wonder if our whole marriage was nothing but a scam.

## Chapter Eleven

# HENDRIX

So far, being on tour is not exactly how I imagined it.

Don't get me wrong. When we arrived in Miami yesterday and were shuttled over to the Kaseya Center, where legends like Beyoncé and U2 have all performed, I was fucking giddy as hell.

This whole thing didn't feel real until I stepped on that stage. Over eighteen thousand empty seats stared back at me, just waiting to be filled. The biggest gig I'd ever done up until that moment wasn't even a third of that, and this was just day fucking one.

We had been traveling all day, but at that moment, I could have strapped on my bass and played an entire set right from start to finish. That's how pumped I was. How fucking honored I felt to be part of this tour.

But yesterday was just a walk-through, and before I knew it, we were whisked back to our hotel for a mandatory group dinner. Asher's idea, apparently. Something about everyone getting to know each other and bonding or some shit.

I know I'm the new guy, but even I knew this was a

total buzzkill. Asher may be a bit of a recluse now, but the rest of the crew definitely was not, and they were itching for a night out. Still, everyone stayed because we all love Asher. Surprisingly, the dinner wasn't so bad. It might have even bordered on fun if I hadn't spent the entire evening listening to Zara laugh at someone else's jokes throughout the meal. Darius was a cool guy, but he wasn't *that* funny.

Afterward, when a few of the techies headed for the club and asked me to join, I surprised the hell out of myself by saying no. Then I surprised myself even more by walking myself up to my room, picking up my bass, and practicing until my fingers went numb.

Because I refuse to fuck this up.

And now it's finally game day. We just finished our final sound check, and I feel like I'm going to puke.

My hands are shaking. My breath is coming out all weird and choppy, and I'm sweating like I'm standing in the middle of the Sahara fucking desert on a hot summer day.

I find a dark corner away from the stage where I can hide, because Christ, this is embarrassing. I'm a seasoned musician. I've been performing on stage since I was a scrawny-ass teenager. The first time my dad took me to a music store, and I saw a dude playing Black Sabbath on a shiny new bass, I knew. I just knew that was what I wanted to do for the rest of my life.

And I've been trying to make it a reality ever since.

I thought I'd get my chance with Edwin and our band, but it didn't happen, and I've been trying to crawl back from that mistake ever since. So now that I'm here, why do I feel this unexplainable dread in the back of my mind like I'm right on the cusp of losing everything?

Like the rug is about to be pulled out from under me?

Like my life is about to change forever?

"Hendrix?"

*Fucking hell.*

I was really hoping to have this mini meltdown all by myself, so, of course, the universe would send her my way.

I'm shoved as far into the corner as physically possible without actually becoming part of the drywall. My feet are wedged in between several of the cords that have been taped to the ground—something that one of the techies wouldn't approve of, but it's fine. Desperate times and all that.

"You going to acknowledge me, or am I gonna have to make it awkward?"

"Acknowledged," I manage to say.

I'll give it to her. She's keeping her distance. Most people would have marched right up and demanded answers.

*What's wrong with you?*

*What the fuck are you doing?*

*Stop being weird and get your ass out of there.*

I'm ashamed to admit, if the tables were reversed, I might be one of those people. Perhaps having four siblings has made me a natural problem solver. I see something is broken, and I immediately want to fix it. It has not, however, made me subtle, and I tend to attack problems head-on.

Zara, on the other hand, seems to be approaching me like a wounded animal. Cautious. Calculated.

I can't tell if it makes me want to run or stay just to see what she does.

My feet stay firmly planted on the ground...or wedged between the wires.

She steps into my line of sight, and whatever assessment she makes doesn't show on her face. But I know her well enough, from studying her all those years ago in the library, to realize Zara doesn't merely look. She analyzes. She observes and examines, furrowing away information in that great big brain of hers. It was just as hot back then as it is now.

"I, uh, was actually looking for someone to help me with something in my clinic? Do you think you could spare a few minutes?"

She's a terrible liar. Takes one to know one, after all.

"Your clinic?"

An amused smile spreads across her lips. "Yeah. The one I have set up backstage. What did you think I was going to do? Run around handing out Band-Aids all night?"

I hadn't even thought about it. When Ridge had us write up the paperwork for the position, he made it clear we were to just give her whatever the fuck she wanted because, in his words, he was *not* postponing this tour over a toddler.

"What do you need?" I ask, running a shaky hand through my hair. Her eyes track it, and I immediately put it back at my side.

"Just some heavy boxes that need to be moved."

"I—"

But before I can even come up with an excuse, she looks up at me with those intense brown eyes and says, "Please?"

How the fuck am I supposed to say no to that? "Sure."

It's thankfully a short trip to her clinic. I do not want anyone to see me like this. She may have lured me out of my corner—god, was I really just huddled in a fucking corner—but I'm still a mess. My palms are sweaty, and my knees feel weak. I hear someone call the ninety-minute mark in the distance. My heart leaps to my throat.

Yeah, I'm a mess.

We walk into the room she's taken over. It's on the small side and directly across from the hospitality suite. It's set up with a portable exam table, locked rolling carts I'm assuming are filled with supplies, and a whole bunch of other shit I recognize but can't name.

But one thing I don't see is a single fucking box.

"What the hell, Zara?"

"Sit," she commands, shutting the door behind her. My eyes immediately go to the exam table. "Not there. Over here." She points to two folding chairs that I must have overlooked.

I glance back at her, but she has that *don't mess with me* look about her that she used to give me when I tried to convince her to cancel tutoring and go party with me instead.

Never happened. Not even once.

I huff out a resigned sigh. I don't have time for this, but I take the seat anyway, pushing it back to create some distance between us. I don't feel like my laid-back self right now, and I need my space.

She must understand that because she mimics my behavior, moving her chair the same distance before plopping down to face me.

"Are you my therapist now?" My right hand started plucking out a rhythm on my thigh, something we played during sound check. It's something I do whenever I'm bored or nervous.

Or stressed.

"No," she answers, letting out a sound of disbelief. "God, no. I'm barely stable. What would make me remotely qualified to be in charge of someone else's mental health?"

"So then, why am I here? Why waste my time? Why lie about nonexistent boxes to get me in here?" I get to the end of the chorus, and my hand cramps. I knew I played too long last night. I shake it out, and Zara's eyes narrow, and I fold it in my lap before she can say anything.

She lets out a frustrated sigh, looking away briefly. "Okay, how about this? Story Time."

I stare at her and blink, because that's a phrase I haven't heard in a while. "Story Time?" A shy smile tugs at the corners of her lips, seemingly pleased that I remember what she's referring to. "All right. But do you remember the rules of Story Time?"

"There are no rules of Story Time."

"Yes, there are. This isn't Fight Club."

"Those were your rules, and they're stupid. How am I supposed to know if a story is"—she makes air quotes—"boring? And what if I need more than two minutes to make my point?"

I simply shrug. "Those are the rules. Can't be changed."

"Yes, they can! You're the one who—" She huffs out a breath. "You're just as insufferable as you were in college."

I shift in my seat as if I'm about to get up. "I can leave."

"No! Ugh. Fine." I grin, feeling myself begin to relax a little, just from the sound of her voice. "Stay."

"Your two minutes start..." I make a show of glancing down at my smart watch and pausing before I finally say, "Now."

She takes a breath and begins. "Okay, so at the end of your second year of med school, you take basically the hardest exam of your life. I won't *bore* you with the specifics, but it's the kind of exam that either breaks you or makes you. For eight weeks, I lived in the library." At the mention of the library, one of those fantasies I've had of her over the years hits me square in the gut. Her body splayed out on a table. Her hair fans the open pages of the forgotten book she abandoned as I spread her wide and thrust—*Get it together, man.* I swallow and focus back on the here and now.

At least I'm not hyperventilating anymore. Well, not much, anyway.

"And that's any different from undergrad? You were there so often, they should have just put a cot in the corner for you to sleep on."

"New rule." She folds her arms across her chest. It presses her tits together, and I have to force myself not to look. "No talking when it's not your story."

"You can't just make—" Her brow arches, and I relent. "Fine."

"Anyway, like I was saying, it was one of the most stressful moments of my life—at least, up until then. But I got through it, and when I woke up on the morning of the exam, I felt good. Confident, even." If this is her point, she's seriously missed the mark. "I met Tanner at—"

"New rule," I interject, not giving a shit that I'm interrupting her. "No talking about douchey exes during Story Time."

She stares at me and simply replies, "All right."

I stare right back. "Okay, then."

It takes her a moment, almost as if she's still digesting the moment, but finally, she shifts in her seat and speaks. "Anyway, I got to where they were administering the test, and as soon as I walked up to the building, I froze. I couldn't move. Tan—" She stops herself from saying his name. "Certain outside forces possibly added to my stress in that moment, and I ended up having a full-blown panic attack. It was the first time something like that ever happened to me."

"Wait." I hold up my hand. "What do you mean by 'outside forces?'"

"It doesn't matter," she answers quickly. "And you're breaking the rules."

"Fuck the rules. What did he do, Zara?"

She lets out a long sigh. "He told me I was embarrassing him and needed to pull myself together."

"God, that guy's an asshole." I just shake my head. "You know that, right? Because nothing about that moment was embarrassing. It's natural to freak out when shit gets stressful."

"I know."

"Especially when it's something you've been working toward for a really long time."

"Yes."

I didn't realize my gaze had drifted down to the ground until I felt her eyes on me, and I understood the double meaning of what I had just said.

Did she intentionally turn this around and connect it back to me, or was that a coincidence? Either way, I let out a deep breath, and just as I'm about to lift my gaze to look at her, the door bursts open, and two of the crew members barrel in.

They come to an abrupt halt when they see us.

"Uh, sorry, Doc. Didn't know you had anyone in here. We can come back," the scrawny dark-haired guy says as the tall blond one looks at him with wide eyes, holding a wad of toilet paper to his nose.

"No." She rises to her feet. "It's fine. Bring him over here." She points to the exam table and then turns back to me, giving a warm smile. "We good?"

"Yeah." I gaze into her eyes, suddenly feeling like a heavy weight has been lifted off my shoulders. "We're good."

I hate to say it, but I'm going to anyway.

I don't understand how this band survived this many tours without a full-time doctor.

Maybe it's just this particular tour or the people on it. But we're only on day one, and I've dealt with a bloody nose caused by two very clumsy crew members, a dehydrated security guard, and a near panic attack by one very hot bass guitarist.

When I walked past Hendrix earlier, I almost didn't see him. He had done a decent job of making himself nearly invisible in that darkened corner.

He did not want to be found.

And that's what set off the alarm bells in my head.

Hendrix isn't the kind of person to run and hide from challenges. Even in college, when he struggled with biology, he didn't succumb to his fate. He simply dealt with the issue, found a tutor—me—and retook the class. Since our recent reunion, I've noticed that even though the single-minded determination he once had may have taken a hit or two over the years, no doubt due to Edwin's betrayal, it's still there.

It's still driving him to succeed.

And if there's one thing I know, it's how overwhelming stress can feel when you're working toward a long-term goal.

That is what I saw in his eyes in that hallway.

The kind of stress that can paralyze you.

If not properly managed, it can rob you of the very dream you're trying so desperately to achieve. It almost took mine that day outside the testing facility. If I hadn't known what kind of breathing exercises to do, thanks to a roommate back in undergrad who suffered from panic attacks, I might not have made it into the building or through the next two years of med school.

But I did.

And I knew he could too.

So I lied and got him out of the hallway. Once we were safely behind closed doors, I did the first thing that came to mind: Story Time.

It was something I made up during our tutoring sessions to help bridge the gap between what was in the textbook and what made sense to him. I used real-world examples and wove them together with what I was trying to teach him. Soon, it became a sort of game he loved to join in on, only his stories had little to do with science and often involved a heavy amount of flirting. But it was fun.

He was fun.

I never used Story Time again with any of the other students I tutored. Whenever I thought about it, I always found an excuse for why it wasn't suitable for that person or that particular situation. It just never felt right.

And now I know why.

It wasn't that I couldn't find anyone who felt right.

It was that I didn't want to.

Story Time was *ours*.

It's a couple of hours later. The first concert of the tour is in full swing, and based on the deafening level of noise coming from the direction of the stage, I think Hendrix is doing just fine.

I've just wiped down my entire clinic with antiseptic when Elena comes in, sans kid.

"Hey, you busy?" she asks, looking every bit the rocker's wife in tight black pants and a cropped Manic tee. She takes a cursory glance around and gives a faint smile of approval.

"No, why? Everything okay with Marisa?"

"Yeah, she's with the nanny for a few hours," she explains with a shrug. "If I don't hand her over now and then, it sort of defeats the purpose of having one in the first place."

"Is it a requirement that you have one?" I met Selene, the nanny, on the plane yesterday. She reminded me a bit of my mom. They are close in age, and she has the same sweet and sassy demeanor that everyone loves about my mom. Within hours, she'd been named the unofficial grandma on tour, promising baked goods to everyone as soon as she got her hands on an oven.

"No, and this is the first time I've ever had one. When we're home, it's just the two of us. But being on tour is a whole different beast, you know?" I nod because after just twenty-four hours of this, I wholeheartedly agree. It's a lot. And I don't even have a kid. "And at times like this, when I want to watch my husband play, it just wouldn't be possible without a nanny. I could put headphones on her ears and take her out there for a few minutes, but that's about it," she explains. "With Selene, she can be content in the quiet room, and I can enjoy a bit of adult time."

I nod, shrugging off my white coat and placing it on top of one of the rolling carts. "That makes perfect sense, and it's what I would recommend if you had asked me."

"Well then, I guess I'm not doing too badly at this whole parenting thing."

"Nah, I'd say you're doing pretty damn good."

"Nice. Doctor approved! I'm so texting that to Marin."

"That's your sister-in-law? The one from North Carolina?"

"Yeah." She smiles, reaching out to grab my arm. "Did I tell you she's an artist? And she lives on the cutest little island in North Carolina? Come on, I'll tell you all about her on the way."

"Where are we going?" I ask, grabbing my cell, since I'm apparently leaving the clinic.

"To a rock concert, duh."

There are three things I realize almost simultaneously as Elena and I reach the side of the stage.

One—rock concerts are loud. Like, the ear-ringing, chest-vibrating kind of loud. I mean, I knew they would be, but experiencing it in person is really something else.

Two—I actually kind of love it. The noise. The energy. The pure chaos of it all. It makes me feel alive in a way I haven't felt in years.

And three—I most definitely want to have sex with Hendrix Creed again.

There are people everywhere backstage, and I kind of feel like I'm in the way standing here, but Elena seems completely unbothered, acting like the queen she is as she makes eye contact with Zander and blows him a kiss.

The look he gives her...

I find myself blushing and needing to turn away. Good god, I don't think a man has ever looked at me like that. Like he wants to devour me.

Like I'm the center of his whole damn universe.

I turn my attention to the rest of the band. Darius is pounding away on the drums. Despite being a goofy guy, he looks so professional and natural with a drumstick in his hand. Asher looks every bit the rock god he is. His voice is a dream, and everyone is captivated by him.

Everyone but me.

My eyes go straight to Hendrix.

And I can't turn away.

He's wearing black jeans that look like they were made for him, and given the money that was put into this tour, maybe they were. The tight black tee, now slick with sweat, clings to his washboard abs like a second skin.

This is the first time I've ever seen him play.

In college, I often saw him lugging a guitar bag around, but that was the extent of my encounters with Hendrix the musician.

Until tonight.

He looks completely absorbed in the moment. Focused. Happy.

His posture, the way he holds the bass, and how skillfully his fingers work the strings—he makes it all seem effortless, even though I know it's anything but.

He's truly a master of his craft.

It's sexy as hell.

As if he can sense me staring, or possibly drooling, he glances over, and our eyes lock. My breath catches as he takes me in.

Is there some sort of masterclass they make these guys take? Rock Star 101: How to Smolder? The Art of Eye Fucking? Because, holy hell, I feel the heat of his gaze lighting me up from the inside. My skin feels like it's on fire.

I resist the urge to fan myself and inflate his ego. It's big enough as it is. He smirks as if he can read my thoughts and turns back toward the stage.

"I know, by the way," Elena practically screams in my ear since it's so damn loud.

I turn to her and try to gauge her meaning, but her eyes are focused on her husband, her hips swaying back and forth to the music. "You know what?" I ask her, although not nearly as loud.

"About you and Hendrix?

"YOU WHAT?" I don't even bother leaning into her ear. I'm pretty sure everyone around us heard that.

*Oops.*

She laughs and motions for me to take a few steps back. I do, but it does little to muffle the sound. It does, however, give us a bit of privacy and somewhat blocks our view of the four hot and sweaty rock stars.

We can see them, but they can no longer see us.

Small mercies, because I do not want to be having this conversation knowing he could, at any time, look over at me with those sex eyes of his.

I lean into her ear and loudly say, "How do you know? *What* do you know?"

"What?"

"HOW DO YOU—" I stop myself and save my voice, because this is never going to work. Partially because Elena's eyes are still glued on Zander, and she's only giving me half her attention. I pull out my phone and open the notes app. She watches with a curious smile as I begin typing.

*How do you know? What do you know?*

I hand the phone over to her and wait as she quickly reads, responds, and hands it back to me.

*Zander told me. Hendrix told him.*

My eyes fly up to hers. He is the one who told me to keep it quiet. What the hell?

She motions with her hand to keep reading. Oh, right.

*But, to be fair, Hendrix can't keep a secret or tell a lie to save his life. And once Presley figured out you two went to school together, it sort of all came out.*

I start typing again.

*Why does Hendrix and me going to college together matter?*

I have to tap her on the arm to get her attention. She's already fallen back under the spell of her husband's sultry voice. I had no idea until tonight that Zander did backup vocals for the band. But then again, Manic had somewhat fallen off my radar over the last couple of years.

I inwardly sigh. I could say that about a lot of things, actually.

Something brushes against my arm, and I jump. I look up to see Elena holding out my phone and laughing. I guess she isn't the only one lost in the music.

"Sorry," I say, taking the phone back.

I skim through the old messages until I reach the new stuff she's written.

*He told Pres about a woman from college that he hooked up with at a party. Hendrix is no saint, but he doesn't get around THAT much. There was only one person it could be.*

I focus entirely too much on the fact that Hendrix is not sleeping with a new girl every night. I force myself not to ask her for details, like just how often is he getting around? Every other night? Weekly?

*God, Zara. Shut up.*

I type out a normal question, one that doesn't include Hendrix's sex life, or at least his sex life with anyone else.

*So you, Presley, and Zander know. Does anyone else know?*

The expression on her face as she reads it makes my eyes widen. She looks up at me, lips pressed together, and shakes her head. But it's not the kind of head shake that makes me think she's saying, *No, Zara. Absolutely nothing to worry about. Your secret is safe.*

No, she's frantically shaking her head back and forth like, *please, don't make me say it.*

I fold my arms firmly across my chest and nod toward the phone.

She lets out an exasperated sigh, and I see her mouth the word, "Fine." A strand of her dark-brown hair falls in front of her face as she leans over the phone, and she absently pushes it away. She begins typing, and after what feels like an eternity, she finally—reluctantly—hands the phone back.

My eyes widen. She's penned a new novel right here inside my phone. It's that long.

*Okay, so don't freak out.*

That's never a good start.

*But this may have all come out during a family dinner.*

*The Creeds are known for having these huge family dinners. Totally informal and...*

I skip ahead.

*Anyway, I wasn't there that night because I needed a night to myself, so I got all of this secondhand from Zander. But, apparently, Presley made the connection while they were all around the dinner table and just sort of blurted it out.*

Oh god. I don't like where this is going.

*Luckily, it was just the kids. Hendrix's parents were in the kitchen.*

Thank God.

*But Asher happened to be there that night. Random, right?*

Fuck my life.

*Oh, and Lance and Tilly (that's Hendrix's mom) came in right at the tail end. So yeah, they know too.*

My hands fly over the keyboard.

*Is there anyone who DOESN'T KNOW?*

When I hand it back to her, she actually looks up like she has to think about it for a minute. But then she laughs as I playfully smack her arm, my lip twitching in amusement.

She types significantly less this time, and when I get it back, I snort.

*Not sure. Want me to go around and ask? Oh! How does this sound? "Sir, we're conducting a poll. Were you aware of the rumor that our esteemed doctor and new bass guitarist engaged in coitus before the start of the tour? Yes or no?"*

I roll my eyes but can't contain the smile that spreads across my face. I don't remember having this much fun with a friend in a long time. Aside from my sister, I don't remember having an actual friend in a long time. Not since I got married.

*As your doctor, I must insist you refrain from using the word coitus from here on out. It's bad for your health.*

When I hand it back to her, she bursts out laughing, but then sobers slightly as she begins to write again. Her eyes find mine, and there's an emotion behind them.

Soon, she hands the phone back.

*All joking aside, I want you to know this because I now consider you a friend, and I don't keep secrets from my friends.*

*I see the way you and Hendrix look at each other, and I know how confusing being on tour can be for people. It's easy to forget that real life exists outside this little bubble, and eventually, we will go back to that. So just make sure whatever you start here can survive when all this is over.*

I read over her words at least twice.

She sees the way we look at each other? I mean, I'm sure how I look at him is obvious. I wouldn't doubt that half the women in this stadium gaze at him with a mix of heat and adoration just as I do.

But has she caught him looking at me?

I think back to that moment when he was on stage. That heated gaze, the way our eyes met, and how that single glance made me feel more than anything I experienced in my entire marriage.

I swallow and nervously bite the corner of my lip as I type one last message to her.

*You and I are most definitely friends.* 😊 *And I appreciate you looking out for me. But it's a nonissue. Hendrix and I agreed to keep things professional during the tour. Also, he made it crystal clear that anything more than that would be a giant distraction, and he needed to focus. That's basically "fuck off" in guy speak.*

I can practically taste the bitterness in the words as I type them out and hand the phone back to her.

She takes her time reading my message, but her response is almost instantaneous.

*Yeah, but remember how I said he's a horrible liar?*

## Chapter Thirteen

# HENDRIX

"They say nothing good happens after midnight. Clearly, they've never been to Nashville! Thanks for all the love," Asher hollers into the mic as the crowd goes wild. "Good night!"

We've already done three encores, and this crowd is so wild they'd gladly take a dozen more. But Ash gives a final wave, his shirt long since tossed into the crowd. His hair is slick with sweat, and his tattooed body glistens.

The girls in the front row go fucking nuts, hoping he'll single one of them out to go backstage. But he doesn't.

He never does.

He gives us the signal, a quick thumbs up to the crowd, and Darius and I give a quick wave and make our exit first. I hand off my bass to one of the roadies as someone else removes my earpiece and hands me a towel and a water bottle.

I down that sucker in two gulps.

"Christ, that was bloody brilliant," Darius exclaims,

nearly breathless from chugging his own bottle of water. "I fucking love Nashville."

"I didn't think they'd be so energetic, considering..." I say, just as breathless. The heat from the lights and the buzz from the crowd have me amped and exhausted all at the same time.

"They're known for country music here?" Someone offers us both another water as the crowd roars, and I see Zander and Ash leaving the stage. They're both laughing and slapping each other on the back. "Nah. This city just loves music, period. Can't you feel it?"

I stare blankly at him. "Feel what?"

"The love, mate. That crowd? They're buzzing. Giving us nothing but pure love."

When I stand on the stage, I definitely feel something from the crowd. Whether it's love, I'm not sure. Excitement? Sure. Lust? Definitely.

Whatever it is, it's better than any high I could ever chase, and now that I've experienced it at this level, with twenty thousand screaming fans surrounding me, I don't ever want to go back.

I see a tornado of chocolate-brown hair fly by me as Elena throws herself into Zander's waiting arms. His hands possessively palm her ass, and then they're practically mauling each other, right there, in front of the whole damn crew.

"Fuck," Darius curses. "That's hot."

Asher joins us and promptly whacks the back of his head. "Ease up with the staring, yeah? If Zander sees you, I'll need a new bloody drummer."

"Tell me how, mate? When he's squeezing her peachy little arse like that. Ooh, speaking of peaches." His attention turns sharply away from Zander and Elena, and as I follow his wandering gaze, I see Zara heading our way. She's still wearing her white lab coat, and her silky brown hair is pulled back in a ponytail at the nape of her neck. Just as she notices us, Darius gives a flirty little wave.

"No."

"What?" He glances back toward me. "What do you mean no?"

"I mean exactly that, Dar. No. Zara is off limits. She's too important to the tour for you to pursue for one of your late-night hookups."

I glance back in her direction and see that she's joined Elena and Zander, who have managed to pull apart. Zander sneaks a glance my way, and I give him a slight shake of my head. He nods.

He will keep the girls away until this little matter is settled.

"Woah." He holds up both hands, feigning innocence. "Who said I was going after her?" Asher and I just stare at him, not saying a word. He instantly folds like a house of cards. "All right, fine. Maybe the thought crossed my mind, yeah? But can you blame me? I mean, have you had a look at her? I can't imagine what she looks like under that white coat with all those lush curves—"

"Stop," I growl. I didn't realize I had taken a step forward, but now we're practically nose to nose. "Not another fucking word."

I see a brief moment of confusion before something clicks, and a wide smile spreads across his face. "Oh, I see." He takes a casual step back. "You want her. That's what this is all about. It's not about me or what's best for the bloody tour. No, you want her all for yourself."

I can feel my heart hammering in my chest. I look over at Asher, and his expression is a blank canvas as he just watches the exchange between us. He already knows Zara and I hooked up, but that's about the extent of what he knows. What anyone knows, for that matter.

My family was generous enough not to ask for details that night when it all came out, thanks to my former favorite sister, Presley. They were more worried about how it might complicate our relationship and the tour. Somehow, I managed to convince them it wouldn't—on both counts.

I'm not sure how any of them fell for all the lies I was feeding them, when I barely believe it myself. But I went into this tour trying to convince myself it would all be fine, that Zara Valentine would not be an issue. And now here I am, three stops in, ready to rip the head off our drummer for even thinking he might have a shot with her.

Yeah, totally not an issue.

Fucking hell.

"That's not it at all," I lie. "I'm simply looking out for her. Zara and I are good friends. We go way back, and I know this job is important to her."

Darius's grin widens, clearly not buying what I'm selling. "All right." He nods. "Good to know."

And then he saunters off like this was some sort of challenge. And he won.

"What did I just do?"

Asher pats me on the shoulder. "I don't know, but I don't think you're going to like it."

About an hour later, I rush around my room, grabbing my wallet and room key as I dash out the door. Tonight, the PR team has arranged for us to hit up an exclusive club here in Nashville, and according to Missy or Misty from PR—I can't remember her name—it is mandatory that the entire band attend.

Even the hired gun.

We've been on tour for a little over a week, and it's been nothing short of insane. The crowds are electric, the band is tight, and the music is fucking fire.

And I'm so fucking exhausted.

Zander warned me it would be like this. He said tour life was not as glamorous as Hollywood made it out to be, and I believed him. I saw it with my own eyes when I visited him over the years, but seeing it and living it are two vastly different things.

Hell, I've been so tired that I was late coming into a chorus tonight. In Atlanta, it was like my brain glitched and my fingers stopped working. That, combined with my first-day jitters, and I feel like a damn novice again. I finally had to loosen up on my late-night practicing to get in a couple of extra hours of sleep. Otherwise, one of these days, I am going to face-plant right on stage, in front of twenty thousand people.

That would certainly mark the end of my touring days. And probably the day I become an internet meme.

As soon as I step out of my room, I hear an echo. The door next to me closes almost simultaneously, and I glance over to see Zara standing at the door down the hall.

Fucking. Hell.

She's wearing a short miniskirt and a black low-cut tank top. The skirt sparkles with gold sequins that make her olive skin glow. Her hair falls in loose waves around her face, and she's wearing that same dark red lipstick she wore that night we hooked up.

The day after, I wore her lipstick like a fucking brand.

God, I never wanted to wash it off.

She must feel my gaze on her because she looks up and then does a double-take, clearing her throat. "Hey," she says, a bit startled. "I didn't realize we were neighbors."

"Neither did I." And now that I do, I'm probably not going to sleep a damn wink knowing she's just on the other side of this thin wall.

"You, um, look nice." She gestures to me awkwardly. When did things start being weird between us?

*Maybe after she pulled you into her clinic and helped you get through your shit so you could perform, and rather than thank her like a normal person, you awkwardly avoided her out of embarrassment.*

Right. After that, then.

"You look...more than nice," I say, and feel instantly rewarded when I see a shy smile spread across her face as we walk down the hallway. "I didn't realize you were going to this thing tonight. Were you also forced into it as well?"

"Not forced, no," she answers. When we step up to the elevator, we both reach out at the same time to press the down button. Our hands brush together, and I feel her inhale a quick breath of air before retracting her hand to her side. "Elena suggested I go. I haven't really done much since we left LA."

"Why?"

The doors open, and we both step in, each taking a side so we can face one another. The mirrored walls allow me a three hundred and sixty-degree view of her in that short-ass miniskirt. It's actual torture. Why are there always mirrors? Do they want people to fuck in here?

"I've never really traveled," she explains with a touch of embarrassment in her tone. "My family didn't really have the money for it. Both of my parents are teachers, and finances were always just tight. They took us on small trips all over the state, but that is pretty much the extent of my travel experience."

"You and—" I can't even say the dipshit's name, and she must notice as an amused smile tugs at the corner of her red lips.

"No." She shakes her head. "We went on a short trip to Hawaii for our honeymoon, but I was still in my final year of residency. I stayed on an extra year to specialize in emergency medicine, and then we had our practice to build. Besides, everywhere I wanted to go, he'd already been. So..."

"I've been to a ton of places. Doesn't mean I don't want to go back and share those places with the people I love."

She presses her lips together and gives me a sad smile. "I'm starting to wonder if our marriage was just some sort of weird social experiment for Tanner. Like he'd already been everywhere and tried everything, and nothing was giving him joy, so he thought, 'Well, maybe I'll try being a normal bloke for a while.' Only that turned out to be just as boring as everything else."

I grin. "Did you just say bloke?"

She shrugs. "You hang around a bunch of English guys long enough..."

"A bunch? I only know of two, Darius and Ridge. And Ridge has been living in the States so long that he barely counts. On an unrelated note, if you really want to piss off Asher, ask him what part of England he's from?"

She tips her head back, and the laugh that follows makes me feel like I've won the damn lottery. After the initial awkwardness, I wasn't sure I'd hear it again.

We exit the elevator and head toward the lobby, where PR Misty waits to stuff us into sleek black sedans and whisk us away.

Her eyes perk up! "Perfect! I was looking for you two." She motions for us to follow her, walking at a pace that can only be described as brisk and stepping out into the sweet Tennessee spring air.

We barely cross the threshold before the cameras begin to flash.

Shit, I forgot about the press.

Typically, when we enter and exit hotels, we use a VIP entrance in the back to avoid paparazzi and the Manic Fanatics who camp out, hoping to catch a glimpse of us. However, in this case, the PR team wants us to be seen.

Something about keeping the wolves happy or at bay or whatever.

Knowing this doesn't stop me from pulling Zara tightly against my side as we walk to the car, allowing me to shield her from the frenzy.

I don't miss the barrage of questions thrown my way, though.

*Hendrix, will you be taking over for Evans permanently?*

*Is this your girlfriend?*

*Do you feel you got your spot on this tour because of your family's connection to the band?*

That last one makes my hackles rise, my fist clench,

but I do as my PR training instructed and ignore them all, helping Zara into the town car as I quickly follow.

It takes me a moment to adjust and release the breath I've been holding. However, as soon as I do, I hear Darius's posh British accent say, "Hey, Doc! I saved you a seat. You ready to party?"

*Just fucking great.*

## Chapter Fourteen

# ZARA

I can't remember the last time I went to a nightclub. I think it was in college, maybe, when Violet visited and convinced me to go because she wanted to try out her new fake ID.

Regardless of how long it's been, I know with crystal clarity that I've never been to a place like this. Stepping into this club feels like entering an alternate dimension. And that says a lot considering all the bougie shit I've encountered this week.

Velvet is nestled in one of Nashville's trendiest neighborhoods. After we are dropped off in the back alley, we're escorted through an inconspicuous door manned by a burly-looking bouncer.

Although this club is ultra-exclusive, we are still led upstairs to an even more exclusive private VIP area. It is dripping with opulence and adorned with velvet curtains and plush leather sofas. There is even blackout glass to gaze down at the main floor.

I feel like a voyeur standing here watching everyone below.

"You look lonely over here." I startle at the sound of Darius walking toward me. He hands me a glass of champagne and joins me, gazing out over the crowd. The lights glow as the people below move to the beat.

It's hypnotic.

"Not bored," I tell him. "Just surprised, I guess."

"Oh?" He's a little more relaxed now than he was during all the times I've been around him before. It's like he's dropped some superfluous wall he keeps up around everyone else. And right now, he's giving me a glimpse of the real Darius.

I kind of like it.

"Well, I guess I thought if I were ever at a private club with a bunch of rock stars—"

He smirks. "We'd be drowning in pussy and knee-deep in coke?"

I laugh, nearly choking on my champagne. "Something like that."

"We used to be like that. Well, minus the coke. None of us has ever been into the hard stuff—except Mitch. But he was into a lot of stupid shit that eventually caught up to him."

I can tell that his former bandmate is a sore subject, so I decide to sidestep it altogether.

"So this is what you do now? Just hide up here and... talk?"

He must see me looking at the crowd because a mischievous grin spreads across his face. "Are you bored, Doc?"

"No! I—"

"Is this night of frivolity not up to your standards?" A rueful smile spreads across his face, and I realize he's teasing me.

"I guess I just thought there would be more..." I huff out in frustration. "Dancing."

"Oh, so you want to dance?"

I bite my bottom lip before finally relenting. "Sort of. It's been a while since I've had the opportunity. But I don't exactly want to go alone, and there is absolutely no one who can go with me who won't be mauled by half those girls—"

"I'll do it." He shrugs.

"What?"

"Even with all the social media I do, I rarely get recognized. Perks of being the drummer. Always in the background," he explains. "And it's so dark, I doubt anyone would notice me, anyway."

"Are you sure?"

"Hell yeah." He sets down his drink on a nearby table and holds out his hand, and that's when I see him. Hendrix stands not too far away, talking to Zander but glaring at me. "Come on, Doc. Let's go have some fun."

For some reason, as I look away from Hendrix and take Darius's hand, I suddenly feel a twinge of guilt, which is crazy.

We agreed to keep this professional, right?

So why do I feel his eyes on me the whole way to the door?

About halfway down the stairs, I have a slight moment of panic.

I did not think this through.

Do I want to dance? Yes.

The way the music is pulsing and the lights are flashing, how could I not? I just didn't think about the fact that I would be dancing with Darius.

Up close and personal. With his body...so close to mine.

He pulls us into the throng of people, and true to his word, no one seems to give a fuck. No one tries to rip his clothes off or beg him to sign their boobs. They just carry on, completely swept up in the beat.

When we're somewhere near the middle, he stops, and I don't even have time to be nervous. This man's confidence leaves no room for it. He pulls me close, his hands snake around my hips, and then we're dancing, just like that.

I learn fairly quickly that Darius is a damn good dancer. He's the perfect blend of playful and sexy that I need to feel comfortable. That is, until he flips me around and pulls me flush against his chest, and suddenly everything gets way more intimate.

My heart hammers in my chest as he grinds his hips against me and leans down to whisper in my ear. "Do you think he's watching?"

I tense in his arms. "What? Who?"

I feel his deep chuckle vibrating against me. "Come off it, Doc. I know you and Hendrix have something going on. Bloke practically bit my head off when I mentioned you after tonight's show."

"He did?" My heart starts racing as I tilt my head to the side to see him grinning down at me.

"He did."

I don't know how to handle that information, or the

fact that Darius is out here on the dance floor practically flaunting me in front of him.

I glare up at him. "So...you want to make him jealous because he embarrassed you?"

"No." His eyes gleam with amusement. "No. I'm solid. A bandmate tells me to back off, and I listen. We don't fight over women. Besides, I wasn't looking for anything serious. Just a bit of fun."

"Okay..."

"But he doesn't know that." He lets that sink in momentarily as he runs his hands all over my body. It feels good. It really does.

But it doesn't feel right.

*He* doesn't feel right.

"So I'll ask the question again," he says as my eyes venture up to the blackened glass. "Do you want to make him jealous?"

I swallow the nervous thrill that runs down my spine. God, it's so wrong. We said we wouldn't do this, that we'd keep things professional. But then I remember the way he looked at me when I stepped out of my room. There's no denying it. He still wants me.

And I've never stopped wanting him.

"Yes."

"Excellent. And you'll protect me when he comes down here swinging for me?" He turns me back around so I'm facing him, but we're still just as close.

"Sure."

"A little more enthusiasm would be appreciated, Doc. I'm your wingman after all."

"I don't think wingmen are supposed to get boners when they're on the job."

He laughs, dipping his head into the curve of my

shoulder. "Can't be helped, love. I'd have to be dead to not get hard when dancing with a beautiful woman like you."

"That was a compliment, I think."

"Oh, it was definitely a compliment. Which is why I must be an absolute arse for passing you up."

"You make it sound like I already said yes. How do you know I'd ever be interested?" I raise an eyebrow in challenge.

"Oh, you'd be interested," he says confidently. "I'm not even trying right now, love. If I did, you wouldn't be able to resist. And you'd be thanking me for it by morning. One hundred percent satisfaction guarantee."

I roll my eyes. "One hundred percent, huh?"

"No complaints so far." He shrugs before his gaze cuts just over my shoulder. "Oh, here we go. He's coming down the steps. You ready?" My stomach drops to my feet, but I nod. "Okay, brilliant. I'm off to the bar."

"What?" I grab him before he can pull away. "What do you mean you're off to the bar?"

"Doc, he looks like he's ready to rip out my spleen and shove it down my throat, and as much as I love you, I'd rather you be the recipient of all that rage—if you know what I mean." He winks.

It takes me a minute to catch his meaning, but a flood of heat creeps up my neck when I do. He laughs. "You're welcome!" he says over his shoulder as he walks away, and I'm left standing in the middle of the dance floor by myself.

All by myself.

Shit. What do I do now?

Do I stand here and wait?

No. I should dance, right?

I look back at the stairs to see if I can spot Hendrix, but he's no longer visible. I've never really danced solo. But I guess this is as good a time as any?

Before I can gather the courage, I feel someone's arms wrap around me from behind and pull me close against their body. For a split second, I think it has to be Hendrix, but then I look down and the hands aren't right. The tiny knuckle tattoos and silver rings he usually wears are absent, and the cuffs of his shirt are blue instead of black.

Oh my god, I'm being groped by a random, pervy stranger.

I freeze and then try to pull away. But this seems to embolden the guy. That, or he's not paying enough attention to care.

Either way, he doesn't stop, and I feel trapped.

Everything starts to blur. The music suddenly feels too loud. The lights are too bright and...

"Hey! Get your fucking hands off her!"

I turn just as Hendrix rips the guy off me. The second his hands are no longer on me, I bolt and feel like I can breathe again.

"What the hell is your problem, man? We were having a good time!" The guy is trashed. His words are slurred, and his eyes are glassy. The people around us start to notice the commotion.

I take another step toward Hendrix.

"Yeah? Does she look like someone who was having a good time?" He gestures to me as the guy's gaze follows. "Did you even ask before you put your hands all over her?"

Drunk Guy doesn't have an answer for that.

"Leave." Hendrix doesn't even spare him another glance, but the lethal edge to his voice has the guy running off into the crowd faster than I can blink. The attention we've attracted seems to disappear just as quickly as people begin to focus back on the music and the people around them. "Are you okay?"

He's tentative, and his words are gentle, as if he doesn't know whether he should touch me. I just nod. He opens his mouth like he's going to ask another question, but decides against it. It's kind of hard to hold a conversation with the distance between us, which is probably why he holds out his hand and says, "Come with me."

He takes my hand, and we weave through the dance floor. I assume he's taking us back upstairs, but instead, we head in the opposite direction toward a curtained entrance where a bear of a man in a suit stands.

"Good evening, Mr. Creed." *He knows his name?* "Just the two of you?"

Hendrix just nods.

"Right this way."

I have no idea what's going on. But I blindly follow anyway.

The big guy escorts us down a hallway. The lighting is dim, but there are expensive-looking chandeliers and artwork that likely cost more than my car. More velvet curtains adorn the space. Some are closed while others remain open, which provides my first clue about where he's taken me.

It's another VIP lounge. Only this one is far more intimate.

Instead of expanding the entire top floor, these spaces have been sectioned off into small rooms with walls separating them. They're big enough to fit three or four people, maybe?

Or perhaps just two.

There are maybe eight in total, four on each side, and I can't figure out why we keep passing empty rooms until we reach the end of the hallway. But then it dawns on me. The way he addressed Hendrix by name. The guys are being treated like royalty tonight, and he's making sure we're giving as much privacy as possible from the other guests.

My cheeks flame. What does he think we're going to do in here?

Oh my god. Is that what these are for? Little pleasure dens for the club's guests to use for a quick fuck?

Hendrix and I enter the small space. In the middle is a sleek black marble table, surrounded by supple leather club chairs and a stylish sofa.

"There is champagne chilling just over there." The man gestures to one side of the sofa, where an ornate silver champagne bucket, complete with its own pedestal, is located. "But if you need anything else, there is a call button on the small table beside the sofa. Otherwise, you will be undisturbed."

He quietly exits. The curtain draws shut and then... we are alone.

I can still hear the deep, pulsing rhythm of the club music, but in here, it's muted. It seems to be at just the right volume to allow conversation while also providing a blanket of privacy from those around us.

We both find our way to the sofa, and I look up to find Hendrix staring at me.

"Do you want any champagne?" he asks. "Or I can call back Lurch and get you something else."

I snort out a laugh. "Did you just call him Lurch? Like from the Addams Family?"

"He's certainly built like him, and seriously, what was

that guy's last job? Guard at Buckingham Palace? He didn't crack a single smile."

"Well, can you blame him? Look at what he does all night. Waiting on a bunch of entitled assholes while they do all sorts of kinky things in these little sin bins, and he stands out there keeping watch. I'd be a sourpuss too."

Hendrix blanches a little. "You don't think that's why I brought you here, do you? I mean, that is what most people do. You're right. But I just wanted to get you off that dance floor and away from—" His breath shudders.

"No, I didn't think that." I did, sort of. "And you're right. I did need a breather after—" My voice trails off.

"What happened?" he asks. "Where did Darius go? Did he ditch you?"

Now, this part will be difficult to explain. I chew on my bottom lip, trying to find the right words. "Not exactly, no."

"What exactly does that mean? Because one minute he was all over you—" He stops mid-sentence, as if he can barely stomach the words coming out of his mouth. "And the next, he's over by the bar surrounded by a bunch of women."

"When did you—"

"Just before we walked off the dance floor, I looked over and there he was, completely oblivious to what had just happened to you."

"It's not his fault," I explain, quickly continuing before he can argue. "He saw you at the top of the stairs. He knew you were coming."

"So he did ditch you, then?"

"No." I let out a sigh. I am not explaining this well. Mostly because I don't want to explain it at all. I was sort of hoping there would be no words involved. Just some dirty dancing that might lead to perhaps something even dirtier in a dark corner or an empty supply closet. That happens outside of romance novels, right? "He was trying to make you jealous. For me."

"For...you?"

I give a slow nod as he stares at me intently. "I wanted to make you jealous."

"Why?"

I throw up my hands. "I don't know," I tell him. "Nothing I do when I'm around you makes any sense. Do you know how many one-night stands I've had? One. The occasional fuck buddy in college, sure. But I've never been spontaneous enough to throw caution to the wind like that. And now here I am in a swanky nightclub while touring the country with a—"

He silences me with a kiss.

I gasp in surprise at the feel of his lips on mine, but before I have a chance to react, he's pulling back. "Is this okay? I should have asked first."

"Yes!" I grip the front of his shirt and yank him closer. "God, yes."

He lets out a brief chuckle just before his mouth slams against mine, and shit. I forgot what it's like to kiss Hendrick Creed. Some men see kissing as a stepping stone to the main event. But not him. Not Hendrix. For him, kissing is a full-body experience. And you had better be ready because this man likes to take his time.

He kisses me until my lips feel swollen. Until I'm breathless and my heart is pounding wildly in my chest. He kisses me like I'm his last dying wish, and when he leaves this world, all he wants is the taste of my lips on his.

One hand grips the back of my neck, while the other

curves around my waist, pulling me onto his lap. My sequin skirt rides all the way up. Never breaking our kiss, he starts to explore my body. He drags the tips of his fingers over my thighs and then slips them under my skirt to cup my ass. He stills.

Slightly breathless, he asks, "Are you not wearing any underwear?"

"Lace thong."

I feel his fingers find the edge of the delicate lace, and I watch his eyes darken. "I want to rip these off you and stuff them in my pocket as a souvenir."

"And then what?"

The hand that was around my neck settles around my waist, while the other starts to wander from my backside, over my hip, and toward...

I suck in a breath.

His thumb grazes the center of my thighs. It's barely a whisper of a touch over the now soaking wet lace of my thong, and I'm already trembling in anticipation.

"And then—" My phone starts ringing in my purse.

*Are you seriously fucking kidding me right now?*

I'm staring at him. He's staring at me.

His hand is still *right there*.

I swallow nervously. "I..." Fuck, this is all suddenly so very awkward. "It might be an emergency."

He double-blinks as the lust haze begins to lift. He's looking at me like he just remembered all the reasons why he didn't want to start this up again.

Yup, reality is a cold-hearted bitch. "Right. Shit."

It gets even more awkward as I try to shift myself off him, avoiding his very obvious and large erection.

This better not be a telemarketer.

I quickly dig through my purse, pull out my phone,

and look at the caller ID. Shit. Definitely not a tele-marketer.

"Elena?" I don't even bother saying hello. I see the look of concern on Hendrix's face. "What's up?"

"It's Marisa. Can you meet me at the side entrance? There is a car waiting. We need to head back."

"I'm on my way."

Duty calls.

*Chapter Fifteen*

# HENDRIX

It's Saturday morning, and we are now in New Orleans. I'm sitting at a table all by myself—breakfast forgotten—in the private dining room the hotel has set up for us. And I'm staring at the entrance like a fucking stalker.

It's been over twenty-four hours since that night at the club. Twenty-four hours since we kissed, and I had my hands wrapped around...

"Okay, man?"

I blink once, twice, and finally look up to see Zander standing in front of me, wearing a shit-eating grin. "What?"

"I said, Are you okay, brother? You're staring at that door like I used to stare at that Playboy I stole from Macon's room when I was fifteen."

I chuckle, shaking my head. "Boy Scout Macon used to jerk it to Playboy?"

"Even Macon was a teenager once. And he was never a Boy Scout. You have to have parents who give a shit to take you to stuff like that." He plops down in the chair next to mine with a giant cup of steaming black coffee in his hands.

"Seriously, add some half and half or something to that. You're creeping people out."

"Quit changing the subject," he says, rolling his eyes. He leans back in the chair, stretching his long legs in front of him. Like everyone else, Z is dressed down for the weekend in a pair of black joggers and a hoodie with a North Carolina surf shop logo on the front. "What's up with you and Zara? Elena won't tell me anything. Some bullshit about the girl code. And here I thought marriage vows trumped all, but what do I know?"

I ignore everything else he said. "She's talked to Elena?"

His mouth quirks. "Yeah. She's been glued to our kid since we left the club on Thursday night. Made sure she made the flight okay yesterday and has barely left our hotel room since."

"I thought you said it was just an ear infection." He had texted me and the rest of the guys that night to inform us that Marisa was okay. Z's little family had become an important part of Manic, and it showed, especially when its littlest member was down for the count.

Everyone was worried.

"It was—is—but it took a while for her fever to go down, and we were worried to take her on the plane. Zara has been a godsend. Is there such a thing as a live-in doctor? Because I would seriously consider it to save my wife's sanity. She gets so stressed when Marisa is sick."

"Is she doing better now?"

"She's starting to. The antibiotics Zara gave her just started to kick in, and her fever is down, thank fuck, but we're gonna stay in today and let her rest. I just came down here because I needed to walk."

"Yeah, you're like a dog. You need fresh air and exercise at least once a day."

"Twice if I'm good." He laughs and then takes a sip of his coffee. A silence settles between us before he turns to me and says, "Before I say what I'm about to say, just know I love you, man. But things have changed, and Elena and Marisa are now my whole world, so...if you fuck up things with Zara and send her packing, at least one of them will be really upset. And then I'll be upset, and—"

I hold up my hand. "I get it, Z. Don't fuck the doctor. Again."

"No, man," he argues. "That's not what I'm trying to say."

I scoff. "Then what was that whole 'I'll kick your ass' speech about?"

"First of all, I didn't say I would kick your ass. No violence was threatened. Second, I was just trying to tell you to tread carefully. I am gathering that this thing between you two is more than just one night."

I glare at him.

His grin is so wide, he could practically be a cartoon character. He's enjoying this way too much. "And while this may be new territory for you, it doesn't mean you don't know what to do—"

"That's exactly what it means. I literally don't know how to..." I don't even know what to call it. Date? I haven't dated anyone since high school, and that was mostly out of necessity to fit in. Since then, I've never really met anyone that I found even remotely interesting enough to put forth the effort.

Until I met a shy tutor during my senior year in college.

But I walked away then.

Would I walk away now?

"What do I do?" I finally say.

Zander makes a big show of setting down his coffee mug. He then weaves his fingers together and pretends to crack them all, like some supervillain in a children's novel. "Listen closely, and let me teach you the ways, young padawan."

He's bringing out the Star Wars references?

Dear god, what have I done?

Two hours later, I'm standing in front of Zara's hotel room, trying to gather the courage to knock on her door.

Fuck, this woman turns me inside out.

I still remember walking into my first tutoring session, and all the confidence I thought I had for impressing girls instantly vanished the second I saw her. It was like I reverted back to middle school, and the mere sight of a girl made me sweat.

And when I saw her in Edwin's hallway, I knew nothing had changed.

Whatever good intentions Zander had, his quick and dirty guide to dating only seemed to make me more of a wreck.

Because now I knew all the ways I could fail.

And apparently, there are many.

What is it about someone that makes them stand out?

Among the billion other people on the planet, what is it that makes you turn your head and think, yes...*that's the one*?

I am not a player. Or at least by my definition, I'm not. Since I lost my virginity to Sara Silva in the back of my Land Rover in eleventh grade, I've been with a decent number of women. However, I'm not the kind of person who spends every night trolling apps for someone new. I enjoy spontaneity, and I've never had issues finding a willing partner when I desire it.

I've just never wanted anything beyond a night or two.

Until her.

I continue to stare at the door. If I don't do something soon, like fucking knock on it, someone is gonna walk down the hall and see me standing here. And since this whole floor is nothing but VIP suites for the band, their assistants, and Ridge, I'm bound to get hell for it.

I sigh. This is usually around the time when I would call myself out for being a pussy, but my sisters told me I'm not allowed to use that word when referencing anything weak, because, in their words, *the pussy is powerful.*

They're not wrong.

The way Zara's pussy strangled my cock when she came all over it...

My hand flies up to the door, and suddenly I'm knocking.

Mission accomplished.

I guess I just needed to find the right kind of motivation.

A few seconds later, I hear footsteps and then a lock

turns. The door opens just enough for me to see her face. I awkwardly wave. "Hi."

A warm smile spreads across her face as she pushes the door wider. "Hi." She's dressed casually today as well, in jean shorts and a gray V-neck T-shirt. Her hair is pulled back in a long braid over her shoulder.

Fuck, she's gorgeous.

When I'm checking her out, I happen to notice the computer, paperback, and plush throw she has laid across her neatly made bed. She has the same stunning view of the river as I do, but I'm beginning to wonder if that's all she's seen of this beautiful city.

"Are you planning on staying in all day?" I ask, gesturing to the introvert's starter pack she's got going on over there. God, there are even snacks.

She glances back, revealing a hint of embarrassment. "I...Well, I mean..." She doesn't finish. She doesn't have to. I already know what she was going to say.

She didn't want to go alone.

Well, I guess it's a good thing I'm here, then.

"Grab your purse," I tell her, before waving a hand toward the bed. "This is all just too depressing. I'm taking you out."

"You don't have to." She begins to argue. "I don't want to ruin your plans."

"Cupid, you *are* my plans. Why do you think I'm here?" She stares at me as if she can't decide whether to kiss me or cry. Not wanting to risk tears, I forge ahead. "Now, get a move on! We have lots to see."

## Chapter Sixteen

# HENDRIX

We start just outside the hotel where we are staying at the Four Seasons, which is situated along the Mississippi River. It's a typical day in May for New Orleans, hot and humid, but thankfully not unbearable, and a slight breeze helps cool everything down.

Or at least it should.

But walking next to Zara seems to raise the temperature at least ten degrees. Because the heat between us is off the charts. Every time her hand brushes against mine, I feel my pulse spike. I want to hold her hand, but I don't know if that's weird or even if we're there yet.

Zander, my self-proclaimed dating guide, said physical touch is important, especially outside of the bedroom. It creates intimacy and trust.

Big words coming from a guy whose whole relationship was based on a lie. Zander met Elena right after he signed an NDA with Manic. He was required to keep it quiet until the band decided to make the announcement. For the first few weeks of their courtship, she had no idea she was falling for an up-and-coming rock star.

As we make our way to the French Quarter, we grab iced coffee and chai from a street vendor and pass by a musician playing jazz on the street. I drop a twenty in his case. On the next block, there's a guitarist.

Another twenty goes in his case.

By the fourth block, I've dropped nearly a hundred dollars, and I'm happy to do it. There is some incredible talent on these streets. But the world seems to go on around them, barely stopping for a moment or two before wandering off again. This kind of art should be treasured. Appreciated. Preserved.

Zara has been quiet for most of this time, but she finally turns to me. "You really love music, don't you?"

"Yeah, I really fucking do."

A church bell rings in the distance as a streetcar passes. "Have you always wanted to be a musician?"

"Not always, no," I answer, taking a sip of my coffee. "At one point, I was like any other kid and wanted to be an astronaut or a fireman. But that Creed DNA eventually kicked in, and I found my way to the bass."

"So is everyone in your family musically inclined?"

A large tour group is headed our way, and I grab Zara's hand and pull her close. "No. Well, yes."

"Which one is it?" She laughs.

"It's both, I guess you could say. We all have the ability, but not all make use of it. My older brother, Cash, for example. He's an incredible pianist, but you'll rarely see him play."

"Why?" she asks, not seeming to mind that I haven't let go of her hand. I keep it there. It's nice.

"I don't know, honestly. He once told my mom he fell out of it because he was simply too busy. He's got a demanding job, and being a single dad..."

"But you don't think that's the reason."

I shrug. "Seems like an excuse. If you really love something, you find the time. You *make* the time."

Her expression falters, and I know, without asking, that my words have somehow affected her. It's like watching the light in a room dim. I hate knowing I made her sad. But what I hate even more is the asshole who gave her a reason to be sad.

*Fucking Tanner.*

She hasn't mentioned him much, and I wonder how he's taken to the news that she is going on tour with someone he despises.

*I round the corner into the kitchen but stop short when I hear a familiar laugh.*

*Fucking Tanner Price.*

*Last time he was here, I had to listen to him brag about how he fucked another one of his TAs. When I told Edwin I didn't want him over here again, he said, "He's my friend, Hendrix. We go way back. I can't just cut ties with him. Our parents hang out."*

*That was several months ago, so I was sort of hoping he'd reconsidered my request and kicked the guy to the curb.*

*Guess not.*

*"Why do you even put up with him, Edwin?" Tanner says in that condescending tone I can't stand.*

*"What do you mean?"*

*"You could be living with us in the house my parents*

*bought, but instead you're slumming it with Hendrix Creed?"*

*"I'm not slumming it," he snaps. And just when I think he's gonna defend me, he says, "My parents bought me this house. It's twice as nice as yours."*

*"And you choose to share it with him? He shouldn't even be allowed to shine your damn shoes, let alone share a kitchen with you."*

*Damn. You're hurting my feelings. I roll my eyes and walk away. I don't need to hear what else Tanner Price thinks about me. Edwin and I have plans. Big plans, and nothing he says is going to get in the way of that.*

*We're going places, and in a few years, I won't even remember his name.*

*Can't say the same for him.*

Neither of us has forgotten the other's name. I sneak a glance at Zara.

Definitely not for the reasons I expected, though.

"What about you?" I ask, trying to change the subject and lighten the mood. "Did you always know you wanted to be a doctor?"

"I think I always knew I wanted to do something in STEM," she replies, her voice already sounding lighter. We pass a magic shop with a sign that boasts the best tarot readings in the city. I've seen the same declaration three times in five blocks. "But it wasn't until I was in high school and I saw this guy collapse in the middle of the mall that I knew I wanted to be a doctor."

"Does every doctor have an origin story like this?"

She laughs. "Some, yeah. Others...others just want the prestige." My guess is Tanner falls into that category.

"So was the guy okay?" I ask, tugging on her hand so we can turn the corner. So far, we have been just sort of strolling down Bourbon Street, too busy talking to really stop anywhere. But I have a destination in mind that I think she'll like.

"Well, that's the whole thing. He wasn't okay. God, it's been two decades, and I can still remember exactly how my heart felt when I saw him fall. It was like a tree crashing in the middle of a forest or like that game you play where you have to close your eyes, fall back, and hope someone catches you."

"A trust fall?"

"Yeah, exactly. It was super crowded that day cause of the holidays, which was a blessing. He fell into a startled group of shoppers, and they broke his fall. Anyway, it was the first time outside of a TV show I had heard the words 'Is anyone a doctor?' And then this woman shouted, 'Here!' The crowd split, and she ran and kneeled at his side."

"And little Zara was hooked."

"Yup, and it wasn't even about the heroism or the honor of it. I just kept picturing that man collapsing and thinking, what if that had been my dad or my mom...or someone else I loved? And I just knew I wanted to be the one who could raise my hand in a crowd and know what to do."

I keep walking, but I feel like I've just been kicked in the chest.

This woman is too good for me.

Here she is explaining how she became a doctor

because she couldn't stand the idea of not knowing how to care for and save her loved ones. And my current life goal is to what? Get my chance in the limelight so I can finally one-up Edwin? Prove to the world I'm more than my last name?

"Oh! Is that an art gallery?" she asks, pointing to a building a bit further down the street. I hadn't even realized we had reached Royal Street.

"Yeah," I nod. "Actually, that's where I wanted to take you. There are a bunch on this street."

"Really?"

She's beaming up at me, and damn, if that isn't the best feeling in the world—like sunshine or playing a brand-new bass for the first time. It feels like...something I can't quite define yet. "Yeah, I remember you loved art back in college, so I thought I'd take a chance that you still did."

"I can't believe you remember that."

I remember a lot of things.

I remember how she used to doodle on her notepads during our tutoring sessions. I recall the day when I finally asked her about it and saw her face turn red. I'd never seen her embarrassed about anything before. When she finally showed me the doodles, she admitted she loved art but was a terrible artist. I, in turn, told her I loved to sing even though I couldn't carry a single note.

She drags me down the street, and for the next two hours, with a break in the middle for lunch, we explore every art gallery we can find. I don't think I realized how different each one would be. Neither did she, judging by the way her eyes widened when we entered the one with the neon-colored modern art, complete with matching frames.

It was so damn bright in there. They should consider giving sunglasses at the door.

Every gallery we go to, I feel like I am learning something new about Zara. She loves watercolors and black-and-white photography the most. She will stand in front of a candid photo of an old man playing chess and say something insightful, like, "What do you think his life was like?" and suddenly I will find myself staring at him, wondering the same damn thing.

She is so curious. It's infectious.

Everything about her draws me in, and there are whole chunks of time that pass where I simply watch her move from one canvas to the next, soaking up every detail.

As if she were a priceless piece of art.

Because that's what she's starting to feel like.

*Priceless.*

"You ready?" she asks as we step out of a small photography studio. She actually bought a few prints to put up in her new room when we get back to LA. I remember her apologizing for the lack of furniture and the bare walls. At the time, I just assumed she hadn't moved everything over yet.

I didn't realize that was all she had after the divorce.

"Here." I hold out my hand. "Let me take your bag."

"Oh, you don't have to," she protests and then motions to my right hand. "I saw you rubbing your wrist when we were in there. Is it sore?"

I shake my head. "No. Well, a little. I've been practicing a lot at night. That, combined with performing, it's a lot. My hands haven't seen this much action in years." And then I grin. "Well, except for maybe for this one night about a month ago…"

Her cheeks flame red. "Oh my god, I can't believe you just said that! And on a public street!"

I chuckle and take her bag. This time, she doesn't argue. "Cupid, this is the French Quarter. I doubt there isn't much these streets haven't seen or heard."

We turn a corner and change directions. She doesn't ask why, and I cherish that bit of trust she's given me. We meander down a couple more blocks, and I drop a few more bills for some amazing performers, prompting Zara to tug on my wallet and say, "How many do you have in there?"

I laugh, and I realize that if I had to count how many times I've laughed today, I would have lost track.

We finally make it to our destination, and as soon as that green and white awning is in our sightline, her eyes light up.

"Really?"

I shrug, trying to play it cool. "You can't come to New Orleans without stopping here."

"Oh my god, I am going to eat my weight in beignets."

"Don't forget the coffee. I know you're not a huge fan of it, but I hope you'll make an exception this one time."

"How do you know that?"

"You ordered a chai this morning."

"Oh, right." She nods, like it's the most obvious answer in the world.

"And I might have stalked you a little during breakfast this last week," I add. "Does your doctor know about your croissant addiction?"

She laughs, then rolls her eyes. "Just wait until you see me devour a beignet."

Ten minutes later, we're seated at a table inside—I love air conditioning—and have just placed our order.

Because it's still early in the season, Café du Monde is busy but not swamped.

"Thank you for taking me out today," she says. "I thought I was okay spending the weekend in my room, but this was really special."

"You're welcome," I reply. "But you should know I didn't do this as some sort of favor. I wanted to spend the day with you. In fact, you should probably think a little less of me that I considered faking a cold just to have an excuse to come see you in the clinic."

She laughs. "I'll lower my opinion accordingly."

"As you should."

Her next question seems somewhat hesitant. "Can I ask you why?"

"Why what?"

"Why do you want to spend time with me?" She glances up at me hesitantly. "Is this just two friends catching up or—"

"I don't generally feel up my friends in a VIP lounge, Cupid."

Her cheeks flush, and it has nothing to do with the heat outside. It feels like a win because it's a physical confirmation that the other night affected her just as much as it did me.

If that call from Elena hadn't interrupted us, how far would we have gone?

Would she have let me fuck her right there in that club? Let me spread her wide and bury my head between those lush thighs. Let me worship her until she was screaming my name so loud the whole club could hear. Those thoughts alone have been driving me crazy ever since.

"Then what are we doing here, Hen?" she presses. It's

the first time she's called me that, and the familiarity of it feels nice. Intimate.

"I don't know," I answer honestly.

"You said you didn't want any distractions," she reminds me, uncrossing her legs so she can lean forward. We're now eye level with each other. "You said we should keep it professional."

I swallow, and my throat feels suddenly dry. I knew we would have to talk about this. I just didn't expect it to be so soon. But then again, this is Zara, and she doesn't like riddles or questions without answers. She likes to have all the cards on the table, preferably in a nice, neat row.

It's what made her such a good tutor.

"I don't know how to be professional with you, Zara," I confess. "I didn't back then when we were in college, and I certainly don't now. What I said to you in your office is still true. I need to stay focused." She opens her mouth to offer some sort of protest, but I press on. "But it's become crystal clear to me that when I'm around you, I'm distracted regardless of whether we're keeping things professional or not."

"So?" She doesn't finish her sentence, but I can practically hear the question mark dangling at the end.

"So I'd rather be distracted with you in my bed than distracted and worrying about who might be trying to get in yours. 'Cause seeing you on that dance floor with Darius is not something I want to repeat."

"Darius isn't interested in me," she tries to tell me. I give her an unconvinced look, arching an eyebrow, and she laughs. "Okay, he's not interested in me anymore. And you're missing the point entirely, anyway."

"And what's that?"

"*I'm* not interested in Darius," she says, tilting her head to give me a rueful smile. "Or anyone else."

I cover my heart and, feigning pain, I say, "Ouch, Cupid. That hurts. I just bared my heart and soul to you."

She rolls her eyes and laughs. "You did not. Saying you want to sleep with me again is not a declaration of love."

"Oh shit. My bad." My grin widens. "Did I not make myself clear? I'm not asking for an encore. No, I want season tickets. This"—I motioned between us—"is happening a lot."

Her expression sobers slightly. "I don't know if I'm ready for anything serious. My divorce just happened, and..." She stalls, and I'm terrified her next words might be that she's not over him.

"We don't have to put a label on it," I say, not giving her a chance to continue. "Let's just keep things casual for now. We're on tour. If this isn't the time to have a little fun, I don't know what is."

She looks hesitant, but I can see her coming around. "When you say casual, does that mean—"

"It definitely means exclusive. No more dancing with Darius or any of these other idiots."

She gives me a shy grin. "Okay."

"Okay?"

"However," she says, looking over my shoulder just as our server arrives with a large platter of beignets and our two coffees. She glances at the powdered sugar confections, and a mischievous grin spreads across her lips. "You may change your mind once you see me demolish one of these in public."

Without a second thought, I reach down and shove nearly half of a beignet in my mouth. Powdered sugar goes everywhere—my mouth, my beard. A cloud of it settles on my shirt and the table below. Zara's eyes go wide, and she bursts out laughing. Her hand flies to her mouth, but it's too late. People look over and grin at us. She whips out her phone and snaps a picture of me looking like a stuffed ghost. Finally, after I chew, I manage to say, "Your turn, Cupid. Do your fucking worse."

## Chapter Seventeen

# ZARA

*I am so damn nervous.*

*I don't remember being this nervous on my first day of med school or the morning of my wedding. But put me in an empty apartment with my college crush, and I'm nearing critical meltdown status.*

*I can't believe I invited him over. I can't believe he said yes.*

*I should have asked my sister for more advice.*

*Like, where does she keep her stash of condoms? Or what if he wants to do kinky stuff? Should that be discussed ahead of time? What even is kinky stuff?*

*My sex life hasn't exactly been wild in recent years.*

*Okay, ever. My sex life has never been wild.*

*In fact, there was a time during my marriage when I seriously debated whether there was something wrong with me. Tanner and I never seemed to work together, and I was aware of his reputation. He had plenty of other satisfied women out there, so if it wasn't good with me, it had to be my fault, right?*

*At some point, we just sort of gave up.*

*Oh god, what if Hendrix thinks I'm bad at it too?*

*My eyes dart over to him as I root around in a kitchen drawer for a bottle opener for the wine. Wine that I don't even want. I just needed something to do when we got inside the apartment, so I opened my mouth and offered him wine.*

*Thank God my sister actually had some.*

*I don't know how to do this. I don't know how to have casual sex anymore. I'm not even sure I know how to have sex anymore. What if Tanner has broken me and I...*

*Hendrix's hand closes over mine, stilling it. I was so lost in my thoughts that I hadn't even heard him step into the kitchen. But now he's right behind me, his body pressed against mine.*

*My heart starts to race for an entirely different reason.*

"Let's forget the wine, yeah?"

*I close the drawer as I silently nod and turn to face him.*

*I am of average height for a woman, but I feel incredibly short standing in front of him. He has to be at least six two or six three? And his eyes are such an intense blue. Even in the dim light of the kitchen, I can see the tiny flecks of gold scattered among all that indigo.*

*Beautiful. That's what he is. Utterly beautiful.*

*And for the moment, all mine.*

*The revelation gives me a momentary surge of confidence, and I rise onto my tiptoes to gently press my lips against his.*

*There is nothing soft in the way he reacts. His hand slides around my waist, and suddenly, I find my ass on the cold marble countertop. He steps between my thighs, slants his mouth, and kisses me like he's been waiting his whole damn life for the privilege.*

*He grips my hair in his hands, angling my head so he*

can lick and kiss his way down my neck and collarbone. By the time he reaches around to unzip my dress, my breath is ragged, and my thighs are slick. The straps slip off my shoulders, and the fabric pools around my waist. When he grabs the backs of my calves, I assume he wants me to stand so he can finish unzipping it, but instead, he just slides me to the edge of the counter.

"Spread your legs wide, Cupid. I like seeing you like this," he says with a grin.

"Like what?"

His eyes wander over my lace bra and the red fabric of my dress pooled around my waist. "A little disheveled. A little wild."

I have to admit, I do kind of like it too. And as soon as that thought takes root, I find myself saying, "Take off your shirt."

I fight the blush creeping up my neck. I instantly start to worry I've been too bold. But the cocky grin that spreads across his face washes away all my doubt. "All right."

He left his suit jacket in the car, and I watch as he slowly works each button. You'd think the white tank he has underneath would be a bummer, but it's not. That thin fabric leaves little to the imagination, and I finally get my first look at the tattoos on his arms and the chiseled abs hiding underneath.

Dear god, is he auditioning for an action movie I'm unaware of? I've never been able to use the word rippling in real life until this moment, but that's how I would describe his body.

The crisp white fabric flutters to the ground, landing in a heap on the tile, and then his eyes return to mine. My stomach flips.

"Anything else you want, Zara?"

*I secretly love it when he calls me Cupid, but hearing my name on his lips, still slightly swollen from kissing me, is so incredibly hot.*

*The bravery from earlier has faded slightly, so I find myself giving a nod. He smirks, his hands ghosting up my thighs. "Don't be shy now. Tell me what you want."*

*I want to tell him to take the lead. To just do whatever he wants to do. But that's what the old Zara would do. Or at least the version I became when I married Tanner. The version of me who stopped asking questions and pushing for answers. Who became complacent. Who stood on the sidelines rather than taking charge.*

*I do not want to be that person anymore.*

*"I want you to make me come," I tell him, feeling my voice shake and hating myself for it. Hating that part of me that still feels small.*

*But Hendrix doesn't seem to notice. He just smiles as his fingers hook onto the waistband of my panties.*

*"And exactly how would you like me to do that?"*

*No one has ever asked me what I want in the bedroom. It's empowering. It's sexy, and most of all, it's healing.*

*As my confidence swells with each heated exchange, I raise my heel and place it on his shoulder and apply a bit of pressure. A devilish grin spreads across his face as he takes the hint and slowly drops to his knees. It's the hottest thing I've ever seen.*

*And then he looks up at me through hooded eyes and says, "It will be my fucking pleasure."*

"Zara." Hendrix's sexy voice calls to me. So deep and rough.

"Mmm?"

"Zara."

Wasn't he just on the kitchen floor? I remember the way he looked at me, like the very idea of eating me out was making him crazy. I rub my thighs together just thinking about it, and suddenly I feel an arm snake around my waist.

"Jesus, Zara. You're killing me here."

A hand caresses my cheek, and my eyes flutter open. The light from the window feels blinding, and I blink several times, trying to catch my bearings.

And then I see him.

Hendrix. In my room, my bed. Wearing clothes?

"Did you have a good dream, Cupid?" he asks, sounding smug.

I blink a few more times, taking in the room around me. No kitchen. No counter. I glance down. Definitely no sexy red dress.

"I, um..." I lick my lips, my mouth feeling dry, but he just grins and holds out my phone, which I now notice is vibrating.

"Your mom is calling. Also, you said my name in your sleep."

"I did, huh? My mom?" Talk about conversational whiplash.

He laughs. "Yep. Second time she's called too, so it's probably important."

I snort. "No, she just doesn't like to be ignored." I try to wipe away some of the sleep from my eyes before grabbing it from him. Then I look at the screen. Oh, goodie. She's FaceTiming me.

I swipe to answer and am not surprised at all to see not only my mom, but my sister teaming up on me in a group call. Seriously, who holds a group call at—I check my watch—noon? We slept in until noon?

Hendrix heads to the bathroom to make himself scarce. He's still wearing the same clothes he had on yesterday when we explored the city.

"Hi," I answer. Oh, I sound rough. My voice has taken on that raspy quality only achieved through hard-earned sleep, and now that I'm looking at myself in the camera, the visuals aren't too great either.

I quickly try to tame my hair and wipe away the mascara remnants under my eyes.

"Are you just waking up?" my mom asks. At the same time, my sister says, "Oh my god. Is that your room?"

I promised to call them when I got settled in and tell them how everything was going, but I never did. I'm not avoiding them. I actually like my family—a lot. And I replied to all their text messages, so they know I'm alive and everything. But things have been so busy that I've never really gotten to the point where I feel settled.

"Yes," I answer, giving the room a cursory glance. It is quite grand. Not as flashy as the hotel in Nashville. My room—sorry, suite—was twice this size and reminded me of when our class learned about Hearst Castle, and I went home convinced California had a king and a queen like a fairytale, because only fairytales had castles. That was obviously before I learned how a capitalist society actually worked. "To both of those questions."

My mom clutches her heart, looking panicked, and goes for the most obvious reason for my late morning slumber. "Please tell me you're not doing drugs."

Vi snorts out a laugh as I try not to roll my eyes. "It is my day off, Mom. I am allowed to sleep in."

"Well, we've barely heard from you in a week. How am I supposed to know?" I can hear the hurt in her voice, and now I feel guilty.

"I know, and I'm sorry. It's just been so busy and—"

The toilet flushes, and I freeze. What are the chances they didn't hear that?

Zero to none is my guess.

Violet's eyes go wide, but she quickly tries to regain her composure to save me the embarrassment of explaining exactly who is in my bathroom.

Did I mention that I love her?

My mother, however, doesn't give two shits about embarrassing her children, especially when it comes to our dating lives, and she goes right for the kill. "Sleeping in, huh?" A wry grin spreads across her face.

"Um, yep." I scoot down in the covers like I'm six years old again and hiding from the monster in my closet. I don't know why I feel embarrassed. Hendrix and I didn't even do anything.

Last night, at least.

Not that I wouldn't have been open to it. So *very* open to it.

But, oddly enough, the night turned out to be quite PG. After our messy beignet adventure, we went in search of new shirts and then wandered around some more. We strolled through the historic neighborhoods and visited those cemeteries you always see on TV. By the time we had dinner and headed back to the hotel, it was late.

When I invited him to my room, I had every intention of stripping that man down and licking every inch of him. But he seemed to be in no rush and instead ordered us dessert and put on a movie. Before I knew it, it was morning.

It ended up being the best date of my life. And nothing even happened.

Of course, it didn't look that way at all.

Not that my mom is the judgy type. Despite her strict upbringing, Maya Garis Valentine is definitely one of the cool moms. While she taught us how to make chocolate chip cookies *and* baklava, she also educated us about women's rights and the power of no. She demonstrates that you can cherish the past while embracing the future.

"Alone?" she presses.

My sister rolls her eyes. "Clearly, she didn't, Mom. So can you stop tormenting her?"

I really love my sister.

My mom lets out a reluctant sigh. "Fine."

"Good." Vi nods. "Now, bring him out. It's time for inspection."

Correction. I loved my sister, as in past tense. As in no longer. She's dead to me.

"What?" I sit up, the blankets slipping to my waist. Unlike Hendrix, I changed into a pair of leggings and a hoodie when we got back.

My sister frowns. "I hope that's not what you wear to bed at night."

"I agree." My mom gives a firm nod. "Men don't like all that fabric. Gets in the way." I gag. Thoughts of my parents in bed with very little fabric flood my brain. "Besides, it's too hot. You'll wake up sweaty."

"Aren't you the one who taught us never to change ourselves for a man?" I ask, realizing just how epically I had failed that particular lesson during my marriage to Tanner.

"I did. A man or woman..." She tosses that in for my sister's benefit. Always an ally, my mom. "Should love *you*. Not the person they want or think you should be. That isn't love. It's just manipulation in pretty packaging."

A door creaks, and I turn.

"Is that him?" Vi asks.

"Where?" my mom echoes. "I can't see! Flip the camera! Unless he's naked. Is he naked?"

A hesitant Hendrix pokes his head out, and our eyes meet. *Sorry*, he mouths with a tiny smirk. My shoulders are already shaking in silent laughter.

Can't fault the guy for flushing the toilet after he pees. Considering some of the dates my sister has complained about over the years, that trait alone makes him marriage material.

"My mother would like to know if you're naked."

"Um, no?" He glances down at his athletic shorts and the maroon New Orleans shirt we bought him after his other one got covered in powdered sugar. "I am not."

"She'd also like to know your thoughts on hoodies in bed. Yay or nay?"

He stares at me as if I'm asking a trick question before he finally replies, "Depends on what's underneath."

"Nice," Vi says while my mom simply laughs. Hendrix walks over to the other side of the bed—his side, I guess, since we shared it last night—and surprises me by plopping down right next to me. He then scoots closer, not caring in the least that he's now in plain view of both my mother and my sister.

There's a long moment of silence. Then, my mother

lets out an audible curse. I smother a laugh with my palm while my sister mutters, "Jesus, I need to go get a glass of water."

Hendrix turns and gives me a look that says, *What'd I do?*

"Seems like you have an effect on all the Valentine women."

"Well, my mom always told me I am quite the charmer." He smiles, and I swear every straight woman's panties within a twenty-mile radius simultaneously bursts into flames.

"This is Hendrix," I say as they both stare unabashedly at him. "This is my mom, Maya, and my sister, Violet."

"You're the new bass guitarist," my mom exclaims.

Hendrix's lip quirks. I doubt he expected my sixty-five-year-old mother to be up on Manic at Midnight news. "Temporary, but yes."

And you know my daughter—" my mom starts to ask, but my sister cuts in.

"Are you guys matching?" Okay, she can live.

I look down at the hoodie I'm wearing. It is the exact same color as Hendrix's T-shirt and bears the same simple New Orleans block lettering on the front.

"Oh, yeah. We went to Café du Monde," I begin to say, before adding, "It's this popular place in New Orleans—"

"Yes, yes, I know the one. I've seen it on TV. They sell the coffee and the fried pastries with the sugar on top."

I am suddenly hit with a wave of guilt as I realize just how many places my mom has seen but never visited. She has family in other countries she's never even met, and here I am, just a few years into my thirties, getting ready to travel all over the world, while my mom has barely left the Bay Area.

How I'd love to change that one day.

"Well, when we were there, we had a bit of an incident."

Hendrix leans in. "What your daughter is too embarrassed to say is that she made quite a mess."

"*I* made a mess?" His lip twitches as he tries to keep up the charade.

"They had to call in a cleanup crew after she finished all those beignets. First time ever, actually. They took pictures."

I push him so hard that he nearly falls off the bed, breaking into a fit of laughter as he instantly springs back.

"Okay, I may have started it," he fesses up. "But she one hundred percent bested me."

"She's always been a bit competitive." Vi laughs. "Whatever you do, don't ask her about her fourth-grade spelling bee."

"That thing was so rigged," I mutter.

"So where are you guys headed next?" My mom is looking at Hendrix and me as if she's already planned our wedding, named our kids, and picked out a nice house nearby where she and Dad can retire.

And she wonders why Vi doesn't tell her anything about her love life.

"Texas," we answer in unison.

"We'll spend a week there," Hendrix elaborates. "Wednesday is Houston, and then we go on to play Dallas on Saturday."

"And when are you in LA?" Violet asks.

"Two weeks, I think?" I say, and before she can ask, I add, "Yes, I got you a ticket—and a backstage pass!"

"Yes!" She throws a fist in the air. "And don't worry, Mom. I'll get you that pic."

"You've always been my favorite."

"Hey!" I say at the same time Hendrix asks, "What pic?"

"My mom is obsessed with Asher," I tell him with a sigh. "She's been begging me to get a picture of him ever since I stepped onto the plane."

"Oh, well, hell. I can get you one. I have a ton. What's your flavor, Mrs. V? Hot and sweaty right off stage? Candid? Blooper reel? I've got 'em all."

"Never mind," my mom deadpans, focusing all her attention on Hendrix. "He's my favorite."

Then, I spent the next thirty minutes listening to them bond over their mutual affection for Asher Knight.

## Chapter Eighteen

# HENDRIX

Something weird is going on tonight.

I noticed it the moment we arrived at the arena. A small crowd of VIPs stood lined up behind a rope to watch us, and as usual, the instant we stepped out of the SUVs, they erupted with excitement.

They screamed and cheered. I swear some people were even sobbing as if the Messiah himself had just arrived. Girls held up glittery homemade signs with Asher and Zander's names surrounded by hearts. Darius paused to take photos with a kid holding drumsticks. Manic Fanatic shirts were on display everywhere.

And then it happened.

"Hendrix!"

"Oh my god, it's the hot new bass player!"

"Hendrix! Over here!"

"Sign my shirt!"

"Sign my tits!"

And it didn't stop there. All the backstage pass holders suddenly seemed to notice I existed, pausing to take selfies with me and ask for my autograph. One girl even slipped her phone number into my pocket.

That quickly went in the trash.

On stage, I heard my name called more times than I could count. It felt like I was living in some sort of parallel universe.

Finally, after we finish the last encore and everyone has left the stage, I turn to Darius and Asher before they head to their dressing rooms to change.

Zander is already long gone.

Probably balls deep in his wife, no doubt.

"Did something happen?" I ask as techies seamlessly move around us like a well-oiled machine. I kind of feel bad being in their way, so I need to make this quick.

"What do you mean?" Asher asks, chugging a bottle of water.

Now I feel embarrassed if no one else seems to notice it. "I mean, uh…" I grab the back of my neck. "Someone asked me to sign their tits today."

Asher nearly chokes on his water, sputtering a laugh. The water dribbles down his chest, past what seems to be a family crest, maybe? I've never asked. "Welcome to the club. I'm asked that at least twenty times a show."

"Did you?" is all Darius contributes to the conversation.

"No!" I shake my head. "I'm—" Seeing someone? In a relationship? Off the market? Fuck, I don't have a clue how to finish that sentence, so I just step right over it. "Anyway, stuff like that's never happened to me. I'm new, and so far, I've been pretty invisible, except to the few reporters who hounded me about my family connections."

"Fuck those guys." Asher's tone is bitter, his accent a

little thicker. "Tell them to piss off and be done with it. That's what I do when folks ask about mine."

At the same time, I thank him, and Darius says, "That was probably my fault, yeah?"

We both turn and give him a blank stare. "What do you mean it was your fault?"

He shrugs, the fabric of his tight black tank top straining. I thought I was in pretty good shape until the first time I saw Darius Payne. He's built like a brick. Tall, with the solid muscle of a linebacker. Like Asher, he came from wealth, but he's not bitter about it.

All the original members went to the same boarding school—that's how they all met—and instead of bonding over how they were all going to be future billionaires or some shit, they decided to start a band.

It turns out that the little rebels were actually kind of good. Really good, actually. But even though they've all come a long way from their boarding school days, they're all still rich boys at heart.

Even Asher, who tries his damnedest to hide it.

"Do you not have any social media presence?"

"Not really," I answer. "I probably should, but I had to manage Zander's for a while before we hired someone at the agency, and I just got burned out on the whole thing."

"Okay. Well, remember New Orleans? How I was filming content for mine?" Darius says.

Unlike me, Darius is serious about making content. I have to give it to him. From what I've seen, he's pretty good at it. He's careful about what he posts, like during Sunday's concert when he made sure to get all of our permission before posting a video to his account, and he's always kind to his fans.

It must be a lot of work, but unlike Asher and Zander, who shy away from the attention, Darius seems to enjoy it.

"Yeah," I answer. "What about it?"

"So, it was supposed to be just a behind-the-scenes video where I walked around and introduced various crew members, showed off the green rooms and the hospitality suite, and then, of course, let them get a glimpse of the band. I didn't think much of it at the time, but you"—he points at me—"were in the wardrobe, and I think they were grabbing a different shirt for you or something and..."

I try to think back to that moment when he dropped in and asked me to say hi to his followers. "I was shirtless?"

He just nods. "And the internet went wild, mate."

"Why? Asher takes his shirt off all the time. Hell, he's not wearing one right now." I motion toward his bare chest. He chuckles, clearly amused by this whole thing. Honestly, he is probably just happy to not be the center of attention for once.

"Exactly. You never take off your shirt, so it was sort of like that episode where the Mandalorian takes off his helmet for the first time. Very thrilling. Kind of forbidden." I roll my eyes. "Right. Well, the video has a few million views, which is proper good, yeah? My videos tend to attract a lot of attention anyway, but—"

I gape at him. "It's been three days."

"You're welcome?"

"For what? Making my abs go viral on the internet?"

"No." He laughs. "The video is fleeting. It's your name they'll remember. The rest of the story, though? That's up to you."

It takes exactly fifteen minutes for my siblings to start blowing up my phone after I exit the stage. I've barely changed out of my sweaty clothes before the messages start rolling in.

PRES

Dude, your man chest is everywhere.

MERC

You've actually gone and proved me wrong—bass players can be famous.

MYLES

Well, at least we know all those hours staring at himself at the gym paid off.

ME

You know, I don't need to take this abuse. And at least one of us is famous...

MYLES

Oh damn. I think that dig was directed at me.

MERC

It totally was.

PRES

I'd be offended for you, Myles, but so far your acting career hasn't done shit for me. So I'm having a hard time feeling sympathy.

CASH

If I have to see this video pop up on my feed one more time...

ME

Do you think I control the internet now, Cash? Also, since when do you scroll social media?

CASH

I'm not seventy fucking years old. I may be the oldest, but I'm not geriatric. Even I doomscroll from time to time. Also, I work in the industry. I have to stay relevant.

ME

Really doubt pencil pushers need to stay up on the music trends...

PRES

Don't ever say doomscroll again.

MYLES

Agreed.

PRES

And if you say you're on the apps, I will throw myself off a cliff.

CASH

FML.

ME

Wait, how are you guys just now finding out about the video? It's been out for days.

MERC

We know. We saw it.

ME

What?

CASH

Dad kept us quiet. Ridge said it seemed like you hadn't seen it, and Dad wanted to keep it that way as long as possible.

ME

Why?

MERC

So you could stay focused.

ME

I'm always focused.

MYLES

What is it like to have a bunch of girls screaming your name?

ME

Are you asking because your career sucks and you want to live vicariously through your big brother?

PRES

OH DAMN.

MYLES

That's it. I'm taking Pres to the Oscars.

PRES

Hell yeah, bitches.

CASH

You guys are fucking children. Speaking of, I've got to go pick up my actual child from Nikki's.

MYLES

Say hi to the Wicked Witch of the West for us!

PRES

It's the East, Myles! Get it right!

**MERC**

I thought we were calling her Maleficent now?

**PRES**

We were, but then I watched that movie with Angelina Jolie and decided Maleficent might be one of those misunderstood villains. And Nikki definitely IS NOT. So back to the Wicked Witch of the EAST it is.

**ME**

Why East?

**PRES**

Because the West Coast is better. Obviously.

**CASH**

You know this is the mother of my child you're talking about.

**PRES**

And...

**CASH**

And...no comment. I've got to go.

**MERC**

He hates her just as much as we do. He's just more diplomatic about it.

**MYLES**

I've got to go too. I'm prepping for a big audition—for my career that does NOT suck.

**ME**

Good luck, man. Love you.

**MYLES**

Love you too.

Somehow, I managed to get changed during all that and pack up to head back to the hotel. Just as I'm sending a goodbye text to Pres and Mercury, I nearly plow into Zara halfway between my dressing room and the clinic.

Lucky, I guess, since I was on my way to find her, because tonight, I've decided we are going out.

We've barely seen each other since Sunday. After we got off the phone that afternoon with her mom, I barely had enough time to run back to my room to grab a shower and change. We then managed to squeeze in a late lunch at the hotel restaurant before we were whisked away to the arena for sound check.

Ever since, we've been like two ships passing in the night.

We got a bit of time on the plane, but aside from that, it's been extra practice sessions and a photoshoot for a magazine spread. Meanwhile, she's been dealing with heat exhaustion and a summer cold outbreak.

Given how much she does, I honestly don't know how the band has made it this long without a doctor on staff. This woman works her ass off.

My arms grip her shoulders, steadying her as she looks up at me wide-eyed. "Sorry!" she says, startled. "I didn't see you."

"No." I shake my head and lamely wave my phone. "It was my fault. I was texting my siblings and clearly wasn't paying attention."

"Siblings? As in all of them? At the same time?"

"Yeah, we have a group chat. It's currently called the Creed Council of Chaos."

"Currently?"

I grin. "It's had many names. It's sort of a competition to see who can come up with the best one."

She laughs. "And who came up with this one?"

"Presley."

She cocks her head to the side. "Why do you sound bitter about that?"

"I'm not bitter," I answer a bit too quickly.

Her brows lift. "Oh my god, you are! This really is a competitive thing. Wow, the Creed siblings are becoming more and more fascinating by the day. Let me guess, you were the last one to name the group before Presley booted you out?"

I wrap my arms across my chest. "I don't want to talk about it."

She snorts out a laugh. "Okay, but before we drop what I'm sure is a very sensitive subject for you, can you at least tell me what it was called?"

She gives me a pandering stare, and I sigh. "I feel like you're not supporting me here, Zara."

She reaches out and places a hand on each of my biceps, gently rubbing my arms over my T-shirt in a playful, *there, there*, sort of way. The enormous effort she's making not to crack up is impressive. "I'm sorry," she says sarcastically. "You're right. You definitely deserve support during this difficult transition. Losing is hard."

"Fine," I relent, just a second before she gives in and giggles. It's fucking adorable. "It was called"—I pause for dramatic effect—"Creed Me Up Scotty!"

First, I think she didn't hear me. The silence that follows would definitely explain it, but then her eyes go comically wide, and she just shakes her head in disbelief. "That is so bad!" Her giggle is a full-blown cackle now.

"It's not that bad!"

"No, it is. It's pretty terrible."

"Okay." I throw an arm over her shoulder as we begin

to make our way down the hallway. "But you weren't there when Cash chose *Creedence Clearwater Revival*. Like, that's just a band name. There's nothing remotely original about it."

"At least it's not an insult to Star Trek."

"Never took you for a Trekkie, Cupid."

"Oh, I'm not, but my dad is."

We pass a few crew members who greet us by name. A couple of guys seem to notice how my arm is draped around her, and I have to hold myself back from shooting daggers in their direction when they linger a bit too long on Zara.

"The basketball star?"

She gives me a pointed look. "Who also happens to be a science teacher. People are multifaceted, remember?"

"Most people," I agree. "But I'm not. I'm a musician, and that's about it."

She comes to an abrupt halt and turns. "Oh, I don't believe that for a second," she says. "You are so much more than your music, Hendrix. And I can't wait to discover all the many layers that you're made of."

She hooks her arm in mine, and we start back down toward the exit. But I'm still stuck on her words, because I'm suddenly left wondering what will happen when she peels back that first layer and discovers there's nothing underneath.

Because music is the only thing that makes me special.

Without it, I am nothing.

"You must really like her if you're FaceTiming me for fashion advice," Presley says as I step in front of the camera. I've propped my phone on the dresser and am now waiting to see if she approves of the black jeans and matching tee I picked out.

She just stares.

"What?" I look down and then back up again. "It's not bad, is it?"

"No," she agrees. She's sitting cross-legged on— Wait...is that my sofa? I don't know why I'm surprised. I gave her a key to my house. She probably moved in the second our plane left LAX. At least she's alone. I do not need mental images of her and her boyfriend in my house. "It's not terrible. But it's not great. You're basically wearing the same thing you wear to perform in."

"How would you know? Are you looking up our concerts? Oh my god," I gush. "Are you proud of me, Pres?"

"More like making sure you don't embarrass the family." She motions with her finger. "Do you have a vest or a jacket you could throw on over that?"

I raise an eyebrow at her. A vest? "We're in Texas. It's like four hundred degrees outside."

She shrugs. "So?"

"So?"

"Zander would wear his jacket."

"Let's not talk about Zander's weird obsession with

that thing, okay? Not all of us carry around a leather jacket like it's a treasured blankie from childhood."

"I actually see Elena with it more these days." She pauses, giving me an appraising look. "What about the jeans? What color options do I have to work with?"

"Are you asking if I have a pink or purple pair in my suitcase?"

"Oooh, do you?"

I slow blink because I can't tell if she's fucking with me or not. "No. No, I do not."

"Dammit. You are no fun. What about gray or—"

"I have about five more that look exactly like this, Pres." I point to the jeans in question.

She rolls her eyes. "And you used to give Zander a hard time about his obsession with black."

"They make my ass look good." She makes a gagging noise. "Oh, I do have a faded pair that looks sort of gray."

"Wear those. And then—"

My phone beeps, signaling a new text message. I lean in to read it, my sister making a disgruntled remark about my face being too close to the screen, but I don't care.

Because the text message is from Zara.

ZARA

Can't make it. Sorry.

My brows furrow. "What's wrong?" Presley asks.

"What could make a woman cancel a date at the last minute without any explanation or warning?"

Now her brows are bunched together as she tries to come up with an answer. "Everything was fine the last time—"

"Perfect," I tell her. "Everything between us has been fucking perfect." A little sporadic thanks to our crazy schedules, but we made up for it with texts and plans for later in the week.

She bites the corner of her lip before saying, "Then it's not you. It's—" Something else.

"I gotta go, Pres. Thanks for the help."

I'll take it from here.

I never should have answered the phone. That was my first mistake.

My second was not hanging up the moment I realized he was alive and wasn't in mortal peril.

But I didn't do either of those things. No, I stayed on the phone and listened as he berated me for my childish behavior, reminding me that I asked for this and that all this negative attention was my fault. He didn't ask for a divorce after all. I did.

*Are you trying to make me jealous, Zara? Is that what this little stunt is all about?*

The *stunt* he was referring to isn't the tour I'm currently on, although he is still plenty pissed about that. His parents were forced to issue our divorce announcement early because of it. I doubt anyone but their rich, snobby friends gave a shit.

No, what was sparking this current tirade was the internet footage he'd seen of Hendrix and me, arm in arm, as he helped me into one of the cars that night we went to the club in Nashville.

I think it's gained some popularity over the past few days because Hendrix has also received some attention thanks to a viral video. I haven't seen the video that caused all the fuss, but Elena told me about it. Something about a behind-the-scenes tour Darius did for his social media that attracted a lot of attention after he caught Hendrix without a shirt.

It doesn't surprise me. That man is cut like a fine Greek statue. It does, however, make me slightly jealous knowing millions of women are drooling over him. Will he change his mind about our arrangement when he realizes he can have his pick of practically anyone?

It's those feelings of uncertainty, piled onto years of emotional baggage Tanner just dug up, that have me canceling my plans with Hendrix. I don't even give him a reason why.

What is wrong with me?

Instead of sending a follow-up text to apologize for my abruptness, like I should be doing, I instead toss my phone onto the bed and hopelessly stare into the hotel mirror.

If I hadn't answered his phone call, I would have used this mirror to check my makeup and accessorize the cute dress I picked out. If he hadn't called, I'd be smiling at the woman staring back at me.

But right now, when I look at her, all I see is failure.

I see a woman who was taught to be fierce, yet she allowed a man to make her feel weak.

A woman who became so fragile that she blamed herself for her husband's mistakes.

A woman who believed she was too smart to ever fall for someone like *him*.

What if I'm just making the same mistake? After

everything I went through, can I learn to trust someone else? Can I trust myself?

A knock at the door interrupts my doom spiral. I freeze, uncertain whether to answer it. I didn't order room service, and it's too late in the day for anything else.

"Zara?" I hear Hendrix's concerned voice, and without hesitation, I walk toward the door to unlock it. I pull it open and see him scan me from head to toe, checking for injuries or illness, no doubt.

"Hi," I say, fidgeting with the hem of my sweatshirt. I hadn't even gotten dressed before Tanner called. I probably look like an absolute mess, with my frizzy, air-dried hair and the oversized basketball sweatshirt I stole from my dad last Thanksgiving.

"Hi," he replies. "Are you okay?"

"Yes," I say a little too quickly. "No. Maybe?"

"Can I come in?" His words are so hesitant, as if he's speaking to a baby deer. God, it's me. I'm the fucking deer.

I nod, my eyes sweeping over his tall frame as he passes by me. He looks so damn good. Dressed in black jeans and a T-shirt, his outfit is downright elegant compared to mine.

He settles into one of the overstuffed chairs across from the bed. I'm not sure if he's offering me space or simply needs some of his own, but I take the bed anyway, crossing my legs as I face him.

"I'm sorry for—"

He raises a hand in the air. "I didn't come here for an apology, Zara."

"Okay, but you deserve one."

"You know, my mom once told me that women are

basically conditioned from birth to apologize for everything," he says. "Regardless of who is at fault."

"And why did your mom tell you this?"

He chuckles. "Don't worry. It wasn't because she was correcting my behavior," he says, and then shrugs. "Although she probably wouldn't like the way I interrupted you just now. That was rude of me. She has three sons, so she's always made it her mission to ensure we're decent human beings. Decent men."

"And that's why you won't let me apologize for canceling a date?"

"Okay, I can see you're gonna make this difficult for me. How about this? Story Time." A small smile curves his lips, and I love that after all these years, this is still our thing. "One bright summer day, you're walking down the street on the way to the grocery store. You're minding your business, and up ahead, there's a guy. He's on his phone, doing whatever...and isn't paying attention to what's ahead of him. You try to step aside, but Phone Dude moves at the same time and slams into you. He looks up. Your eyes meet. What do you do?"

"Story Time doesn't involve questions."

"Humor me," he replies.

"I..." My initial reaction is to say I would obviously give that guy a piece of my mind and tell him to watch where he is going, but then a memory pops into my head.

*Tanner and I are at a charity gala. I feel like a fish out of water. The dress his mom picked out for me is heavy, and*

*the shoes are too tight. Everyone keeps congratulating Tanner on finishing his residency. They say nothing to me. We're heading to the bar so Tanner can refill his drink, when a man knocks into me from behind. Pain tears into my shoulder.*

*I look up. "Fucking hell," the man curses, glancing at his stained jacket. I clutch my injured shoulder as he looks at me expectantly.*

*I glance over at Tanner, hoping he'll say something, but he doesn't. He doesn't stand up for me or ask if I'm okay. Suddenly, I feel embarrassed. "I'm so sorry. It was entirely my fault." I say.*

*And the worst part is, I believe it.*

The words must be clearly written all over my face, because Hendrix doesn't wait for me to respond.

"I know you want to apologize for canceling on me, but there's no need," he says, his voice low and full of emotion. "I know you wouldn't have done so if there wasn't a good reason."

"Are you sure?"

He grins. "My mom also taught me this other valuable lesson, probably more than once, since I was a little shit growing up. It's this crazy notion that the world doesn't revolve around me. Crazy, right?"

I can't help but laugh.

I'm starting to think I'd like his mom.

"It comes in handy in certain situations, like, say, for instance, when you get a vague text from a woman canceling a date." I grimace, biting my bottom lip. I feel that instant need to apologize again. Jesus, maybe his mom is on to something, after all. "Someone else might assume they did something to cause the cancelation, while I can take a moment, rationalize that it's not always about me, and realize you might just be having a bad day."

*This is where you tell him about your bad day, Zara.*

He stares back at me, patiently waiting for me to respond. He doesn't say it, but I get the feeling he would sit there for however long I need, just soaking in the silence while I find the courage to talk.

This man is nothing like Tanner.

In my heart of hearts, I know this to be true. And yet, when I think about taking this leap with him, opening up to him about my mistakes and the fears that cling to me because of it, it feels scarier than any kind of physical attachment we could form.

"Tanner called," I begin, and I see his posture stiffen just ever so slightly. "Like most of our conversations lately, it was less than cordial. He accused me of trying to make him jealous and said that even though we are divorced, I will always be attached to his family, and I would do well to remember that."

"What the hell does that mean?" The gentle-natured Hendrix has vanished. He leans forward in his seat, his hands clenched into fists.

"Just that I am expected to carry myself with decorum and that gallivanting around the country with a bunch of rock stars—"

"Or perhaps one specific rock star?"

I nod. "Yes. He did mention the video of us in front of the hotel last week."

Hendrix rolls his eyes. "Decorum? The absolute hypocrisy of that family, I swear."

"What do you mean?"

He tilts his head and gives me a curious expression. "Tanner used to hang out at our house from time to time during college. I overheard some wild shit during those four years."

"Like what?"

"Let's see." He taps his fingers against his thigh. "Tanner got caught sleeping with a professor during our junior year. And his dad had to pay off a lot of people to keep it quiet."

My chest tightens. Not from jealousy. I fell out of love with that man a long time ago. It's more to do with how much I didn't know about him and how well he hid it from me. "Honestly, nothing surprises me about that man anymore."

"So I'm guessing you know about his dad's affair?"

"No, but it wouldn't shock me to learn that he had one."

"Oh, I'm sure he's had several, but this one was with a campaign staffer? And he also got caught. Not very stealthy, those Prices."

I stare at him blankly. "What? When?"

He gives me a pensive gaze. "Uh, well, the band was just starting to make a name for itself, so maybe two years after I graduated."

"That would have been a year for me." And exactly one year into med school. Right when things started to get serious between Tanner and me. "Why didn't he ever tell me? It seems like something you would share with your girlfriend, right?"

"I don't think Edwin was even supposed to tell me,"

Hendrix confesses. "He heard it from his dad and just couldn't help himself when it came to that sort of thing. He loved spreading others' misfortunes, and at the time, it sounded like Senator Price was on the outs, but he must have cut some sort of deal or got people to look the other way, because the truth never came out."

This news settles uneasily in my gut. I didn't start dating Tanner until after I stopped tutoring him, and even after that, he kept things casual. I knew his reputation, so I didn't think it would become anything more. But then, something changed, and almost overnight, he wanted to be exclusive.

I thought I was special.

I thought he was special.

But maybe it was just a lie.

I try to convince him I'm feeling better, and we should try to make our dinner reservation. "I can just throw on a dress," I tell him. "And if I'm quick with my hair and makeup..."

But he's having none of that.

"Stop trying to make me happy by saying what you think I want to hear, Zara. Tell me what *you* want, even if it's a little time alone." His gaze is purposeful. "I'm not some spoiled little man-child that's going to take it as a personal affront if you need a few hours to yourself."

I snort. Man-child. That's one way to describe my ex. He definitely whines like one.

"I want—" I stop and take the time to think about it. What do I want? As sweet as he is for offering it, I know the last thing I want is for him to leave. "I want room service," I finally say. "Specifically, a burger. With lots of french fries."

He laughs. "Anything else?"

I press my lips together, feeling heat crawl up my neck. "I really want a bubble bath."

He clears his throat, trying so hard to be a gentleman as his eyes dart around the suite, looking at anything but me. "Yup. We can do that. For you, I mean. Anything else?"

"Ice cream," I answer, wondering if I've ever seen anything as adorable as a blushing rock star.

Thirty minutes later, I'm staring at a feast of food that is spread out on the small table in my lavish suite. "I distinctly remember asking for a burger. Not the whole damn menu."

He shrugs, like it's not a big deal that he just dropped a small fortune on this meal. "I wanted to make sure I had all my bases covered, in case you didn't like the burger."

"All the bases are fully covered, Hen." I wonder if he likes it when I call him that. I look over and see a tiny smile curling his lips, and I think I have my answer. "I think there is enough food to feed everyone on this floor."

He shakes his head, dropping into one of the dining chairs. "Nuh-uh. I know who else is on this floor, and those fuckers aren't setting foot in this room. They'd never leave, and this is the first night I've had you all to myself in days. So..." He waves a hand at the mountain of plates. "Eat up, Cupid."

"I sure hope you're helping," I say, taking the seat next to him.

He places a hand on my thigh and gives it an affectionate squeeze. I feel butterflies in my stomach, and I swear, I'm blushing. "Do you think I ordered all this to sit back and be a spectator? Fuck no. I've got my eye on that wrap over there." He points to what looks like a Caesar chicken wrap. "And that lobster mac and—" I swipe it off the table before he even finishes his sentence.

"Dibs," I declare.

"Did you just call dibs? Are we back in the middle school cafeteria?" He laughs.

"No!" I exclaim, acting offended. "But this grown-ass adult can still call dibs. And look who now has herself an entire serving of lobster mac and cheese!" I proceed to dig into said mac and cheese, and dear fucking god in heaven, it's delicious.

"You know, I'd be more put out over the mac and cheese if I didn't find this side of you so damn sexy." My fork stops mid-bite, and I just stare at him. "This is the Zara I remember. The girl who loved to banter with me back and forth. Who made up an entire game just to teach me science? Fuck decorum and whatever the hell Tanner's family thinks of you, Zara, because they never knew you. They never even took the opportunity to learn. And as far as I'm concerned, you have far more class than they'll ever have."

He digs into the chicken wrap while I'm briefly stunned by his words. They're no different from anything I've been telling myself since the day I decided to get a divorce.

But hearing him say them strikes a chord, maybe because things could have been different. If...

"Story Time," I find myself saying. My voice is rough and full of emotion.

He gives me a warm smile but doesn't respond with any of the funny retorts he usually says when we play this game. He simply stares at me with those beautiful blue eyes and waits for me to continue. "Once there was this tutor who fell for one of her students."

I watch as his lips part in surprise. Is he about to

point out the rule against discussing exes, or is he beginning to realize that this story is about...

"It was just a crush. Or at least, that's what she told herself. He was a relentless flirt, and it was only natural that she'd start to feel something from all that attention. But as the weeks went on, she began to realize that what she felt for him was...more."

"Zara." He breathes out.

"Story Time isn't over," I remind him with a shaky laugh, and he instantly quiets. "But she was scared, you see? Because they were so different, and she just couldn't imagine a world in which someone like him could ever want someone like...me."

He looks at me with a gaze so intense, it burns. Finally, he swallows and says, "Story Time?"

I simply nod.

"Once there was this dumbass college student who fell head over fucking heels for his tutor." He reaches out and takes my hands as my breath catches because there's no way. Because back then, he was just flirting. It didn't mean anything to him.

Did it?

"He would flirt and tease her because he was too scared to actually tell her how he felt. Then the weeks ran out, and their time together came to an end. And rather than do what his heart was telling him to do, he convinced himself he was doing the right thing by walking away."

"Why?" I ask, not caring if I'm breaking the rules. I need to know.

"Do you want the real reason or the selfish, made-up reason I told myself at the time?"

"Both, I guess?"

He takes a deep breath and lets it out slowly. "I guess the real reason is I was scared. Still am, if you want the super honest truth. But at the time, I convinced myself I didn't need the distraction. That I would be holding myself back by getting into a relationship when Edwin and I were just putting the band together."

I tilt my head. "You tend to use that excuse a lot."

"Yeah, and look how far all those years of focus have taken me," he grumbles. "I feel like the only part of me that's closer to gaining any notoriety in this field is my damn abs."

I run an appreciative hand down his chest. "It is a nice set of abs. But definitely not the best part of you." His smile turns wicked, and I can't help but laugh. "I'm talking about your musical talent!"

"You sure?"

"I'm sure," I answer. "Besides, it's been too long since I've seen those other parts of you, so I wouldn't really be able to say." I raise my eyebrow in an obvious challenge.

"Are you saying you need a refresher?"

I give a casual shrug. "I do need a bath."

"Fuck, Zara." His eyes darken. "That's not a good idea."

"Why?"

"Because you've had a bad day, and if I get in that water with you, I'm gonna want to touch you. Everywhere."

*Everywhere.* A shiver runs down my spine.

"You said I should tell you what I want, right?"

He holds my gaze. His voice is raspy and deep when he answers. "Yes."

I rise from the table and hold out my hand. "Tonight, I just want you."

## Chapter Twenty-One

# HENDRIX

"*I just want you.*"

*I'll give you anything. Everything. I'm yours,* I wanted to tell her.

But I didn't. Because not even a week ago, she told me she wasn't ready for something serious. And words like that?

Definitely serious.

Fuck, I am so in over my head.

When did this change happen? When did this stop being a casual hookup with an old flame and turn into something I'm scared of losing?

But then I know my answer. Zara's not just some old flame. She's a raging fire. She's a goddamn inferno, and I've been holding a torch for her since I was twenty-two. She's the reason I've never been able to date. She's why I've never been able to settle down with anyone else.

Because that's exactly what it would be. Settling.

Zara will always be my first choice.

Fucking hell.

My gaze drifts to the closed door that separates us. I

left her in the main part of the suite to finish her ice cream, while I came in here to set up the bath. I grew up in a house with three women, so I've been around enough girly shit to know what goes into a proper bubble bath.

Plus, this isn't exactly rocket science.

Any man who claims otherwise is just fucking lazy.

I check the water temperature before reaching for the fancy basket of bath stuff the hotel provided. There's high-end bubble bath, skincare, and who knows what else in here. I reach for the bubble bath and go to put the basket back on the counter.

I turn around and unscrew the cap. I flex my right hand, noticing a stiffness that's become all too familiar. Musicians are known for getting tendonitis and shit, but damn. I'm only thirty-two. It's too soon for that, right?

It's probably just stiff from playing too much. Honestly, I welcome the ache. It means I'm finally doing what I love. And fuck, do I love it.

The other night, in between concerts, the four of us hung out in Asher's room. The girls joined us, and we hung out and ate pizza. Zander, Ash, and I pulled out our guitars, and everyone else sang along.

It was the most fun I've had with a band...ever.

Now, I know why Zander signed with these guys, despite never wanting to be in the limelight. They're easy to love, and it's going to make it hard to say goodbye when the tour ends.

After a quick sniff test to ensure I'm not about to make the whole bathroom smell like my grandmother's linen drawer, I pour a small amount of the bubble bath into the water. It begins to suds immediately.

The good stuff doesn't require a lot. Hints of lavender

and vanilla begin to fill the room, and when the tub is about halfway, I dim the lights and head out to fetch...

"Jesus," I blurt out, my voice cracking a little like it did in middle school at the sight of Zara half naked. Well, almost half naked.

She looks up in alarm, trying to figure out what caused me to curse, but then sees me staring at her in nothing but an oversized T-shirt and gives a shy smile. "I didn't want to drag all those clothes in there."

"Very pragmatic of you, doctor." She rolls her eyes and begins to fiddle with the hem of her shirt. It raises the hem slightly, revealing more of her smooth skin. It's distracting, but not enough for me to notice that she's a bit nervous.

It's a stark contrast to the woman who so pointedly told me exactly what she wanted less than twenty minutes ago.

"What's going on in that head of yours, Cupid?" I ask, taking a step forward.

"Do you—" She pauses for a second like she's second-guessing herself. "Do you really like knowing what I want...in the bedroom?"

Her question confuses me for a moment. "What do you mean?"

"I don't want you to feel like I'm being selfish, or worse, think I'm not enjoying myself."

I close the distance between us. "Yes, I really do. I'm a direct sort of guy, Zara. I like knowing what you want. What you need and"—I smirk—"what you like. In and out of the bedroom. Want to tell me where this is coming from?"

"Tanner seemed to be offended anytime I asked for anything or told him to try something different."

Fucking hell. "Tanner is a selfish prick who didn't deserve you. Any decent guy not only appreciates pointers but gets off on having a confident woman in the bedroom. I love knowing I am touching you exactly the way you like it."

"And what if all I want is to touch you?" Her voice is low. Sultry.

If I weren't already half hard for her, I would be now.

"Then, I'd say we should take this conversation into the bathroom," I say, a second before I bend at the waist and haul her over my shoulder. She shrieks like a banshee and flails. I slap her ass for good measure. "The water is getting cold."

I stride into the spacious bathroom and set her down on the counter. She lets out a little yelp when her butt lands on the cold white marble. The thin cotton panties she's wearing aren't doing shit to keep her warm.

But I'm about to remedy that.

She becomes a captive audience the second my hand reaches over my shoulder to grab the back of my shirt. When it drops to the floor, she's practically salivating. It's a hell of an ego booster.

That video of my abs could get a hundred million views, and the only one I care about is the girl staring at me right now.

She makes me feel like a real rock star.

"What do all your tattoos mean?" she asks, her eyes wandering over the many works of art I have all over my body. I take a step closer to her so she can run her fingers over them.

It makes my whole body shudder.

Last time, when we were naked, we were basically strangers again, and neither one of us wanted to walk down memory lane when we had such limited time together.

So we spoke with our bodies rather than our words.

Now that we have the time, she wants the answers she'd never been able to ask. "A lot of them are music or family related. This one"—I point to the bold script on my forearm that bears my last name—"being the most obvious. All of us have one, even Zander. But there are other family-inspired ones too. The waves that cover most of my shoulder and bicep are for my parents because they remind me of home. And over here..." I point to the M and the backward P with the crown on top.

"Your sisters," she says with a smile. "That's sweet."

"Is it still sweet if I tell you they forced me to get it?"

"I doubt anyone could force you into anything. What about this one?" She points to the one on my chest, close to my—"Is that a..."

"Cherub?" I supply, feeling suddenly incredibly embarrassed. "Uh, yup. Ready for the bath?"

She hops off the counter and stalks toward me as I move toward the bath. Fuck, why didn't I think this through?

*Because you were thinking with your dick and not your head.*

That night in her apartment, the room was dim, and we were so high on lust for each other that she didn't seem to notice. Not that I think she would have said anything. It had been years, and the idea of me having a random angel tattoo on my body wouldn't have rung any alarm bells.

But, now?

Maybe if I just strip off the rest of my clothes, she'll be so distracted by my hard-on, she'll forget all about it.

I reach for the fly of my jeans, and before I can even start to unbutton them, I hear her say, "Don't even think about trying to distract me with your dick right now, Hendrix. Why do you have a cupid tattoo on your chest?"

I let out a heavy sigh as my gaze meets hers. "You heard what I said earlier, Zara. I was the stupid ass college student who walked away. Doesn't mean I forgot."

Her eyes widen, and for a second, I think she's going to cry. Fuck, *don't cry*, I silently chant. And then she moves, and before I can blink, her mouth slams against mine. It takes me but a moment to react, and then I pull her close, and I'm kissing her back.

She pulls back and shit, is she crying? "It should have been us," she murmurs. "Back then, it should have been us."

My heart squeezes, because it's the same thought I've secretly had every time I picture her with that dick-for-brains Tanner.

It should have been me.

But it wasn't.

"It doesn't matter," I say against the hollow of her shoulder. "We're here now."

She meets my gaze, that worried look returning. "What if I'm not ready? What if it's too soon?"

I swallow the lump of nerves forming in my throat and gently hold the back of her head. "Then we just take it one day at a time, okay? No labels, remember? It's just you and me figuring this out as we go."

She gives a nod before reaching up to kiss me again, and this time, I don't need a second. When her lips meet mine, I settle into the feel of it like I was meant for this. Meant for her.

"Come on." I reluctantly pull back. "I owe someone a bath."

I bend down to check the water, grinning as I notice the way she checks me out. The water has chilled slightly, so I add a bit more hot water while Zara watches me with a brazen intensity.

It's moments like this when her confidence comes peaking back out that I know she'll be all right, that whatever he did to tear it down isn't permanent.

And it's also a reminder of just how much I want to punch that guy in the fucking face.

But I'm not focusing on that right now.

I've been waiting days to spend another night alone with her, and I'm making the most of it.

Which reminds me...

"I'll be right back," I tell her. The blank stare she gives me makes me chuckle, so I follow it up with. "Get naked."

The night I stayed over in her suite in Nashville, I found myself fumbling around the next morning in a half-asleep stupor, trying to locate her ringing phone. Instead, I stumbled upon something else.

In a drawer in her nightstand.

I'm hoping it's found its way back into this hotel's nightstand as well.

I stroll into the suite and head straight for the bed, picking the same side as before, and—

"There you are."

I grab the little purple toy from its hiding spot and head back to the bathroom just in time to see Zara's naked body slip into the water.

"You are so damn beautiful."

She turns, the tips of her hair stirring the bubbles around her. "You said that last time we were together."

"And I meant it last time." I stalk forward, and her eyes widen when she sees me place the vibrator next to the tub. I grin. "I also meant it all those times I thought it in college, but never said it. You've always been beautiful to me."

My words seem to carry a deeper meaning because she does that thing that I'm learning is so Zara, where she pauses as if she's absorbing each word individually and then considers whether she wants to share what she's thinking.

She must decide against it because the next thing out of her mouth is, "You know stealing is against the law." Her eyes find the purple toy.

"It's not stealing if I plan to give it back. And I think you'll enjoy what I have planned to do with it." I start to slowly undo the button of my jeans and enjoy the way she watches every movement as if it's the most fascinating thing she's ever seen.

And then she licks her lips, and my fucking hand starts to shake in anticipation.

I get my zipper down, and my pants and boxers drop to the ground in record time. Thank fuck I had the foresight to ditch my shoes and socks before I came in here to prep the bath.

"Jesus, Zara. The way you're looking at me..."

"Sorry. I just forgot how...big you were."

She's killing me here. I step into the tub behind her. One of the many perks of this suite is the enormous tub. Being as tall as I am, I wouldn't be able to join her otherwise. I slide into the water, careful not to let any spill over the edge. It's the perfect temperature, and as I anchor one leg on either side of her, I lean forward and whisper in her ear, "What did I say about apologizing?"

"To stop?"

I slide a hand along the wet skin of her waist under the water and pull her until her body is flush against mine. It's a combination of bliss and pure fucking torture as her perfect little ass wedges itself against my rock-hard dick. Her breath hitches. "For things you aren't responsible for? Absolutely. And besides, did I say I didn't like the way you were looking at me?"

"No."

"No. In fact, I think you can feel just how much I liked it." I grind my hips, and she groans. "I really want to make you come." My voice sounds hoarse as I scatter a few kisses along her neck and shoulders. I know we've been in the water for exactly four seconds, but I'm dying to touch her. I've been thinking about it nonstop since that night of the engagement party. "Will you let me?"

"Are you seriously begging me to let you get me off? Shouldn't I be doing that?"

"I'm not begging...yet. But I will if you want me to." I reach back and grab her little purple wand. "And trust me, this will be just as much fun for me as it is for you. Also, I didn't take you for the vibrator-in-my-luggage type of girl."

She looks back, and her cheeks turn pink. "I'm not. My sister bought it for me. A divorce present, I guess you could call it."

"And have you used it yet?"

She presses her lips together and nods.

I lower the toy under the water and drag it down the

side of her body. She shudders. It's not even on yet, and she's already so responsive. "And who do you think of when you touch yourself with it, Zara?"

"You," she whispers.

"That's fucking right, you do." I slide it over her stomach, circling her hip, pulling her a bit higher so she's basically sitting in my lap. "Do you fuck yourself with it?"

Her head falls back on my shoulder as I make my way between the apex of her thighs. She groans impatiently as I hold off getting to the final destination, waiting for her answer.

"Yes."

With it still off, I lightly brush the head of the vibrator against her clit. She arches her back, and I feel my cock rub between the cheeks of her ass. Fuck.

I resist the urge to buck my hips. If I do, this will all be over a lot sooner than I have planned.

"Is that what you want me to do, Zara? Do you want me to fuck you with this vibrator?"

"Yes. God, yes."

I cup her chin with my free hand and kiss her deeply, grinning against her mouth as she lets out another gasp of pleasure as I finally flip the vibrator on and rub slow, tight circles around her clit. Next time, it will be my tongue doing this because the taste of her has been haunting me for weeks, and I can't wait to have another taste.

I rarely do oral. It's not that I'm a selfish lover. It's the fact that STDs are a real thing, and I've never wanted to put my mouth anywhere near someone I've only known for a handful of hours.

But that night with Zara was different.

Even though I hadn't seen her in years, I didn't want to fuck her like a stranger.

I wanted to fuck her like she was mine.

"When you were touching yourself, what were you imagining me doing to you?" I ask, kicking the vibrator up a notch and using it to tease her tight pussy.

"You were doing that," she says with a shaky voice, and I know her well enough to know that little shake is partially due to lust, but also a little bit of nerves too. From that first night we were together, when I caught her panicking in the kitchen, I realized that talking about sex is hard for her, especially when it comes to what she wants. It's an odd contradiction to how she conducts herself in her daily life, and it ignites a rage deep inside me, especially now that I know the reason why.

"This specifically?" I ask, sliding the tip of the vibrator inside her. She gasps and I groan as she grinds her ass into me. I use my free hand to pin her body in place. If she keeps doing that, I'm gonna blow.

"N-no," she answers, albeit a bit breathy. "You were— I was remembering the kitchen."

I grin. "So you like me on my knees then? Is that it, Zara?"

"Yes."

I push the vibrator in about an inch. Maybe a little more. Then I pull back and do it all again, teasing her entrance.

"Shit, Hen—"

I push it in further this time, but take my time. She's squirming in my arms and rubbing that perfect round ass all over my cock. There's water sloshing, and the bubbles that are left are sticking to our skin.

It's fucking perfect.

"You want to know a secret?" I say, peppering her shoulder with more kisses. "I've gotten off to that memory of me on my knees, with my head buried between your thighs so many times, I've lost count."

And then I turn the toy up another notch and bury it to the hilt. She screams out my name and arches her back. It's nowhere as large as I am, thank you very much, but it's deep enough to hit her G-spot, and she's feeling it.

I slide it out and thrust it back in. Her hand moves toward her clit and then steadies, like she's unsure if she's allowed to touch herself in my presence.

I just shake my head, adding it to the list of things I want to kill Tanner Price for. Reaching for her hand, I weave our fingers together and slide them down between her legs. "Touch yourself, Zara. I'm dying to see how you get yourself off."

She's tentative at first. Just shallow strokes, but when I jack up the power to the vibrator and start fucking her in earnest, she finally lets go.

And holy shit, is it a beautiful sight.

Her head tips back, and her lips find mine. She kisses me like she's drowning, and I'm her only source of oxygen. Her hips start to move, feverously rocking against my cock as she chases her orgasm.

The friction of her ass cheeks sliding along my cock, watching her splayed out on top of me, rubbing her clit while I fuck her pussy with that vibrator.

It's all so fucking hot. It's all too much.

God. Fuck, I think gonna...

She cries out, her body convulsing just as my balls tighten and I come, shooting jets of cum into the bathwater. My breath is ragged as I turn off the toy and place it next to the tub.

My head falls onto her back as I run a hand over her belly. I can feel her heart racing.

And then she starts to laugh. "You ruined our bath."

"I'll make it up to you in the shower."

And I do.

Twice.

## Chapter Twenty-Two

# ZARA

The second time I wake up with Hendrix in my bed, I am definitely not wearing a hoodie.

And thankfully, neither is he.

In fact, the only thing he's wearing is a shit-eating grin as his eyes roam over my naked breasts peeking out of the ridiculously high thread count sheets. He rolls onto his side. "Hi."

"Hi," I respond, mirroring his position.

"Think we can go a whole morning without your mom calling this time?"

"Shhh!" I exclaim, causing him to laugh. "She'll hear you."

He wraps an arm around my waist and pulls me closer. His hand slides down my hip, over the curve of my ass until he's gripping the back of my thigh. He hikes my leg over his.

"Let's do breakfast in bed," he suggests. "We don't have to be downstairs until noon, and I'm not ready to share you yet."

"Okay."

He gets up, not bothering to cover up. God, he's got a great ass. He heads over to the small desk where he left the room service menu last night and gives it a cursory glance, then picks up the phone. Before I can argue, he's ordered half the menu again, along with a pot of coffee and chai for me.

"I could have just told you what I wanted."

He shrugs, already heading back to the bed. "Yeah, but that would have taken up too much time. And I have things I need to do."

"Oh?"

His grin is positively wicked.

My stomach flips.

It's unreal how much I want this man.

Last night, we were naked for hours. After the bath, we took a shower where he got me off with his fingers and then his tongue. When our skin was finally pruny and clean, we wrapped each other in fluffy white towels and dried our hair. As soon as we left the bathroom, I pushed him onto the bed and showed him he wasn't the only one who looked good on his knees.

We went on and on like this for hours, but we never had sex.

It was like he was saving it.

Or savoring us.

He lifts the covers and slips in beside me. His body is ridiculous. Hard, lean muscles wrapped in an array of black ink that are simply mesmerizing. I don't have a moment to worry about morning breath or bedhead because he's already cupping my jaw and kissing me like I'm perfection.

He definitely makes me feel that way.

"I want you," I say.

I feel his grin against my lips. "I'm right here."

"You know what I mean."

He pulls back, and his eyes sparkle with amusement. "I don't, actually. You need to be specific, Cupid."

I really wasn't sure I believed him at first when he said he liked it when I told him what I wanted, but the way he's looking at me now with such intense heat in his eyes makes me know he's telling the truth.

He really gets off on it.

It makes me feel powerful.

It makes me feel sexy.

"I want you to fuck me."

*Holy shit, did I really just say that?* Judging by the wolfish grin spreading across Hendrix's face, I'd say so.

The hand that's resting on my hip starts to roam, sliding down the curve of my ass. The metal of his rings feels practically chilly on my heated flesh as he gives it a hard squeeze. "With my fingers?"

"No."

He leans forward and places a tender kiss on my collarbone, then the curve of my neck, and moves to the shell of my ear before he whispers, "With my tongue?"

Goose bumps dance across my skin. "No."

He nudges my shoulder and rolls me onto my back. I feel the delicious weight of his body on mine as he plants a hand on either side of my head to hold himself up. His cock is so close to where I want it to be that I could practically feel my pussy contracting, like it's begging to be filled.

He must notice the proximity as well, because his

eyes flutter shut for a brief moment, and when they open again, they're practically molten.

"What about your naughty little vibrator? Want me to fuck you with that again?"

"No." I swallow, remembering the way we both fell apart in the bath last night. Knowing I made him come from just watching me was empowering. "I want you inside me, Hen. I want you to fuck me."

"Fuck." His voice is so low, husky. "Say it again."

"I want you to fuck me."

"Say my name, Zara. Who do you want to fuck you?" He reaches between us and palms his cock. He gives it a few light pumps. I think I actually lick my lips in anticipation because he lets out a groan, followed by a curse.

"You, Hendrix. I want you to fuck me. Only you."

That must be the winning combination because his mouth is suddenly on mine, and he's hauling me onto his lap. My legs instantly wrap around his waist, and just as he's lifting me up and all of me is about to be reunited with all of him, he freezes.

"Shit. Condom." He puts me back down and runs a hand down his face. "I can't believe I almost forgot. I know that sounds cliché as hell, but I never do. I have some in my room. I can throw on some clothes and—"

"I have an IUD," I tell him with a tentative shrug. "And I haven't had sex in almost—" I try to think back to the last time Tanner and I were intimate. "A year, maybe? Well, except, you know. And I was tested during our six-month separation, just in case he..." I take a deep breath, unable to voice the words. I had my suspicions at the end, but I was never able to find any proof.

His eyes widen ever so slightly, but he doesn't comment on it, except to say. "I was tested right before we left for the tour. All of us were. I'm clean. But I don't want to do anything you're not comfortable with. I can easily run to my room, or—"

I smile. "You're forgetting you're in bed with the on-site doctor. I happen to have a medical bag just over there." I point to the giant duffle I carry with me everywhere. "That is stuffed with supplies, including emergency condoms."

"I'm surprised you still have some after Darius learned about your stash."

I snort. "I cannot confirm or deny whether he's asked for any. Patient-client confidentiality and all. Sorry."

"All right. Well, you keep your secrets, then."

"At least I can," I tease.

"That's a low blow, Cupid." He chuckles as he tries to get off the bed, but I grab his hand to stop him.

"I'm okay," I tell him. "Without, I mean."

His brow furrows as he searches my face for any sign of doubt. "Are you sure?"

I nod, reaching for him. His arms instantly wrap around mine. "I trust you, and it's not like before when we weren't planning on ever seeing each other again. This time we're sticking together. Just the two of us."

"Just try to get rid of me, Zara. I dare you."

I give a shy smile. "So...we're good?"

He flashes a wicked grin, fisting my hair as he pulls me close. "Yeah, we're so fucking good."

His mouth presses against mine, and when he kisses me, I feel like I finally understand what it means to be kissed breathless. I remember my roommate in college coming back from a date once and describing the way her date kissed as being an out-of-body experience.

I couldn't relate.

Back then, kissing had just been...kissing.

But Hendrix could definitely make the heavens sing and the earth shake with the way his mouth moves against mine. It is fucking divine.

He pushes me down onto the mattress and settles between my legs.

"We're going to go slow. You make me lose my head, and I was being a little too hasty before." He's referring to when I was in his lap, and he's probably right. With his size, I will more than likely need a little time to adjust, but I doubt I would have thought of that in the heat of the moment. I was ready to hop onto his dick like it was a pogo stick.

"Sure you don't want me to go down on you first?"

I dig my nails into his bare ass. "If you don't fuck me before room service arrives, I will murder you."

He chuckles, palming his dick as he starts to rub the fat head over my sensitive clit. "Okay, okay. You don't have to beg, baby."

I'm too lost in the feel of his cock rubbing me to focus on the fact that he called me baby. Or the fact that I liked it.

"God, you're so fucking wet. All this for me?"

I angle my hips, needing him inside me. "Yes."

"If your pussy wasn't so damn tight, I could just slip in, but I remember just how well you squeezed my cock, so we're gonna take a little at a time. Okay?"

I want to scream, *hell no*, and tell him just to shove it all in and fuck me already, but the rational part of me does actually remember how tight of a fit it was. So I just nod instead.

The way his large palms grip my hips makes me feel

tiny in comparison to his large frame as he angles me just right and pushes in.

"So tight," he grits out.

"More," I beg.

I wrap my legs around him, digging my heels into his ass as I squeeze my inner walls around him.

"Fucking hell, Zara." He slides in deeper, and we both moan. "Do that again." I do, and his eyes practically roll back in his head.

He's just as big as I remember, but it's easier to take this time around. Either my body has a good memory, or all those orgasms last night prepared me in advance, because after a moment or two, I'm begging him to move.

"You sure?" Always so attentive.

"Yes!"

He thrusts deep, and I cry out as he buries himself to the hilt.

"So good," I murmur.

"So good," he echoes, before he pulls me back into his lap. I adjust myself, preferring my legs to be on either side of him, so I can straddle him. He's patient as I make myself comfortable, scattering kisses on my shoulders as he runs his hands over my breasts to pinch my nipples.

For several minutes, we're like this. Just taking our time as we explore each other's bodies. He kisses me as I slowly rock back and forth, feeling the pleasure build like a rising tide.

Until I feel like I'm burning from the inside.

Our kisses turn fervent as my body demands more.

*More, more, more.*

"That's it, Cupid. Ride me." My hips start to move as my back arches and my tits bounce. "Yes. Fucking ride my dick."

I'm lost to the feeling of his body in mine.

He pulls one of my pebbled nipples into his mouth and sucks hard as I let out a fevered moan. His hands are everywhere. On my ass, rubbing my clit. Finally, when he must be getting close, he pulls back and says, "Touch yourself, Zara."

And then he grabs my hips with both hands and pushes us forward until my back hits the mattress again. He grabs both of my ankles and throws a leg over each shoulder. Oh my god, I've never had sex like this before. It's wild and unhinged. It's passionate and intense.

His hand grabs my waist, and then he starts fucking me like a man possessed.

I cry out. I scream. I call out his name and probably a deity or two.

"I'm gonna come," I cry out as his hips slam into me. "Oh fuck, I'm gonna come."

"Good." He grins. "Let me see it, Zara. Let me feel it," he growls, and if I wasn't close before, that certainly would send me over the edge. "Come all over my cock."

My back arches, and I let out a scream that is probably far too loud for a hotel room, and with a few final flicks to my clit, I let go. My body starts shaking as every nerve ending in my body starts to detonate.

My pussy is still convulsing when Hendrix lets out a guttural groan, his whole body shuddering, as I feel him release deep inside me.

His eyes meet mine, and I feel my stomach clench. God, he's even hot when he comes.

Just as he's leaning down to kiss me, there's a light knock on the door, followed by a timid voice on the other side that says, "I'm just going to leave your food by the door."

We both stare at each other for a beat and then burst out laughing.

"Hungry?" Hendrix asks.

I give him a heated look and grin, pulling him closer. "Starved."

Our food is cold by the time we get to it.

*Chapter Twenty-Three*

# ZARA

"Viva La Vegas, bitches!"

"Jesus fucking Christ," Hendrix mutters under his breath as he attempts to cover the grin curving his lips.

Darius has half his body sticking out of the top of the Escalade's sunroof, yelling at the top of his lungs at the entire Vegas strip. I don't think he's had a drop of liquor. He's still riding the high from their performance tonight.

And damn, what a performance it was.

The guys were electric tonight.

It was a slow night at the clinic, so I was able to sneak over to the stage and watch. I don't think I'll ever get used to seeing Hendrix perform.

He is an absolute professional. Even when he appeared to have missed a riff, he just kept on going, not showing a single sign of distress on his face.

A part of me was worried the attention would change him. That all the adoration from the fans and the girls would change *us*. But he handles it like he does every-thing else: with gratitude and grace. He signs T-shirts, poses for pictures, and always pays special attention to aspiring musicians.

It makes my heart swell to see him manifesting his dreams. But a small part of me wonders if there's space for me in this new life he's creating.

Do I want there to be?

"Darius!" Zander laughs, grabbing the back of his shirt to yank him back into the seat. "What the hell do you not understand about staying under the fucking radar, my man? You're gonna cause a damn riot!"

Sitting across from us, Asher just smiles and shakes his head. I'm honestly surprised he agreed to go out with us tonight. Unless it's PR-related, he usually stays at the hotel. "I say we just toss him out the window like a bloody sacrifice, yeah?"

"Agreed," Hendrix and Elena say at the same time.

I glance out the window and watch as the flashing lights of Vegas go by. It's so bright, and there are people everywhere.

The group could not believe I'd never been here.

"Didn't you grow up in California?" Zander asked.

"Um…yup. California native."

"Isn't Vegas like a short drive from the Bay Area?" Elena asked, making everyone laugh. She was obviously the newest California implant. East Coasters tend to forget just how big our state is.

"Not short," I answer, unless you consider nine hours short. "But drivable, yes. Not exactly on my parents' list for family-friendly destinations, though."

"Right then. We're going out!" Darius declared.

"No nightclubs!" we all shouted. Darius and Vegas sounded like a bad combination. Of all the guys, he was the least tame, and this was, by no means, a PR-sanctioned event we were planning.

But when he told us what he had in mind, the guys quickly got on board.

Now, we're cruising down the strip in a tricked-out Escalade on our way to a private location for a group activity I never thought I'd be doing.

It's been a little over a week since we were in Houston, and every day has felt like one of those cheesy montage reels they do in a rom-com. The two main characters have finally hooked up, and it's just sex, breakfast in bed, and endless laughter. Followed by more sex.

That is what my life feels like right now.

Every moment we're not working, we're together.

We never even discussed it, but after that first night, he didn't bother going to his room when we got to Dallas. He just followed me to mine, and we've been together ever since.

And it feels...*good*.

"All right, so this is a mandatory participation kind of night, yeah?" Darius gives each of us a stern, take-no-shit look. "No spectators."

Zander gives his wife and me a glance before turning to address Darius. "No one's gonna be forced, Darius. This isn't the sort of thing you get peer pressured into."

I chew on my bottom lip for a moment before making eye contact with Elena. We lock eyes for a second, and then her lips curl into an amused smile.

I nod.

"We're in," we both say at the same time.

"What?" Hendrix and Zander echo back.

"We're in." Elena shrugs, raising an eyebrow at her husband. "What? You thought I'd chicken out?"

"No, I just—"

"It's not like it's my first time."

"No, but—" He swallows, and the look he gives her is primal. "Fuck."

I turn away and find myself staring right into Hendrix's concerned gaze. "You sure? 'Cause you know it's—"

I laugh. "Permanent?"

He gives a smirk. "Uh-huh."

"Did you know that when you got that little cherub on your chest?"

His denim blue eyes soften as he holds my gaze. "Yes," he answers. "I did."

Before I can form a reply, Darius announces that we've arrived, and everyone erupts in a boisterous cheer.

The SUV comes to a stop, and as usual, we're behind the building, so at first glance, it is not all that appealing. The driver pulled right up to the nondescript steel door to prevent us from being seen, so I barely have a moment to look around before we're ushered inside.

When Darius announced his intentions for us tonight, he quickly roped PR Misty to help with his plans. With her magic connections, she was able to get us into one of the top tattoo studios in Vegas tonight.

*Just us*, as in they shut the whole place down.

But I guess when one of the biggest bands comes calling, it's sort of a big deal. Plus, I'm sure they're going to be walking away with a lot more than what they'd make on any other given night. And then some.

We're headed down a hallway when Hendrix says, "Hey Zander, remember when you got a tattoo for your brother's bachelor party? This is kind of like that."

"Yeah, only no one's getting married," he says with a smirk over his shoulder.

"I mean, you could." He shrugs. "Again, I mean. Since you two didn't bother to invite any of us the first time around."

I hear Darius behind me say, "Oh damn."

I snicker out a laugh.

"Or you could," he counters. "Seeing as I'm already married and you're not."

"Wait, what?" He almost trips as his gaze darts to mine. "He's not...I don't—"

"Yeah, wouldn't that be fun, guys?" Zander says over his shoulder. His grin is downright evil. "We all get tattoos, and then head to the little white chapel so Hendrix can have his very own Vegas wedding."

"What the fuck?" His eyes are like saucers, and I swear he's sweating out of his ears. "I have no idea what he's talking about."

"But I wanted an Elvis impersonator!" I whine.

"You do? Wait, you're fucking with me, aren't you?"

I grab his arm, laughing. "Come on, Romeo. I'm gonna get your name tattooed on my neck!"

"Okay, now I know you're messing with me!"

"I now understand why females carry the babies. We're obviously physically superior," Elena says as she watches her husband make the tiniest grimace as the tattoo artist works a deep line of ink into his skin.

"So rude," he mutters.

"Did you see me flinch?"

"I didn't realize it was a contest," he answers with a smirk. "Also, I believe I've told you at least a thousand times that you're physically superior."

"During sex, yeah."

Hendrix chuckles in the chair next to him. All the guys decided to get matching tattoos to commemorate the tour, so they went with the tour logo. It's a star with two interlocking Ms in the center.

"I meant more like when you gave birth to our beautiful daughter, but sure. Sex too."

Now, it's Elena who laughs.

She has already had her turn, and I have no idea what she got. All I know is that it was in an area that required her to go into a private room, and when it was finished, the tattoo artist came out, but Elena and Zander did not.

When they finally emerged thirty minutes later, Zander was grinning ear to ear as he discreetly slipped the artist a wad of cash.

Guess he really liked her tattoo.

I still haven't made a firm decision on mine. I've picked something out. I'm just questioning my choice.

What if I change my mind later?

What if I have regrets?

When I was married to Tanner, I knew something so off the cuff, like a tattoo, would never fly. Body art and piercings were for other people. Not a senator's family.

So I never allowed myself to think of the possibility.

Until now.

Now, I appreciate the idea of doing something spontaneous, of having this little souvenir from this wild time in my life when I traveled around the world with a bunch of rock stars.

"All done." The guy working on Hendrix gives his wrist one final wipe down and asks him to look it over before he covers it up. I still can't believe he had any room left, but right there, below his Creed tattoo, is a bold, five-point star with two interlocking Ms for Manic at Midnight.

He inspects his new ink, and I notice a flash of emotion cross his face before he replaces it with a broad grin. "Looks good, man. Thanks."

I'm not sure why, but seeing his expression in that moment really solidifies it for me.

My decision is made.

There will be no second-guessing. No regrets.

About ten minutes later, the guy—his name is Dex, I think—has his station wiped down, sanitized, and set up again. He looks up and gives me a wink. He's probably in his mid-twenties and already covered in tattoos. I thought Hendrix had a lot, but this guy has him beat. "You ready?"

"Um...yep."

Hendrix hasn't asked what I'm getting. I think he's letting it be a surprise, or he's giving me space to make the choice on my own.

Either way, he gives me an encouraging smile as I walk the few steps to Dex's space. The studio has an open concept, with six artists evenly spaced out behind a huge counter that separates the lobby. Each artist showcases their own unique style. Some display floor-to-ceiling sketches, while others have plants and photos of their friends and family. This all helps distinguish and divide their spaces. In the back, there are private areas for clients who might need to remove clothing.

Speaking of...

"I, um..." My throat suddenly feels dry. "I was thinking of getting it...here." I point to my hip.

"Sure," he nods, not seeming to care in the least. I guess he sees naked body parts all the time. "We'll probably need to head to the back, though, since you'll need to lower your jeans."

I hear a chair scraping against the linoleum as someone stands, and suddenly Hendrix is right behind me. "What now?"

Dex looks over my shoulder, and an amused grin spreads across his face. "This is your girl?"

"She is," he answers, with absolutely no hesitation.

My stomach flips like I've just been asked out to the junior prom. *I was never asked out to the junior prom.*

"He can come back," he tells me, before adding with a flirty wink, "If you want him to." Now, he's just fucking with him.

Hendrix practically growls behind me, placing a possessive hand on my hip.

"I want him to," I answer, before tossing a glance over my shoulder.

I find Elena standing next to Zander as he's finishing up. She looks up at me and gives me two enthusiastic thumbs up and mouths, *Good luck!*

I might need it.

We both follow Dex behind another curtain to a hallway that has a few closed doors.

"We each have our own private room back here too. Seems kind of redundant, but the owner likes to have us all out front and on display whenever he can."

"Well, it is Vegas," I say awkwardly as he ushers us into a small room that resembles his station up front. Several rolling carts line the walls. They're similar to the ones in my clinic, minus the plethora of stickers. A couple of chairs are scattered around, and the familiar padded table sits in the middle. A bunch of sketches adorn the walls, ranging from old-school pinup tattoos to detailed cartoon characters and gruesome-looking monsters.

He probably thinks my simple design is boring in comparison.

Hendrix must sense my nervousness because his hand slides over mine, and I instantly relax. I'm so glad he's here with me.

"You ever going to tell me what you're getting?" Hendrix finally asks. I wondered how long he would last before the suspense finally got to him.

While the guys were busy getting their tattoos, I went to the lobby and chatted with the artist at the counter. She helped me flip through some flash books to find something I liked, and then she was even kind enough to use the design as inspiration to draw something for me on the fly.

Now, I have an original piece of art to adorn my body.

And Hendrix is going to lose his mind when he finds out what it is.

"You'll see," I tease.

"All right." Dex points to the table. He's gone back into his professional mode and is no longer teasing Hendrix. "I need you to slide your jeans and underwear about halfway down. I can tuck a towel under the waistband.

"Okay."

"I'll get shit ready over here while you do that so your man doesn't try to murder me, yeah?" *Okay, maybe a little bit of teasing...*

I snort out a laugh. "Yeah."

"Cool."

He turns his back and begins to do...whatever it is tattoo artists do to prepare, while I position myself on the table. The paper crinkles beneath me as I move to undo the fly of my jeans.

Hendrix sighs as he gazes down at me. "I know I'm gonna find this ridiculously sexy in a day or two, but right now, I just want to let you know this is pure fucking torture." He looks up and levels his gaze on the back of Dex's head like he's making sure he's keeping his word about keeping his back turned.

I smother a grin as I slide my jeans down, and he runs a hand over his face. "Noted."

"Whoa." He stops me from going any further. "That's enough. Any further and you're going to be showing him things only I'm allowed to see."

"Only you, huh?"

His fingers brush over the sensitive skin of my hipbone. "That's right. Only me."

"All right." Dex's loud voice interrupts the moment, and as Hendrix steps back, I see him turn just in time to see Dex carrying over the stencil.

His eyes widen, and they snap back to mine.

"Seriously?"

I nod. "Well, it is *my* last name."

Dex helps me find the right placement for the small and delicate-looking cupid. "No, baby. Valentine is your last name. Cupid is the name *I* gave you. So you know what that means, don't you?"

I lick my lips and grin. "That we're matching now?"

"No," he says, his blue eyes blazing. "It means that you're mine."

PRES

Hen, we're gonna need an ETA on your arrival.

MERC

Agreed. Also, you got our tickets, right?

MYLES

Can we bring dates?

CASH

I'm the one handling your tickets, asshats. And no, you can't bring dates. VIP tickets don't grow on fucking trees.

PRES

Yeah, if I can't bring my boyfriend, you can't bring some rando from Tinder.

MYLES

What about Grindr?

CASH

No dates!

MYLES

Damn. All right. Guess I'll just…mingle backstage then.

MERC

Ew, Myles. Just no.

PRES

Hen! Answer me!

We're on our way to LA, and my phone has been buzzing incessantly for five minutes straight. I'm trying to ignore it as I work up the courage to ask Zara if she wants to have dinner with my family when we're in town. But when I glance down at my screen and see the mile-long text chain from my siblings, I seriously start to reconsider.

Maybe she's not ready for the Creed family yet.

I'm not even sure I'm ready for the Creed family yet.

Fucking hell.

ME

Jesus. Give me a second. I was busy.

That's a lie. I haven't done a single thing since we took off except stare out the window while my mind catastrophizes all the ways this conversation with Zara could go wrong.

*She tells me she's not ready.*

*She says she doesn't want that kind of relationship with me and never does.*

*She realizes how attached I've become and ends things.*

*I die miserable and alone.*

My right hand nervously plucks out a rhythm on the arm of the chair until my fingers cramp up when I see her exit the bathroom. I grab my phone and am met with a slew of next messages.

> **PRES**
> Busy? Sure. 😉
>
> **MERC**
> Busy with what???
>
> **MYLES**
> Why do I feel I'm missing something?
>
> **CASH**
> I don't care about any of this.

> **ME**
> Nothing.

> **PRES**
> Really? Because I heard you have a GIRLFRIEND!

"Hey," Zara greets me with a bright smile. "I can't believe how short this flight is."

"Yup. Almost there."

*Stop acting weird and just ask her.*

She gives me an odd look before briefly glancing down at my phone as it buzzes five times in a row.

"That'd be my siblings," I explain, before checking my screen again. "They are excited we're coming to town."

I type back a reply.

> **ME**
> You guys are fucking annoying. Also, WTF. Who told you...Z?

> **PRES**
> Elena confirmed it, but you've been photographed everywhere.

> **ME**
>
> Yeah, I've heard.

I should have known they'd already know about Zara.

They were right. Photos of us were everywhere. Exiting venues arm in arm, entering the hotel holding hands, and even a group shot from the tattoo studio Darius posted with the two of us looking very cozy.

Any idiot could see there was something going on.

But the fact that my family has seen it makes the press being involved a bit more real.

And scary.

In the past, the media haven't always been kind to Elena, and she's had to adjust her entire life because of it.

How would they treat the woman in my life?

She has already been through enough.

> **MERC**
>
> When do we get to meet her?
>
> **MYLES**
>
> Is she hot?
>
> **ME**
>
> I will literally kill you, Myles.
>
> **CASH**
>
> She's hot.
>
> **ME**
>
> Fuck the both of you.
>
> **PRES**
>
> Why are you still here? I thought you left.

Cash has left the group Creed Counsel of Chaos.

Myles has added Cash to the group Creed Counsel of Chaos.

> **MYLES**
> Sorry, Cash, you can't leave. We need at least one grown-up present at all times.
>
> **CASH**
> FML.

Looking up at her, I take a moment to just soak in every detail as she scrolls through her social media. From the scattering of freckles on the bridge of her nose to the stray pieces of brown locks that never seem to stay in whatever claw clip contraption she's got in her hair.

She's so fucking beautiful.

Every day with her feels like a free fall. Like I'm tumbling toward something I'm completely unprepared for. I feel like I should be. I grew up in a house with two parents who are madly in love with each other and love us just as deeply.

I know what love is supposed to feel like. I've seen it in the quiet moments when my dad sneaks a kiss when he thinks no one is looking, or when they'd read each one of us our own bedtime story to make us feel special.

But this? It all feels bigger than that.

I told her I was okay without labels, but god, do I want to put one on us. On her.

I want the whole fucking world to know she's mine, and I am hers.

And that thought alone scares the ever-loving shit out of me.

Because what if she doesn't feel the same?

What if Tanner broke something that can't be fixed?

ME

> FYI, she's not my girlfriend. We haven't exactly put a label on it.

PRES

LAME!

MYLES

Dude.

MERC

Why?

ME

> Because she just got divorced. And we're taking it slow.

And I'm fucking terrified.

"Hey." Her hesitant voice has me looking up into her dark-brown eyes.

"Hey." I give her a warm smile.

She returns it with a shy one. "I was wondering..." She nibbles on her bottom before continuing. "Do you think when we're in San Francisco that you might be okay with having dinner with my parents?" I stare at her blankly and blink, completely dumbfounded. She misreads my expression and immediately starts to backpedal. "It's okay if you don't—if you think it's too soon. I mean, we can just do something else, or—"

I press a finger to her lips, putting a stop to her panicked verbal diarrhea. "I would love to."

"You would?"

I chuckle and nod. "I've been freaking out for the last twenty minutes trying to find the courage to ask you to meet my crazy family, so honestly, this is a relief."

"You're kidding?"

"Nope."

"But...wait. Aren't I going to meet them at the concert?"

"Yeah." I shrug. "But that's not really a proper introduction, is it? I want them to meet you. To get to know you and see how amazing you are."

Her expression softens. "Okay."

"Okay. But fair warning," I say. "My family is crazy."

"My mom asked you for shirtless pics of Asher for her home screen, so let's not compare crazy, m'kay?"

"All right." I shrug. "But don't say I didn't warn you."

"I tried to warn her," I tell Zander with a shrug as we stand back and watch the mayhem.

"In all fairness, I don't think anyone can ever be prepared to meet your family. I had the benefit of meeting them in small doses, and even that was a lot."

Literally every member of my family, minus Myles—where is that little shit?—is crammed into the small room that makes up Zara's clinic in the Crypto.com Arena. While I was doing a meet and greet, one of the PAs gave them a tour backstage, and I managed to head them off just before they got here.

Not that it did any good.

"A doctor!" My mom gushes, turning toward me with her hand on her heart. "So impressive, Hendrix."

I scrunch my brow in confusion and sneak a glance toward Zara. She smirks. "Thanks?"

"And you're so pretty. Isn't she pretty, Hen?"

"Yeah, Pres." I grin, my eyes still fixed on Zara, who I

know is probably hating the attention. Especially since she hasn't had a chance to change and is still in the leggings and oversized sweatshirt she wore on the plane. "She's beautiful."

That earns me a blush. Cash comes to pat me on the back, and I tear my gaze away from her to focus on my big brother. "Good job. I'm proud of you."

"For dating a doctor?"

He chuckles. It's an odd sound coming from my grumpy ass brother. "No, for the tour. You're getting noticed, and it's working."

"It is?"

We turn away from the chatter, and I feel each beat of my heart as I wait for him to reply. "I know Dad doesn't represent you, but we've still been getting calls."

"Really?"

"You don't have an agent, Hendrix. They don't know who else to contact."

"Yeah, well, my last one kind of fucked me over." But that wasn't my dad's fault. It was mine for not listening to him.

"I know, which is why it's important you have someone you trust. And fast."

I state the obvious. "Dad isn't an agent. He's a manager."

"But we have agents on staff. You know that."

Yeah, I did. I knew all of them. I'd worked with all of them when I was my dad's assistant. "I want Saul."

"Zander's agent?"

I nod just as a burst of laughter is heard over my shoulder. I resist the urge to look, but I know it's my sisters and Zara, and damn if that doesn't make me happy.

"Dad recommended him to Z because he's good and honest. I know he won't screw me over. Plus, he's been trying to get me to sign with him for years. I've just been—"

"Stubborn?"

"Yeah. That."

"I'll make it happen. In the meantime, just keep doing what you're doing. Play well, get noticed—maybe a little less for the abs?"

"Jealous?" I tease.

He just shakes his head, and I see the faintest whisper of a smile. It reminds me of the man he used to be. Before Nikki. "Just because I sit behind a desk doesn't mean I couldn't still take you, asshat."

"But you'd have to get the suit dirty." I brush a nonexistent piece of lint off the dark navy blazer. "Seriously, dude. Who wears Armani to a rock concert?"

"Someone with style?" he says as he gives my faded black jeans and hoodie a once-over. "Anyway, I'll be in touch when we have some leads, and hopefully soon we can find you something a bit more permanent. Somewhere you can call home."

My heart hammers in my chest.

This is what I've always wanted. A shot to prove myself.

To Edwin. To my family. The world.

"Sounds perfect," I answer. But does it? I toss a glance in Zara's direction.

Suddenly, I'm not so sure.

## Chapter Twenty-Five

# HENDRIX

It's almost showtime, and I'm so fucking pumped.

Having my family here tonight is chaotic—the Creed family always is—but I'm so glad they are. I wouldn't be the man I am without every one of those crazy fuckers.

We're all headed in mass down to the stage. Zara's sister finally showed up, and I got to meet the infamous Violet Valentine in person. As soon as she came whirling into the clinic with her backstage pass around her neck and sky-high heels, she's been a tornado of energy ever since.

She and Zara may look a lot alike, but they couldn't be more different. It's obvious right off the bat that Violet is a people person and takes the time to greet and fawn over every person in the room without an ounce of nervousness.

When she reached me, she gave me a once-over, as if she was making sure I matched the glimpse she got of me on that video call. Then she gave Zara what I assume was a nod of approval and said, "Don't hurt my sister, pretty boy."

Then she hugged Zara and started talking a mile a minute about LA traffic, backstabbing models, and asshole men.

I back away right around the asshole men part of the conversation.

"Have I told you how ridiculously hot you look right now?" I whisper in Zara's ear. My arm is slung over her shoulder as we make our way to the stage. She looks insane tonight, opting out of the usual jeans and T-shirt she wears under her white coat. Instead, she's got on a tight black miniskirt and a cut-off Manic at Midnight tank. It shows off her midriff and the lace bralette underneath. I have a feeling Elena had something to do with this look, because tonight, she looks like she's with the band. She looks like a rock star's girlfriend.

It's hot as fuck.

"I was thinking the same thing about you," she says, as her gaze roams over the tight black tee and jeans that have become somewhat of a staple for me on stage.

I tilt my head to kiss her. She laughs as I stumble, attempting to walk and kiss her at the same time.

"Gross." Presley pretends to gag behind me.

I grin over my shoulder. "Consider this revenge for all the times I've had to watch you suck face with Jace." Speaking of fuckboys... "Hey, where is Myles? I haven't seen him all night?"

"He's around here somewhere," she answers vaguely. "Probably in a dark corner somewhere."

"Well, I'm so glad he could make it," I mutter sarcastically.

"I'm sure he's proud of you," Zara says, reaching up to kiss me once more. I ignore the teasing from behind me and lean in.

Just as she's pulling away, I hear her gasp and then freeze. "Tanner."

My head whips to where her eyes are glued to the figure ahead of us. He stands out like a sore thumb in his dark blazer and jeans. His blond hair is slicked back in some vain attempt to look cool, and he has a VIP badge wrapped around his neck.

How the fuck did he get one of those?

He searches the crowd, looking a little lost until his gaze lands on me, quickly followed by Zara. Anger flashes in his expression as his eyes scan Zara's appearance. An odd mixture of lust and displeasure washes over him as he takes in the short skirt and her bare stomach.

Then he zeros in on the way my arm is wrapped around her waist. How I've slid my fingers just below the waistband of that tiny skirt she's wearing, because I just can't help touching her bare skin.

And how I'm making no attempt to move them.

His eyes narrow, and he surges forward.

"What are you doing here?" Zara demands.

"I need to talk to you."

"You've said plenty."

"How the fuck did you even get back here?" I demand.

His eyes slowly turn to me, and the look he gives me is pure disdain, like I'm beneath him. But, then again, he's always treated me this way.

Disdain, with just a touch of jealousy.

Only now, there's a hell of a lot more jealousy in the mix.

"I'm a senator's son," he says with a wave of his hand. "Do you think my father can't get me a ticket to some frivolous concert?"

"Frivolous?" someone says behind him. He turns, and Asher is standing there with his arms folded across his chest and a menacing smile. His hair is perfectly mussed, and he's opted for the no-shirt route tonight, showcasing all of his tattoos. It's a stark contrast to the clean-cut vibe Tanner has going on. "This frivolous concert, as you call it, employs over a hundred and fifty people—not including the locals we bring on at every stop.

"Over the next five months, this *frivolous* concert will gross over eighty million. When we come to town, hotels are full, restaurants thrive, and tourism gets a boost. I'd say our frivolous concert is doing more for the economy than your father, who, last I heard, was trailing in the polls by nine percent." He fakes a grimace as he casually shoves his hands in his pockets, and I physically have to hold back laughter. "But what do I know? I'm just a dumb rock star."

I think I hear Mercury mutter, *That was so fucking hot*, behind us, but as her big brother, I try to pretend I didn't.

Tanner's face is flushed with anger. His fists clench tightly at his sides. "No, what you are is a joke." He scoffs. "You think I don't know who you are. Who you really are? Some washed-up Scottish nobleman forgotten by his family, who parades around like some cheap—"

"That's enough." I step in because I'm fucking done with this pretentious asshole and his whole Richie Rich attitude.

Asher raises a hand, holding me off. His expression is calm and collected. He even manages an amused grin as he turns his attention back to Tanner. "It's Lord, actually," he states, taking a quiet step forward, with purposeful intent. Tanner falters. "My title? Well, my father's I guess, but you already know that. Didn't you?"

Tanner's face flushes scarlet red.

"If you're going to trash-talk me, at least get the details right. And since you brought it up, I'm not just a washed-up nobleman. I'm a washed-up royal," he says with a casual shrug, as if it's a totally normal thing to say. "My great-great-grandmother was a cousin to the queen. I'm like thirty-ninth in line for the throne. Mad, isn't it?" His eyes narrow at Tanner. "Fortunately, I don't need to be king to throw your ass out of here."

He motions to a security guard, and Tanner turns to Zara.

"I never wanted you!" he shouts as the guard grabs him. "My father needed to cover up a scandal and said voters would love a Cinderella romance. But you're no princess, Zara."

His words echo through the hall, bouncing around in my head. I can't unhear them.

Can't let them go.

"I'll be right back."

She grabs my hand. I turn around and see the fear in her eyes. "Don't do it," she says. "He's not worth it, and his father will ruin you, Hen. His reach is too far and—"

I silence her with a kiss. It's quick and hard. "I won't let him ruin anything, but I can't let him just walk away after what he said, Zara. I just can't."

She gives one quick nod, and before she has a chance to change her mind, I dart off in the direction that Carlos, the security guard, went, knowing I don't have much time. Our run-in with Tanner cost us precious time, and now we're down to the wire before showtime.

But I have to do this.

I appreciate what Asher did back there, but if I let Tanner leave this building with those words still ringing in the air. I need Zara to know no one is allowed to treat her that way ever again.

Unlike this scumbag, I will always defend her.

I will always be on her side.

"Carlos!" I holler down the hallway. "Hold up!"

He's somehow managed to shut Tanner up for the moment, but the minute they both turn around, he starts back up again. "Oh, seriously? What now?"

"I just need a minute with him," I tell Carlos.

"Okay, but no fighting. Your girl's busy enough without having to patch you up too."

I snort and point a finger over at Tanner. "You think I couldn't take *him*? Besides, that piece of shit is my girl's ex-husband. Pretty sure he'd deserve it."

"No shit? That whole scene back there makes a hell of a lot more sense now." He just shakes his head, giving Tanner a disapproving glare. "You take all the time you need. And by all the time, I mean two minutes." He glances at his watch and winces. "Make it one."

He takes a step back, and I turn my attention to Tanner. The smug look he's sporting makes me want to hit him, despite my promise to Zara.

"So...you here to piss all over your territory and show me what a big man you are?"

Okay, now I really want to hit him.

"What bothers you the most, Tanner? That she's happy? Or that she's happy with me?"

His jaw tics. "It'll never last, you know? This thing between you. If she wasn't happy with me, you sure as hell don't have a chance."

"Did you even try?" I demand, raising my voice in

anger. "Or did you just think your presence alone was enough to keep her happy? Because that's not love. That's devotion, at best. But, then again, I doubt someone like you would even know the difference."

He makes a noise that tells me he doesn't believe a word I've said. Not surprising. I didn't expect him to.

This conversation isn't about him anyway.

"Tell me, how much did you use Zara to get you through med school? 'Cause we both know you couldn't have done it by yourself."

Now that gets a reaction. I swear to god, there is actual steam coming out of his ears.

"That bitch didn't do—"

I move so fast, he barely has a chance to react before I slam his body against the wall. My forearm wedges itself neatly beneath his windpipe, and I hold it there, watching him squirm.

"I think your one minute is up," Carlos interjects, clearly trying to avoid an impending brawl.

"We're just finishing up," I say darkly, easing my grip on his throat. As his lungs suck in air, I pin him with an icy glare. "She doesn't want to see you anymore, Tanner. She doesn't want to talk to you. So this is the last time you show up anywhere uninvited. It's the last time you make demands on her life and how she's living it. And it's the last fucking time you call her names. Got it?"

His eyes are staring daggers at me, but he manages a curt nod before Carlos hauls him away. I allow myself a moment to breathe, to steady my shaking hands.

And then I leave Tanner behind, walk to the stage and forget all about Tanner fucking Price.

It's showtime, baby.

## Chapter Twenty-Six

# ZARA

The morning after the LA concert, I wake up feeling...off.

At first, I think it's just warm in the room. Or maybe it's the hot man snuggled up next to me. But then I quickly realize it's me. I'm hot. Not just hot. I'm burning up. I throw off the covers and feel the breeze from the air conditioner hit my sweat-soaked skin. It makes me shiver.

Shit, that's not good.

I instantly shift into doctor mode.

Hangover? No.

We didn't go out last night after the concert. After Hendrix's family thoroughly congratulated him and told him how happy and proud they were, the two of us came back here and celebrated privately.

A shiver races up my spine that has nothing to do with my current symptoms. The way that man worships my body, like it's his sole purpose in life...I'm not sure I'll ever get enough.

I'm not sure I want to.

Seeing the way he stood up for me in front of Tanner.

The way he was ready to tear apart the world after he admitted what I had been suspecting for a while now.

Our entire marriage was a farce.

I thought it would hurt more, but hearing him say it out loud was, in a way, sort of cathartic. I can move on and not feel an ounce of guilt for it. He never loved me, so why should I mourn something that was never real in the first place?

Especially when what is happening between Hendrix and me *is* real. So real it sometimes scares me.

I felt some of the walls I was holding up collapse last night.

I loved meeting his family. He's so close to them. It reminds me a lot of my own, and I can't wait to introduce him to them.

"Hey." I hear Hendrix's soft voice. His voice is groggy as he wakes, sitting up next to me. I turn to face him, and the warm smile on his face instantly fades. "What's the matter?"

His eyes search my face, down my body, and back up again. I feel gross, and when I self-consciously tug at the tank top I threw on late last night, I realize it's nearly soaked through.

That doesn't make me feel any better.

"I don't know," I answer honestly. "I don't feel well."

His hand goes to my forehead. "You feel warm."

I give him an amused grin as I swing my legs off the bed. "That is not an accurate way to check for a fever."

"Yeah, well, it always seemed to work for my mom."

I rise to my feet, determined to grab my medical bag and a fresh T-shirt, but before I can take a single step, my head starts to spin.

"Zara?" I can hear the note of concern in his voice as

I reach for the side of the bed. His hand is around my waist, guiding me back down to the bed before I have a chance to respond to him.

"Thanks," I tell him. "Can you grab me my—" But he's already halfway across the room to get it.

"On it," he says over his shoulder. A moment later, he returns with my med bag, a new shirt—Is he telepathic?—and a bottle of water.

He kneels in front of me and unzips the bag, then lets me take over, knowing I have the inside organized within an inch of my life. I grab the thermometer, but he swiftly swipes it out of my hand.

"Hey!" I protest. "Who's the professional here?"

"Who's the one who can barely stand?" he counters.

"Fine. I guess it's not that hard." I gesture toward the thermometer and then to my forehead, prompting him to roll his eyes.

"Thanks for the vote of confidence, Doc." He turns it on and holds it close to my forehead, waits for the beep, and then sighs. "Looks like you're not going anywhere today." He turns it around to show me. It's just under one hundred and one.

*Dammit.*

I glance down at my watch. We're supposed to be at his family's house in two hours, and now he will have to go without me.

"I'm so sorry," I start to say, but I have to stop myself because my stomach lurches, and suddenly I'm leaping off the bed and sprinting toward the bathroom.

Just when I thought this day couldn't get any worse.

I make it just in time to heave my guts into the toilet. It feels like I'm there for an hour at least, but it's probably a minute tops. By the time I'm done, I'm physically exhausted. I didn't realize just how weak I was feeling until my body decided to try to exorcise a demon. But now I'm feeling everything, and it all hurts. My whole fucking body feels like it got run over by a truck.

"You okay?"

I hadn't even noticed he was here. But as I flush the toilet and grab some toilet paper to wipe the tears quickly, and whatever else is on my face, I realize he's been here the whole damn time. I think he even held my hair back.

I groan, letting my head fall back to rest against the wall. "You did not need to see that."

"Did you think I was just going to stand out there while you were getting so sick you started to sob?"

I was sobbing? I don't exactly remember that, but it explains the tears.

"I hate throwing up, so I wouldn't blame you. Give me blood and guts all damn day long, but this? No fucking thank you." My voice is hoarse as I make a valiant effort to stand. I can't even get halfway. It's pretty pathetic. Hendrix steps in, wraps an arm around my waist, and lifts me up.

"Well, I guess we make a good team, don't we?"

I swallow, feeling a surge of emotions catch in my throat. "Yeah. I guess we do."

He holds my gaze for a moment before he says, "Come on, let's get you back to bed."

He takes a step toward the door. "Wait!" I exclaim. "Please let me preserve an ounce of dignity. Can I brush my teeth first?"

His eyes sparkle with warmth, and he chuckles. "Sure, but then it's straight to bed."

"Yes, doctor," I quip as he helps me walk the short

distance to the counter. He promptly lifts me so I can sit on it rather than stand another minute on my Jell-O legs.

Grabbing my toothbrush, he lets out an amused *pfft*. "I would rather we take up role-playing when you're not puking your guts out, but I appreciate your enthusiasm."

He slathers it in a bit of toothpaste, wets it, and hands it to me. "So am I the nurse in this scenario? Since you're the doctor?"

"What? No. You're the rock star," he says, as if it's an obvious conclusion. "We're switching roles in this fantasy. I get to wear the white coat, and you'll be the one with the bass strapped to your hip." He pauses and swallows. "Fuck. Maybe this was a bad conversation to start. Now, I'm getting hard at the idea of you holding my bass."

I lean over the sink and spit out my toothpaste. "You could always teach me," I suggest. "That would be one way of making your fantasy come to life. Or at least part of it. And if you're really into wearing my lab coat, I could let you borrow it." I look at him in the mirror's reflection, my gaze running up and down his muscled frame. "Pretty sure you'll rip it Hulk-style the second you put it on, though."

I double-blink, and Hendrix laughs. "You're imagining it, aren't you?"

"Yeah," I confess, my gaze stuck on his in the mirror. "Why is that so hot?"

"'Cause you're obsessed with me. Obviously," he says with a cocky grin as he helps me off the counter. After I take a few wobbly steps, he bends down and swoops me up into his arms.

My stomach flutters, and this time, it has nothing to do with being sick.

Yeah, he might be right.

I think I am a little obsessed with Hendrix Creed.

After he gets me settled back in bed, he does what he does best and orders way too much room service, saying he doesn't know what will *jive* with my stomach.

Honestly, I'm not sure anything will.

I haven't had to dash back into the bathroom yet, but it's only been an hour, so I'm not holding my breath. For now, though, I've managed to keep down the little bit of water I drank to take the Tylenol for my fever.

And now, I'm enjoying the view of a freshly showered Hendrix walking into the main part of the suite in nothing but a low-slung towel and a knowing smirk. "See anything you like?"

"Maybe if you drop that towel a little lower," I tease, even though my words lack the conviction they usually do. I don't think I could follow through with any of the lewd thoughts going through my mind right now, even if I tried.

For someone whose job is to care for sick people, I'm a total hypocrite when it comes to being sick myself. At work, I always emphasize the importance of rest and downtime when a patient is unwell, but when I'm the one affected, I just want to get it over with. Rest? Who has time for that?

Yes, I know. I'm a terrible patient.

"Honestly, I'm mostly jealous that you're clean," I

confess. "Even with the new shirt you got me and clean teeth, I still feel disgusting."

"Well, that's easy to solve. We can get you in the shower after we eat," he says over his shoulder as he rummages through his suitcase. "Or rather, after I eat and we cross our fingers and spoon-feed you broth and crackers one at a time."

"We?" I focus on that one word he keeps repeating. "What do you mean, we? You have to leave for your parents' house in less than an hour."

"I'm not going."

I sit up straight and instantly regret it. The room tilts, and I clutch the side of my head as a spike of pain shoots through it. "What do you mean you're not going?"

I feel the bed dip as he comes to sit next to me. He's now wearing a pair of gray joggers. His chest is bare, and that little cupid tattoo is staring back at me. I've lost count of how many times I've touched and traced it with my fingertips. Kissed it with my lips. Licked it with my tongue.

It's different from mine. It's bigger. More masculine, if you can imagine a baby angel being such a thing. But every time I see it, I picture a younger version of him walking into a tattoo studio and sitting down in a chair to have it inked on his skin.

And thinking of me the whole time.

It humbles me.

It makes me feel things I probably shouldn't feel a month in, especially not after my recent divorce. But I can't help it.

I have questions I want to ask him when I look at this tattoo. Questions I'm too afraid to vocalize...

*Did you ever think we'd see each other again?*

*Did you wish for it?*

*Or did you just hope this little cherub would ensure you never forgot?*

Because I didn't. I never forgot.

"I mean," he replies, gently running his hand through my hair. "I texted my family and told them you were sick and that we couldn't make it." I open my mouth to respond, but no words come out. "Did you really think I would just leave you here?"

*Yes. Kind of,* I want to say.

"I'm not used to being taken care of. Well, not anymore," I amend. "Growing up, my parents were the perfect duo. She was the panicker, always jumping to the worst possible conclusion. I couldn't even sneeze without her rushing me to the doctor. But my dad was the practical one, stepping in when shit went sideways and someone needed to keep it together. They took care of us, and I always felt protected."

"But you didn't with Tanner?" It's not a question. Not really.

"The first time I got sick when we were dating, I texted him to let him know I wasn't feeling well, and his response was something like, 'Well, good thing you're a med student. Let me know when you're feeling better so I can get those notes you took.'"

"Jesus, Zara. That's cruel."

"At the time, I thought he was just being practical. I *was* a med student. I *did* know how to take care of myself. After we got married, I continued with that same belief. Now I was a doctor. I didn't need the help of my husband, my parents, or anyone else to take care of me when I could do it myself."

"Just because you can do something doesn't mean

you should have to," he utters, confirming the words I've been too afraid to say aloud for far too long. "Everyone deserves to be taken care of. Will you let me?"

Even after all that, I hesitate. "But your family…"

"Will still be there tomorrow. And the next day. They're not going anywhere, Cupid."

"But won't they be mad?"

"At who? At you for being sick?" He scoffs, shifting to fluff the pillows behind me. Then, he gently eases me back down on the bed and runs a sly hand across my forehead, clearly checking my temperature.

He's not fooling anyone.

"Or at me for staying here to care for my sick girl-friend?" As soon as the words are out of his mouth, his eyes go wide. "Not that you're my girlfriend. It's just that they accidentally called you that a few times and—" He sucks in a huge gulp of air, and I can't help but laugh.

"You gonna survive that slip-up?" I tease.

"Probably not. I think I just died a little."

"I actually think I might be okay with you calling me your girlfriend. That is, if you want to?"

Those blue eyes go all round and soft, and then he breaks into a heart-stopping grin. He bends down to kiss me, but my palm shoots out and stops him before he can reach my face. "Oh no, you don't. You're lucky I'm even letting you stay in this room."

"What? Why?"

"I'm not sure if anyone ever told you how germs spread, but kissing is a pretty good way to do it."

"So, you mean, like all that kissing we did last night? Not to mention all the other stuff…"

"Shit. Yeah. Oh my god, what if I get you sick, Hen? What if you miss a concert because of me?"

His face softens, and his hand brushes away an errant piece of hair from my face. "Then I miss a concert." He shrugs. "Tommy from the opening band can fill in for me, and my doctor girlfriend can help nurse me back to health." My insides instantly melt at his use of the word girlfriend. I hadn't planned on making it official with Hendrix, but after spending the evening with his family and seeing how he cared for me this morning, it just felt right. Now that it's decided, I'm definitely on board.

"Okay." I relent.

"Great." His face lights up, just as a light knock can be heard at the door. He grabs the remote from the night-stand and hands it to me. "Pick a movie, Cupid. Because after we eat and I give you a very thorough washing in the shower, we're going to have our first movie marathon as boyfriend and girlfriend."

I feel like absolute shit, but I can't help but grin.

It turns out to be the best sick day of my life.

## Chapter Twenty-Seven

# HENDRIX

It's barely six in the morning, but I'm wide awake. The sun is slowly rising over the horizon, and as the light spills through the curtains, I lie in bed and watch the slow, steady rhythm of her breathing.

*Boyfriend.*

I've never wanted to be anyone's boyfriend.

But Zara is different. She always has been.

Ever since I walked into Green Library and saw her sitting at a table, looking like a damn knockout in her oversized sweater and pile of books, I knew she was going to ruin me.

I just assumed it would be in the name of science.

I had no idea that I'd be ruined for her, that she'd bind herself to me so completely that no other woman would compare.

And now that I have her back, I don't want to be just her boyfriend.

I just want to be hers.

My phone buzzes on the nightstand, and I quickly

reach for it, not wanting it to wake her. I smile when I see a text from my mom checking on Zara.

MOM

How's she doing?

I gently touch her forehead with the back of my hand. She can complain all she wants, but like I told her, this method always seems to work for my mom. And besides, her fancy thermometer is noisy. This way, I can at least ensure she won't wake up.

ME

Better, I think. Doesn't feel feverish anymore. And she was able to eat a little late last night.

MOM

That's good. Probably just one of those twenty-four-hour bugs. Has anyone else been sick?

ME

Not that I know of. She obviously can't talk about specific patients, but she would give us all a heads-up if something was going around.

MOM

Just making sure what's "going around" isn't the nine-month variety. 🤰😏

My eyes widen, nearly falling out of my head as I experience a momentary heart attack.

A baby? Is she trying to kill me?

Zara definitely had the flu yesterday, and I'm not sure we've been having sex long enough to create another human.

The usual shudder that follows that particular thought isn't as terrifying as it typically is though, and I take a moment to consider that. I try to picture Zara coming out of the bathroom yesterday, holding a pregnancy test.

Oh, the idea of it is still terrifying as fuck. But maybe it's also a little exciting?

*Huh, weird.*

I grab my phone and reluctantly leave the warmth of the bed for the chaise out in the living room area. Clearly, this conversation with my mom isn't wrapping up anytime soon, and I do not want to be the reason Zara wakes up.

Watching her nearly collapse yesterday was scary as hell. Hearing her cry in the bathroom as she retched into the toilet felt devastating, because there was nothing I could do except hold her hair back and watch her suffer.

I remember Zander telling me how, as a father, you feel completely helpless during the birth of your child. You gain a new appreciation for your wife's strength and resilience, but at the same time, you'd do absolutely anything to switch places with her so she wouldn't have to endure that kind of pain.

That's how it felt to see her so sick yesterday—and that was just the flu.

I'm so fucking screwed.

ME

I know Zara is the doctor here, but I don't think having a fever is a common pregnancy symptom.

Also, you are just a little too excited about the prospect of me knocking up the woman I've been seeing for less than a month.

MOM

> Okay, you might be right. It's a bit too
> soon, but I've seen the way you look at
> her, Hen.

My heart starts to gallop in my chest.

ME

> And how do I look at her?

MOM

> Like she's the perfect rhythm to your
> favorite song.

Leave it to my mom to make me all emotional on a Thursday morning.

ME

> I don't want to fuck this up.

MOM

> Then don't.

ME

> That's your great motherly advice?
> Don't?

My phone buzzes again, but this time it's a FaceTime call. She does this a lot. She gets tired of typing out her replies, gives up, and just calls us. When we call her out on it, she claims she just wants to see our pretty faces.

I get up and walk to the balcony. I sneak out and gently close the sliding glass door behind me.

"Hey," I say, after I swipe across my screen to answer.

"There's my rock star son." She beams. Her long, silvery-blonde hair is loose. Tiny tendrils flutter with the breeze as she wraps her favorite sapphire blue blanket around her shoulders. The color matches her eyes. "I couldn't go a second longer without seeing your face."

I offer her a warm smile, knowing she's full of shit. "Missed me that much, huh?"

"I always miss you when you're gone."

"Yeah." I grin and shrug, trying to mask how much her words affect me. I miss her when I'm gone too. I miss all of them, and the thought of traveling on a more permanent basis is starting to feel more like a curse than a dream. "I imagine Creed family dinner just isn't the same lately without me there to liven it up."

She rolls her eyes, but I notice the proud gleam in her gaze as she settles into her favorite lounge chair on the balcony. If I listen closely during the pauses between our words, I can almost hear the waves crashing against the beach. "Well, Jace was here, so he kept it lively enough."

I stiffen. "What do you mean?"

She waves a dismissive hand, and I know what she's about to say I won't like. "He had a little bit too much to drink, and some of the things he said—"

"Like what?"

She nibbles on her bottom lip. "I don't think he meant any of it. But your sister did seem embarrassed."

"What did he say, Mom?"

"Some stuff about the band," she states. "How he wouldn't have bothered coming if he knew none of you were going to show up."

"What the fuck?" I'm pacing now. Five steps to the left. Pivot. Five steps to the right. Pivot. "Why would he even care? He's supposed to be there to spend time with Presley and get to know the family. Why would any of the band members—aside from me—be at our family dinner?"

"I guess he heard that Asher came to the last one before you all left, and he was under the impression that it would be a regular thing."

"So he's just using Pres to meet celebrities? Is that it? Another opportunist asshole?" We've had our fair share of those throughout the years.

She sighs. "I don't know. But your father was not pleased. He hates that guy."

"Join the fucking club," I mutter. "Anything else I missed?"

"Um..." She puts her finger to her lips, and her eyes brighten. "Oh! Hollis called while we were all here. Presley put him on speaker, and everyone got to say hello. I was bummed you missed it."

Now that's a name I haven't heard in a long time. "No shit? Hollis Beck? I haven't spoken to him in a long time. How's he doing?"

"Good." My mom smiles warmly. "He's really good. Living in Nashville. I guess that's what made him think of us. He knew Manic was in town and heard you joined the band—"

"Temporarily," I remind her, trying not to let the ache in my chest show on my face. I don't know how, in such a short time, these guys have become like brothers to me. Even Darius, who drives me kind of crazy. How am I going to move on to another band in a few months?

She rolls her eyes. "Yes, temporarily. And since he still had Presley's contact info saved on his phone, he reached out to her, and we all just happened to be there when he did."

"That's great," I tell her, suddenly flooded with a dozen or more memories of my longtime friend. I had a lot of friends throughout the years, but he was one of the special ones, one of those honorary siblings I told Zara about. "I'm glad he did. I know you and Dad have missed him. I certainly have."

"We have," she agrees. "It was nice to hear his voice. Almost as nice as hearing yours, even if it sounds a bit groggy."

I laugh. "Well, you did text me at six in the morning."

"Funny thing about text messages, Hen. You don't have to answer them if you're not awake."

I sigh. "I was awake. I was watching Zara sleep."

"Oh, my sweet boy. You have it bad, don't you?"

"Yeah, Mom. I do, which is why I'm gonna need you to do better with your advice. *Just don't* isn't enough."

She chuckles before taking a long sip of her coffee. It's kind of making me a little jealous, but there's no way I'm going to risk making myself a cup if it means waking up my girl. Not after the day she had.

*My girl.* The thought of that makes my throat feel thick.

"Okay, you want the long version? Here it is. Your father and I haven't made it this far just because we love each other, Hen. Loving each other is honestly the easy part of the equation. If it were hard, there wouldn't be a multi-billion dollar industry profiting from it."

I raise an eyebrow in doubt. "I think you might be confused on why people use dating apps nowadays, Mom."

She shakes her head and *tsks* at me. "Oh, stop. I know exactly why. But for every person on an app just to hook up, another one hopes to find something lasting."

"Okay, I guess I can see your point." I don't really know any of those *other* people, but I've heard of them.

"Falling for someone is the easy part. It's what

happens afterward that is the hard part. Those are the days when you find out if the foundation of your relationship was built on sand or stone."

Now I'm really jealous of her coffee. I rub my temples and sink into one of the lounge chairs. "Can we not talk in metaphors right now? My brain usually runs on caffeine at this hour, and I'm currently on empty."

"Am I going to have to do this much hand-holding with all of you to get my grandbabies?"

I shrug. "Seems like you got one already without doing a thing." Her face pales, and I then realize what I just said. "Mom, I didn't mean...I was just kidding and—"

Her face shifts into something resembling a smile as she waves a dismissive hand. "No, it's fine. I know what you meant."

Silence stretches between us before I ask, "Do you think Cash will ever..."

My mom lets out a long breath. "I don't know. I hope so. I really do, but that woman broke something in him. It will take something or someone extraordinary to put everything back together again."

"Is that what I need to be for Zara? Extraordinary?"

She smiles, a genuine one this time, and it's that sweet, motherly kind of smile only a child recognizes. "Yeah, you do." She takes another sip of coffee, and I see her look toward the horizon. "But don't forget. She needs to be extraordinary for you too. It has to go both ways."

"Is that how I keep from sinking in the metaphorical sand?"

She laughs. "Having a solid sex life doesn't hurt, either."

"God, Mom," I shudder. "Just shoot me dead right here."

"You're gonna be fine," she assures me.

"How do you know?"

"Because," she says, "I've never seen you so invested in something, Hen. And that—right there—is half the battle."

*Chapter Twenty-Eight*

# ZARA

I wake up to an empty bed, which is a bummer. I've grown accustomed to the way Hendrix sleeps, his large body sticking halfway out of the covers because he refuses to stop snuggling up against me, even though it makes him hot.

I, on the other hand, love being wrapped up in all that warmth. He's basically a giant heating blanket wrapped in a sexy six-pack man body. That's why waking up without him is confusing, because I can't tell if I'm cold due to his absence or because I'm once again feverish.

I quickly pat down my T-shirt and...no sweat to be found. That's good.

My stomach feels fine as well. In fact, just as the thought crosses my mind, it grumbles in response.

Okay, two for two.

I swing my feet to the side of the bed and rise. Will you look at that? No dizziness. No headache. I think I might have successfully beaten the twenty-four-hour flu right on time.

I always have been the punctual type.

I head to the bathroom to take care of my morning business, even spending a minute to brush my teeth. When I'm finished, it doesn't take long to find my long-lost boyfriend.

My cheeks heat.

*Boyfriend.*

I wonder when that word isn't going to make me blush?

If I keep waking up to find him sitting in the corner of our suite with his bass held to his bare chest, probably not anytime soon.

He is so damn beautiful.

He's wearing large headphones that are attached to an amp. His eyes are closed as he plays. It's like he's in another world.

I am in awe of his talent. His fingers never stop moving, working in sync to create whatever bass line is pumping through those headphones of his.

There's no doubt in my mind that this was what he was put on this earth to do.

I don't know how much time passes as I lean against the wall and simply watch him. After a while, I notice that he seems to be practicing the same thing over and over—maybe one of Manic's songs that he's not feeling confident enough with. But after what feels like the fifth attempt, suddenly, his right hand sort of freezes up. His fingers curl. He stops, shakes it out, and tries again, only to have the same thing happen once more.

His eyes open, and he stares blankly at the floor. "Fuck," he hisses softly. He tosses the headphones aside and starts to absentmindedly rub his wrist and fingers. He must be lost in thought because it takes him a whole minute before he notices my bare feet and glances up to meet my gaze. "Hey." He smiles, though it doesn't quite reach his eyes. "How are you feeling?"

"Better, I think."

"Yeah?" His gaze sweeps over me, briefly pausing to check out my bare legs in his oversized tee. "You look better."

"What's up with your hand?" I ask, not hesitating to get straight to the point.

"I don't know." He's still rubbing it, and I take a step forward to kneel in front of him so I can take a better look. "It freezes up sometimes. Maybe a bit of tendonitis. That's pretty common with musicians, isn't it?"

"It is," I confirm. "My mom has it."

"Your mom is a musician?"

I smile up at him, realizing how much we still don't know about each other. Considering how hard I'm falling for him, this simple fact should scare me, but the only thing I'm feeling is excitement.

*I can't wait to learn everything about this man.*

"Yeah, she plays the harp. Pretty damn well too."

"Wow, that's badass. Don't think I've ever met a harpist before."

"Maybe the two of you can jam. Wouldn't that be something?" I joke, hoping to lighten the mood as I glance at his hand. "Are you experiencing a lot of pain?"

"It's sore sometimes."

"But no stabbing or throbbing pain you can pinpoint?" I've already taken his hand in mine, checking his flexibility and mobility. It all seems normal, and he doesn't seem to be in any pain as I manipulate the joint.

"No, not that I've noticed. Can I just say it's really fucking hot when you go into doctor mode? Especially when you're in nothing but my shirt?"

I try to suppress the grin threatening to break free. "Don't distract me. And don't change the subject," I tell him. "What does it feel like? When it does this?"

He lets out a frustrated sigh, as if he knows he's not getting out of this conversation. Good, I'm glad he's resigned to his fate now. He took care of me, and now I'm taking care of him. "Like my hand just forgets what it's doing for a second. It's frustrating, especially when it's happened on stage. I feel like I could play these songs in my sleep now—that's how well they're etched into memory—and yet, I'll be performing and suddenly, my fingers just stop responding, and I'm standing there hoping no one noticed."

The expression on his face damn near breaks me. It's clear he's been worrying about this for a while. I want to ask how long, but I'm worried asking him too many questions right now will only stress him out even more.

He's right. It could just be something as simple as tendonitis.

*But if it's not...*

"Hey." I give him an encouraging smile. "Why don't we do this? When we're on break in Seattle, we get it checked out. I have a friend from med school up there who's in orthopedics. I'll contact him ahead of time, explain the situation..." I can almost see the alarm bells ringing in his head. "And stress the discretion needed," I add. His shoulders relax a little. "But I think it's best if we get it looked at. For your peace of mind, at the very least."

He searches my face as if he's trying to unravel my every thought. I can see the unease, the worry, the doubt.

"It's going to be okay." I lift the bass from his shoulders and gently place it in the case. A moment later, I settle into his lap. He wraps his arms around my waist and buries his head in my chest.

"Promise?"

I swallow, feeling my own unease settle deep in my chest. Against my better judgment, I find myself nodding. "Promise," I answer.

It's one promise I hope I never have to break.

## Chapter Twenty-Nine

# HENDRIX

If there's one thing to be said about Lance Creed, it's that the man moves quickly. No grass is growing under his feet, that's for sure. So it's completely unsurprising to me when I get a text from him this morning asking to meet before we leave LA today.

While Zara gets ready in the hotel suite, I dash downstairs where we've agreed to meet and go through all the required paperwork to sign with the Creed Agency. I'm also meeting with my new agent, Saul.

It's been twenty-four hours since I gave my brother the thumbs up to move ahead, and had I not been holed up with a sick girlfriend yesterday, this probably would have already taken place.

Like I said, the man moves fast.

It makes me wonder how much further along my career would be if I had just given in and signed with him like Zander did. But then again, I wouldn't be here with Zara, which makes me think I'm right where I'm supposed to be.

*Look at me being all sentimental and shit.*

We meet in one of the hotel's available conference rooms, and it takes me just five minutes to sign my name where my dad's new assistant has marked. I don't bother to look it over. I've seen this boilerplate Creed Agency contract more times than I can count.

Besides, this is my dad, the man who used to sneak me cookies after bedtime and gave me an allowance each week for doing literally nothing.

He's no villain.

"Now that we have that out of the way, let's get to the good stuff," Saul says, grabbing a folder from his briefcase. Do people actually carry briefcases anymore? Saul is about the same age as my father, but half as cool. He reminds me a bit of Stan Lee, but instead of sunglasses and superhero comics, you get tweed blazers and legal jargon.

"What's the good stuff?" I ask hesitantly.

He opens the folder, and my eyes widen. "Are those—"

"Offers? Yup." He confirms. "And good ones too."

"Barely a month on tour," my dad says, looking at me with a gleam in his eye. "You should be proud of yourself."

I blow out a breath, feeling a little taken aback. "Do they want me or just the media attention I'll bring with me?"

Saul shrugs. "A little bit of both, I'll wager. And I think there are some we can easily weed out because of that. But there are legitimate offers in here, Hendrix. Bands who want you. Not your name or your..." He waves a hand in my direction.

"My abs?" I roll my eyes.

"Media attention comes and goes. Ask Zander, Asher, or anyone else who has been in the spotlight. So ignore all that." He shoves the folder in my direction, and I stare down at the first name on the stack. It's a band I know well. One I would have been thrilled to work with six months ago. Hell, six weeks ago.

Now, all I feel is a hollow sense of dread in the pit of my stomach, especially when I look at their tour schedule: a four-month US tour and a three-month international tour, starting in October. Manic finishes up in September, which means I'd be leaving almost as soon as I got home.

Another seven months on the road.

Would Zara want to come with me? Can I ask her to?

Elena travels with Zander, but it's not quite the same. Her career is portable. She can write anywhere. I can't just assume that any band I'm signed with will need a full-time doctor or that Zara will even want that as a long-term career.

*Fuck.*

I swallow hard and glance up at Saul and my dad. Saul speaks first. "Take some time and look them over, and when you're ready, give us a call."

"Okay."

As soon as I say goodbye and leave that room, my heart begins to race, and it feels like there isn't enough oxygen in my lungs.

I take out my phone and call Zara.

"Hey." Her voice is warm and sweet. My pulse starts to slow.

"Hey," I reply. "How soon do you think you could be ready?"

"Five minutes? Why? I thought we weren't due to leave until noon."

I lick my lips as my eyes dart toward the exit. "There's somewhere I want to take you first. You up for it?"

"With you?" I swear I can hear the smile in her voice. "Always."

I start to feel nervous just as the Uber makes the final turn into the neighborhood. Up until now, I've been able to keep my chill. Zara and I talked about my new agent, and she congratulated me on all the bands that want me to sign with them.

But now I've lost every ounce of chill. Zero fucking chill.

*What if she doesn't like it?*

*What if my sister trashed the place?*

*What if my fears about the cheese are legit, and it really is a hazmat situation in there?*

Once again, the last one is a bit of a stretch, but I can't help it.

Aside from my sisters and my mom, I've never brought a woman to my house.

Even when Zander lived here, that had been our one rule: no hookups in the house. We'd saved forever to afford the down payment on this place, and when we finally got the keys, we wanted it all to ourselves.

In hindsight, that rule worked to our advantage when Zander's face was splashed on the cover of every magazine and newspaper in the country. Our home remained private, and I never had to stress about any of his former one-nighters showing up at my door.

When our Uber driver pulls into the driveway, I let out a small sigh of relief. The lawn is mowed, the house is still standing, and there aren't any packages at the front door, so I know my sister has been doing her job.

I turn toward Zara to gauge her reaction, and as soon as I do, all the insecurity and worry melt away. She's beaming from ear to ear as she takes it all in. From the outside, it's a pretty cookie-cutter California ranch-style home. But from the way she's looking at it, you would think it's a goddamn mansion.

"We all good?" our Uber driver asks.

"Yup." I nod, realizing we're both taking quite a while to leave his car. "Thanks, man."

"No problem."

Zara grabs her small handbag and exits the back seat. I walk around the front of the car, and together we head down the walkway to the front door. I pull out my keys and twist the lock. It's something I used to do several times a day, and now it feels almost foreign.

It's crazy how quickly our lives can change. I steal a glance at Zara. *In more ways than one...*

I push open the door and let her go first.

*Please don't smell. Please don't smell.*

I walk in behind her and—*oh thank fuck.* No funky cheese smell. Just the same earthy fragrance it always has, thanks to the fancy plug-in thing Presley bought me for Christmas.

"I should have suggested you take me here that first night we hooked up." She jokes, looking around the living room. "You have actual furniture. I barely had a bed in the middle of all those boxes."

I stand next to her, nuzzling into the curve of her collarbone. She's wearing a tan sleeveless dress today with sandals. Her hair is secured with one of those claw clips, and I swear she's not wearing a bra just to drive me crazy. "I don't know...I think we made do," I tease. "Besides, I don't take women here."

She turns, her brown eyes meeting mine. "But I'm here. Am I not considered a woman anymore?"

"No." I turn her to face me, tucking a tendril of hair behind her ear. She reaches behind her and removes the clip from her hair, and it falls like a curtain around her shoulders. Gorgeous. "Now, you're just mine. And I wanted you here because I wanted to see you in my space. In my house."

She looks up at me, biting her bottom lip. My cock twitches in approval. "And now that you have me here, what are you going to do with me?"

*Fucking hell.* "Well, I was going to offer you a glass of water."

"I'm not thirsty."

"Crackers?"

She smirks. "Not hungry, Hendrix."

"Do you want a tour?" I shift, trying to tame the raging erection she's causing.

"Sure. Where's the bedroom?"

My eyes dart to the hallway and then back to her. "Zara, yesterday, you were just—"

She places a finger gently over my mouth, silencing me. "I'm fine," she insists. "I've been fever-free for twenty-four hours as of"—she checks her watch—"an hour ago. And I feel fine. That's the beauty of the twenty-four hour flu."

"You sure?"

Her brow lifts. "I am a doc—"

My mouth closes over hers because if she says she's fine, I'm going to trust her. Like she said, or tried to before I stuck my tongue down her throat, she's the doctor. She should know.

We kiss and kiss *and kiss*. Right there in the middle of my living room.

By the time my hands slide under her ass to pick her up, her lips are swollen and red. It reminds me of that night in Nashville when she got down on her knees and sucked me fucking dry.

"Bedroom?"

"Yes," I manage to say.

We make it there, but it takes a while. About halfway down the hall, I slam her against the wall where I fall to my knees, rip off her dress—yep, definitely no bra today —push her panties to the side and eat her pussy like I'm fucking starved.

I don't let up until she screams my name so loud the damn windows shake.

When I drop her onto my bed, she's still breathless.

I am too. But it's more from the sight of seeing her here, in my bedroom. *In my bed.* I try to etch that image into my memory before pulling my shirt over my head. She watches me with hungry eyes as I unbuckle my belt and remove my jeans. Her gaze roams over every inch of skin. Every toned muscle. Every tattoo before finally landing on that little cherub in the center of my chest.

Her cherub. Her cupid.

I can't help but do the same, focusing on the bit of skin just above her panties where that fresh ink is healing. They're not a matching set, her tattoo and mine, and I wouldn't want them to be. She's her own person, and so am I, but I still like how they link us with a single word. A single memory.

*"You're last name is Valentine? Like Cupid?" I ask.*

*"No, like the saint, you dumbass."*

"You're smiling."

"Just thinking about that time you called me a dumbass."

She laughs as I settle my knees between her thighs. "Which time?"

"When we first met," I reply with a sly grin. "And what do you mean *which time*? How many times have there been?"

"To your face? Just the one." Her eyes sparkle with mischief, and I lean down and kiss the wicked grin off her face. She giggles against my lips, and I love that she feels relaxed enough with me that our lovemaking can be playful as well as intense and passionate.

"I should have known from the very start that *saint* was a terrible nickname for you." I slide a palm down the side of her body until I reach the edge of her satin panties and start to tug. "There's nothing innocent about you."

She lifts her hips to aid me in my endeavor. "I thought I made that pretty clear after the dozen or so times you hit on me."

When I finally free her of the last piece of clothing, I rid myself of mine. I drop my boxer briefs on the ground and join her back on the bed. "That was pure college-boy cockiness," I admit. "I just didn't know how to act around you."

Her eyes find mine, watching as I scatter kisses up her thighs, over her belly, and between the valley of her breasts. "You didn't?"

"No. At first, I thought it was just an infatuation because I wasn't used to being turned down."

"So arrogant," she mumbles as I run a thumb over her peaked nipple, and she arches her back as we continue our lazy game of touching and talking. I've never really talked during sex, aside from making sure my partner was enjoying herself. This represents an entirely different level of intimacy I never expected or even contemplated, being this stripped down, both physically and mentally. "I probably would have been more receptive to your advances if I thought you were serious."

"You mean you didn't get that from the offer of sexual favors?" I tease at the same time she playfully nips at my shoulder. I've never been one for biting, but the sensation of it goes straight to my cock, and I find myself wanting to tell her to do it again but harder so it leaves a mark, branding me as hers.

"You didn't actually want to pay me with sex, did you?" She looks up at me and asks. It's not really a question, or at least not one I believe she doesn't already know the answer to.

"God, no," I answer. "I'm not sure what I would have done if you had said yes, to be honest—or why I even said it. I just remember walking into that library and feeling dumbstruck the moment I saw you, and then it was just cocky word vomit after that."

She cups my cheek. I grip her waist. "You were nervous?"

"For the first time ever. Probably should have been my first clue, huh?"

"First clue for what?"

I smile. "That you were special." I kiss her collarbone.

"That you're different." I kiss the slender column of her neck. "That you were meant to be mine."

When our lips meet this time, it's pure passion. Her fingers thread through my hair as I slide my hand from her waist to her ass and give it a hard squeeze.

I've never wanted anyone the way I want Zara.

"Do you know how many times I fantasized about bending you over that table in the library during our tutoring sessions? How many times I imagined fucking you so hard, I'd have to gag you with your own damn panties to keep you quiet."

Her pupils are blown wide as she squirms beneath me, seeking friction. "Do it," she begs. "Flip me over, Hen. Show me your fantasy. But no panties. I want you to hear me scream."

If I thought I was hard before, I'm practically dying now. Having her tell me what she wants is quite possibly the sexiest thing I've ever heard, and it's happening more and more every time we come together.

It makes me so damn happy for her. Seeing someone find the confidence that was once stolen from them is a beautiful thing to witness.

I don't waste any time. I grab her around the waist and flip her so fast that she lets out a little squeal of excitement before I have her face pressed into the mattress and her ass in the air.

"Fuck," I mutter under my breath as I admire the view.

"Like what you see?"

I grip the base of my cock and give it a few lazy strokes before lining it up to her slick entrance. "You're a goddamn dream, Cupid." I slam into her, and the sensation of her tight pussy is overwhelming. It always is, but being this deep is something else. She cries out, gripping the sheets as I run a hand down her spine.

"More," she begs.

"You want more?" All I'm giving her are shallow thrusts, practically teasing her as she whimpers below me and rolls her hips against mine.

"Yes!"

"How do you want me to fuck you, Zara?"

"Hard," she cries out. "Fuck me hard, Hen."

The words barely make it past her lips before I'm doing exactly that. I grip her hips and let go. It's relentless. It's rough.

And it's so damn good.

Sweat begins to drip down my back as I feel myself getting closer, but I won't go over the edge without her. So I pull her back so she's seated on my knees. My hands wrap around her middle, palming her breast just because I can.

"Touch your clit," I tell her, knowing she's close enough that just a little friction on that sensitive bundle of nerves will be enough to send her over the edge.

It's a tight squeeze. She's basically kneeling in my lap, but she manages to fit two fingers between her legs, and as soon as I hear that little gasp of pleasure, I thrust hard at the same time I slam her body down on mine.

My hands tighten on her tits, squeezing her nipples as I pick up speed.

"Zara, fuck." It's a plea, because I am *right there*. I can feel my balls tightening, and I swear my damn vision is starting to blur.

"I'm...I—" The words come out as one garbled moan

before her back bows, and then she's crying out my name, over and over.

Her body writhes as her pussy squeezes my cock so fucking hard, I really do see stars. I come seconds later with her name on my lips and the knowledge that now that I have this woman in my bed, home, and heart, I never want her to leave.

## Chapter Thirty

# ZARA

"Why does your face look like that?" I ask as soon as the Uber drives off, leaving our bags on the curb of my childhood home. I glance at the stucco exterior and slate roof. Not much has changed since I left for college. Mom has planted some new rose bushes, and the concrete driveway has been redone, but everything else looks the same.

The basketball hoop that my sister and dad used to shoot hoops before dinner is still hanging above the garage, collecting spiderwebs and rust. My dad's old SUV remains on the curb, adorned with its goofy "Science is cool" bumper stickers.

"Like what?" He also glances up at the house, but I can't gauge his opinion because of the weird look on his face.

"Like you're..." I search for the right word to describe the deep crease between his brow and the look of panic in his eyes. "Ready to bolt? Or maybe a little constipated? Shit, you're not sick, are you?"

He rolls his eyes and grabs the duffle we packed along with his guitar. "I'm not sick."

"Then what—" Realization hits me. "Oh, you're nervous!"

He stops and looks at me, his cheeks flaming red. Oh my god, that's adorable. "I've never met anyone's parents before. I don't want to fuck it up."

I take a step forward until my nipples brush his chest. He must remember from our earlier sexathon at his house that I am not wearing a bra today because his eyes are cast downward. He swallows hard. Probably not the best idea to get him all riled up before we head inside, is it?

I reluctantly step back, and I swear he exhales for the first time in sixty seconds. Poor man really is terrified. "You've already met my mom," I remind him.

"It's not your mom I'm worried about."

"You're worried about my dad?" I snort, waving a hand. "Come on. Let me go introduce you to my super scary dad."

"That's it? That's all you're going to give me? No pointers? No tips? I tried to warn you about my family."

I tilt my head, feeling amused. "Hen, your family is lovely, and the only negative part of meeting them was that I didn't get to spend more time with them."

"Really?"

"Really. Now, as for my dad." I tap a finger to my lips, trying to decide how best to explain him. Finally, an idea strikes me. "Have you ever noticed how my mom and sister always FaceTime me, but my dad doesn't?"

"Yeah, I always wondered about that."

I smile. I shouldn't be surprised. He notices everything.

I pull out my phone, open my text history with my dad, and hand it to him. He scrolls back a bit and then looks at me. "He texts you a lot. He's really proud of you."

"Yeah, he is," I confirm with a warm smile. "Texting is easier for him. He's pretty introverted, and always having to be 'on' as a teacher and a coach is quite draining for him, so he's quiet outside of work. Texting is an easy way for us to communicate that doesn't stress him out."

"So don't go in there with a megawatt smile, ready to charm the pants off him? Is that what you're saying?"

I grimace. "Is that what you were planning on doing?"

"I don't have a fucking clue, Zara. Just kind of hoping he doesn't murder me if I'm being honest."

I laugh. "Well, think of it this way. You're following up after the worst son-in-law of the century. How hard could it be?"

"You couldn't have started with that?"

I simply shake my head in amusement. "Okay. Just go in there and be yourself. But keep in mind that if he hangs back or acts standoffish, it's not you. It's just him being himself."

He nods. "Right. Got it."

"Now." I glance at the front of the house, where I see a flutter of curtains, and I grin. "We should probably head inside before they start to worry something is wrong."

I take his free hand in mine. It's his right hand, and I briefly glance down at it, noticing his firm grip. I look up at him, and there's not even a hint of pain on his face.

*Not the time, Zara.*

"Ready?" I ask.

"Not even a little bit."

"Great." I laugh. "Let's go."

I really have no idea what he was so worried about.

Like everyone else in the world—except for my ex-husband, that is—my parents love Hendrix Creed.

My mom has been halfway infatuated with him since she caught us together in my hotel suite back in Nashville. But now? Now that infatuation has escalated into a full-blown obsession.

Even my dad likes him. His quiet appreciation of the new man in my life means everything. The way Hendrix not only respects my dad's aloof personality but also leans into it, allowing him to initiate conversation rather than bombard him in a vain attempt to seek his approval —it's perfect.

*He's perfect.*

We are halfway through dessert, crammed into the kitchen where the small, circular dining table sits. It's the same one that's been here since I was a kid, and I can see the nicks and scratches from years of homework and craft projects. The entire house is like this. Worn. Loved. Full of memories.

Sometimes I dream of giving them enough money to remodel or even start fresh, but I often wonder if they would want to. This house is filled of memories— Christmas mornings, birthday parties and movie nights. It's a bit dingy around the edges, but it's not the sparkle that makes a home. I should know that better than most.

It's the memories.

I blink back into reality and smile at the man next to me. Hendrix is on his second helping of my mom's famous karydopita, a Greek walnut cake. He looks absolutely gorgeous in a pair of fitted jeans and a gray Henley. When he finishes his bite, he turns his attention to my mom and asks, "Are you two going to the concert tomorrow?"

He knows they aren't. I told him when we secured tickets for his family. He knew how bummed I was that my mom—I'd never ask my dad to go to something so chaotic—wouldn't be there to see me thriving. Still, I don't say a word and wait to see where this goes.

"Oh no. I don't think I can handle all that fuss at my age." My mom shakes her head and takes a sip of her coffee.

"That's too bad," Hendrix says, setting his fork down on his empty plate. He glances up at the wall clock, and I feel it. Something is about to happen. "I know Asher will miss seeing you."

My mom's eyes nearly pop right out of her head. "You. He...*What?*" I don't think I've ever heard my mom trip over her words before. Ramble? Sure. Give a heated lecture when we show up past curfew? Hell yes. But to be rendered almost speechless?

He's going to have to teach me that trick.

Hendrix grins. "Well, he loves having Zara on tour. We all do. The whole crew adores her, and I was telling him how I was coming over for dinner today. I mentioned how big of a fan you were, and he said how much he was looking forward to meeting you."

"He *did*?"

"Yeah, he—" The sound of a phone buzzing cuts him

off, and he holds up a single finger, which in most cases would be a really douchey thing to do when you're in the middle of dinner with your girlfriend's parents. But when he pulls out his phone, and I see that mischievous glint in his eye, I know it was planned. "Oh, what a coincidence. Do you mind if I take this?"

My mom absently shakes her head back and forth. I think this woman has finally met her match when it comes to meddling. I glance over at my dad. His dark-brown hair has grayed over time, and his lanky frame has softened a bit, but he still has that all-American good looks that made my mom fall hard for him in college. His eyes crinkle at the corners, and a tiny smile is painted across his lips as he watches the scene unfold before him.

Hendrix swipes his thumb across the screen, and the sound of a FaceTime call connecting fills the air. "Oh, hey man," he says, all nonchalant, like he didn't set this whole thing up.

I guess I know why he wasn't worried about my mom.

Not when he had freaking Asher Knight in his back pocket.

"Hey," Asher's familiar voice replies. "How's it going?"

"Good. Zara and I are enjoying an amazing meal with her folks. Her mom made stifado and this amazing walnut cake. I don't think I've eaten this well in years."

My mom beams with pride. She's not very close with her parents, so cooking is her only real tangible link to her mother's heritage that she still clings to, and I know it means a lot to her to hear his praise.

I lean over and wave into the camera. "Hey, Asher."

"Hey, Doc." Instead of the casual clothes I usually see him in around the hotel, he's in his signature rocker look that he wears on stage, except for one slight change. He's wearing a shirt tonight, which is probably for the best.

No need to give my mom a heart attack.

"Karydopita, huh? No baklava? That's always a personal favorite of mine."

My mom's eyes go all big and round when he correctly pronounces the name of the traditional Greek walnut cake she loves to make. Damn, Asher is good, and she's so smitten. "Next time, I'm sure," I tell him, resting my head on Hen's shoulder. He kisses the top of my head.

My mom shakes her head. "Too much work," she admits with a nervous laugh and a wave of her hand. "I'm too old. If we want baklava, we get it from a nice restaurant in the city."

I can tell we're getting off topic, and he wants to get to the point of whatever this is when he suddenly says, "So...what's up?"

"Right. Yeah." Asher seems a bit caught off guard, and his next words come out stilted, almost as if he's reading from a script or rehearsing something. "I was reviewing the list of VIP tickets tonight with the staff..." I highly doubt this is something he actually does. Although after the incident with Tanner, maybe it is. "And it reminded me how disappointed I was when I discovered I wouldn't get the privilege to meet Zara's mother. I wanted to see if I could persuade Mrs. Valentine to join us at the concert tomorrow."

Wow, he's laying it on thick. I seriously want to know what Hendrix promised him to get him to do this. It has to be something equally embarrassing, right? Because Asher isn't the type of guy who exactly needs anything.

If it is, I so want to be there when he comes to collect.

"Hmm, I don't know," Hendrix replies. "She was

pretty adamant about not going. Maybe you could convince her?"

And then he hands her the phone, and my mom is staring wide-eyed at Asher Knight.

"Hello, Mrs. Valentine," he says in that sexy Scottish accent of his.

She keeps staring. It's like watching one of those dog videos on TikTok where the caption is "No thoughts, just vibes." That is my mom right now.

Asher seems accustomed to this kind of reaction because he just rolls with it and keeps talking. "I was hoping I could convince you to come to the concert tomorrow night. I know you've already been offered VIP tickets, so I'm curious. What else can we do to sweeten the deal?"

"She's worried it will be too loud," I say, raising my voice so he can hear me.

"Right." I hear him acknowledge. "Easy enough, that. We can give you headphones that will dampen the sound, like the crew uses. What else?"

"Ask for anything," Hendrix whispers in my ear. "Seriously. I know you said she has reservations about getting there and is self-conscious about her appearance. I want her to *want* to go, not just be talked into it. She deserves to feel spoiled for a night. Don't worry about the cost. Just get her there."

My eyes sting with unshed tears, but I simply nod.

I open my mouth, but my dad, of all people, beats me to it. "She'll need a way to get there. She doesn't like driving at night."

"Done," Asher says. "How does a limo sound? Or perhaps something a little less flashy if that's too—"

"Limo!" She perks up. "I want the limo."

We all bark out a laugh, and suddenly, my mom has found her voice and her ability to advocate for herself. "I have nothing to wear and my hair is a mess, you see?" She runs a palm through her dyed brown hair.

"I think it's beautiful, but there's nothing wrong with a wee bit of pampering. How about a full day at the spa? And some shopping? Zara can join, yeah?"

Well, now the tears are leaking down my cheeks, and I'm nodding. My mom and I have spent plenty of quality time together over the years, but nothing so extravagant.

Not even when I was married to Tanner and had the means to.

I was always too afraid to spend his money—because it was his. And he always made sure I knew it.

"That would be great, Ash. Thanks."

"No need to thank me—"

"I want a picture!" my mom interrupts. "With you. I will put it on the mantel by my harp."

I nearly choke on my own saliva. Is this the same starstruck woman I saw just five minutes ago?

"Well, that's a given, Mrs. Valentine." I swear Asher's brogue grows thicker with each syllable. God, he's a charmer. "Can't allow my number one fan to leave without grabbing a photo, now can we?"

When the call ends a few minutes later, a hush falls over the table, and then my mom lets out the girliest giggle I think I've ever heard. Her hand covers her mouth as her eyes turn into tiny slits. Soon, the entire table is laughing right along with her.

Even my stoic father.

"I'm gonna meet a rock star!" she squeals.

"Uh, hate to break it to you, Mom, but you already did."

"Oh." She waves a hand in Hendrix's direction. "He doesn't count. He's family now."

I feel Hendrix stiffen next to me, and for a moment, I wonder if my mom has overstepped. But when I sneak a glance in his direction, I see it—the deep swell of emotion swimming behind his eyes.

Yeah, Mom. He sure is.

Given what I've learned about Zara's mom and her strict upbringing, I am surprised to find out that we are allowed to share a room.

Surprised and a little terrified.

Especially when Zara comes out of the attached bathroom wearing nothing but a tiny tank top and a lacy pair of panties.

"Are you trying to kill me?" *Or get me killed?* Because her father may be the strong and silent type, but I doubt he'd be cool with me fucking his daughter in the room just down the hall from his.

She steps into the guest room, which she explained used to be her room until her parents converted it after she got married. The former teal walls are now a neutral tan, and the queen bed now features a fluffy white duvet instead of the flowery bedspread from her youth.

"Why would you say that?" she asks innocently, walking toward me with an extra sway to her hips. Yep, she is definitely trying to kill me.

"You wear more to bed when it's just the two of us in a luxury suite," I tell her. "With thick walls and neighbors who don't give a fuck." I lower my voice to a whisper and point to the wall. "These neighbors very much give a fuck, Zara."

She snorts out a laugh, closing the distance between us. I'm sitting on the edge of the bed in a pair of pajama pants. I think this is the first time I've worn them on the tour. I had to dig deep in my suitcase to find them, but I wasn't about to walk around her house in a pair of boxer briefs, was I?

She must notice the change in attire because she smirks.

And then she drops to her knees in front of me.

*Oh Jesus fuck.*

"Zara," I warn.

"Yes?" She answers sweetly as her fingers inch toward the waistband of my pants.

"What are you doing?" *Just shut up and let the woman work.*

"Thanking you."

I close my hand over hers, steadying her hand. "Thanking me? For what?"

Her eyes meet mine, and I can see her playful expression slip just slightly. "At first, it was a thank you for setting up that phone call for my mom. It was such a sweet thing to do, and it means the world to me that she's going to be there tomorrow—even if most of her focus will be on her crush."

I laugh, running a hand through her damp hair. "Not all of us can be *the* Asher Knight."

"That's another thing," she continues. "I was thinking about that conversation in the shower just now. How you told me to ask for anything—the way you worded it. It sounded very personal to you."

"Well, your mom is special."

"Yeah, but then there was Asher. He was a little dodgy too, using the word 'we' instead of 'I.'" I freeze for a split second, but it's enough for her to notice. "Asher isn't the one paying for everything, is he? You just wanted me to assume he was."

I really didn't think she'd pick up on that, but I guess I shouldn't be surprised. She is, after all, a stickler for details. "I figured you'd be more amenable to the idea if it were his money. He does have a lot of it."

"And I'm sure he was more than willing to pay for it. So why didn't he?"

My eyes lock with hers, and I let out a heavy sigh. "Because, whether or not you knew it came from me, I wanted to do something nice for your mom, and I couldn't do that if—not really—if Asher was fitting the bill. It wouldn't feel right."

"Have I ever told you how wonderful you are?" She rises up on her knees to place a chaste kiss on the corner of my mouth. Then my chin. My neck.

"A few times," I manage to say.

"Yeah? What about kind? Have I ever told you you're kind?"

My brain is starting to glitch as her kisses go south. "Maybe?"

Her lips brush my abs, and her tongue swirls around my belly button. "And what if I said I was really, really grateful?"

I angle her head so that she's looking at me. Frazzled brain or not, I have to say this. "I don't want sex to ever be transactional between us, Zara. Despite what I may have said as a dumb college student, you do not need to reward me for giving you something."

Her fingers brush the waistband of my pants. "I know." She smiles. "And, believe me, there is *nothing* transactional about what I'm about to do to you, because I'm gonna to enjoy every single second."

Fucking hell.

I help her ease my pajama pants down, freeing my erection. I'm so hard, I'm in actual pain. "Do you think you can be quiet?" she asks.

*Yes.* Her delicate fingers close around my shaft. *No.* I groan. *Fuck, maybe.*

She gives it several slow, teasing strokes.

"Not off to a great start." She grins up at me.

"I know how to make one of us quiet." I thrust into her hand.

"Is that what you want? To shut me up?" Fuck.

"Yes," I say, even though we both know it won't do any good. She's a moaner even when she has her mouth stuffed full of my cock. Just thinking of it has me leaking into her hand.

Her tongue darts out, circling the tip and cleaning me off before tracing the sensitive underside. My head falls back as I stifle a groan.

"Eyes on me, Hen," she instructs. I do as I'm told, meeting her gaze. She smiles. "That's a good boy."

Never thought I'd enjoy a praise kink, but here we are.

Her mouth lowers back on my cock, and it's pure fucking heaven. I've had my fair share of blowjobs over the years, but nothing compares to this.

The way she looks at me.

The feeling of her hand stroking my inner thigh.

The knowledge that doing this turns her on too.

When my fingers weave through the silky strands of her hair, she whimpers, and her free hand slips between her thighs. I know the instant her fingers make contact with her clit because she lets out a throaty moan that vibrates around my cock.

I almost make a teasing remark about being quiet, but then her cheeks hollow and she sucks me deeper into her mouth.

"Fuck. *Fuck*," I hiss, fisting the duvet with one hand and her hair with the other. It's taking every ounce of willpower I possess to keep that hand steady. Not because she's doing anything wrong. No. She's doing everything exactly right, and it's so good that all I want to do is grab the back of her head and face fuck the hell out of her until my cum is dripping down the back of her throat.

Depraved? Yes. Especially in her parents' house.

But I never said I was a saint.

If I ever needed a sign that this is the girl of my dreams, she reaches up and places her hand on top of mine, the one in her hair, and meets my gaze. She relaxes her throat and gives the faintest hint of a nod.

Permission.

I don't belittle her decision by asking if she's sure. The trust we've built between us is strong enough that I know when she asks for something, it's because she truly wants it.

Not because she's trying to please me.

I tighten my grip on her hair, and I thrust into her.

She moans. "Baby, you've got to be quiet," I tell her as I pick up speed. It doesn't help the noise issue.

But when I see that hand between her legs relentlessly rubbing her clit, I lose the ability to care. She's so fucking turned on, she's practically humping her hand. Her hips are spread wide, her pussy on full display as she grinds herself against her fingers.

*If her dad does kill me, at least I'll have this image to take to my grave.*

Her movements start to get sloppy, and then, like a tidal wave cresting onto the shore, she comes. Her body vibrates, and I feel her deep moan around my cock. It's so intense that seconds later, I feel my stomach clench. My balls tighten, and then I'm spilling down her throat, murmuring her name as I watch in awe as she takes every single drop.

## Chapter Thirty-Two

# HENDRIX

It's just past six in the morning when I sneak out of the guest room in search of coffee. The house is still quiet, but I spotted a Keurig in the kitchen yesterday, so I think I can get away with making myself a cup without waking anyone.

I tiptoe down the hall and around the corner to the small kitchen. Zara's parents' house sort of reminds me of my own. It's smaller and a bit rough around the edges, but the outdated appliances and worn furniture give it a homey feeling that mine lacks.

The decades' worth of family photos lining the walls don't hurt either.

I make my way to the counter in the corner and grab one of the K-Cups from the container next to the coffeemaker. I consider making a cup for Zara, but it's still early. The spa day we arranged for Zara and her mom doesn't start until ten, so there is still plenty of time before she needs to be out the door.

And besides, she deserves her sleep after...

"Good morning, Hendrix."

"Jesus!" I stop myself, but not before I jump a solid two feet in the air at the sound of Jon Valentine's voice behind me. Okay, maybe it's only a couple of inches, but my heart definitely malfunctions a little.

Turning, I find him standing there, looking exactly as he did the day before, wearing a pair of Levi's, a plaid shirt, and a baseball cap.

Did he sleep in that?

"We aren't religious in this house." He smirks. Or at least I think it's a smirk. Is it more like a barely there curve? "Feel free to use the Lord's name in vain at your leisure. However, if you meet Zara's grandmother, it would probably be wise to refrain. I learned that the hard way."

"Noted."

An awkward silence fills the air. I stare at a painting of a blue jay that hangs on the wall just to the left of him, wishing I had taken the time to put on jeans. It feels strange to stand here in his kitchen when he's dressed for the day, and I'm still bumming it in my pajamas.

He moves to the counter, and before I can understand what he's doing, he picks up the K-Cup I dropped and places it in the machine.

"Thanks," I say, still feeling awkward. I'm not used to silence. It wasn't exactly the norm growing up with four siblings. But I appreciate the need for it when the world might feel too loud. So I sit in it. And I wait. Eventually, when my coffee finishes brewing and he hands me a mug, he speaks.

When he does, my heart dies a little.

"It's a hard thing to watch your daughter fall for the

wrong man." He strides purposefully to the fridge, retrieves a small carton of cream, and sets it on the counter beside me. I gaze at it, swallowing hard.

How can he expect me to drink coffee after a bomb like that?

He takes a bowl of sugar from the cabinet above me and sets it next to the cream. "I knew from the very first moment I met him that he was all wrong for her."

Him? Wait. Is he not talking about me? My heart rate starts to level out.

He walks back to the kitchen table and takes a seat. I guess I should make my coffee now, right? I turn and quickly add some cream and a scoop of sugar.

"Tanner was entitled, smug, and the way he treated her..." I hear him take a shuddering breath. "But what are you supposed to do? Your child isn't a child anymore. And I've seen what happens when a parent refuses to support a relationship."

The way he says this last part is revealing. Zara mentioned that her mother had a complicated relationship with her parents. I have a hunch I know why.

I also understand where he's coming from. I would never pick a guy like Jace for my sister, but it's not my choice. It's hers. All I can do is hope she comes to her senses soon and realizes she deserves better.

So much better.

"After they got married, I watched her wither under the weight of that family's scrutiny. She's been better since she filed for divorce, but yesterday was the first time I've seen my baby girl happy in a long time."

"That's not all because of me."

"Didn't say it was."

"Okay." I press my lips together, holding back a laugh.

"I saw the fire back in her eyes. The passion in her voice when she talked about her work on tour was clear. She loves you, but she is also well on her way to building a well-rounded life. Something I believe you want for her too."

I'm momentarily speechless because, did he just say... "She loves me?"

Now, there's no doubt about the smile spreading across his face. "Oh, so we're still in the denial phase? All right. Is it one-sided?"

"What?" I slow blink.

"Have you figured out you love her? 'Cause it's written all over your damn face, son. Maya said she saw it clear as day the first time she spoke to you on FaceTime."

"That was..." New Orleans. The day I toured the city with her. Had I really been..."Yes, I blurt out. "I love her. Isn't it too soon, though?"

"Tanner waited over two years before he proposed, and we all know how well that went. I popped the question over takeout pizza on our six-month anniversary in Maya's dorm room, and sometimes I still can't believe how lucky I was that she said yes."

He stands as I take a sip of coffee. It's shit. I forgot how much I hate K-Cups. It tastes like fucking dirt water. "There's no set time that makes or breaks a relationship. There's no timer that goes off and declares you ready for the next step. You either are or you aren't, and the only ones who can decide that are the two of you."

Then he walks up and opens a cabinet, revealing a cappuccino maker with a knowing glance before retreating toward the hallway.

He looks back over his shoulder. "Have you decided what you're going to do after the tour ends?" he asks.

"Zara mentioned your position with the band is temporary."

My throat tightens, and I shake my head.

He seems to mull that over for a moment, then nods. "Well, for what it's worth, I'm rooting for you."

That makes two of us.

"I'm so conflicted," I say as I stretch out like a starfish on the giant king-size bed in our luxury suite. "On one hand, I'm exhausted, so the break is much needed, but on the other—"

"You're a workaholic who can't take a vacation when it's given?" Hendrix offers with a cocky grin as he walks toward his suitcase. He's naked, still glistening from his shower as he rubs a towel over his damp hair.

"I am not a workaholic," I argue with an exaggerated huff. "I just feel slightly guilty taking a whole week off when we've only been on tour for a month."

"We're halfway through the US leg of the tour. I know it doesn't feel that way 'cause you're now living your new best life as my super-hot girlfriend, and the days are just flying by, but we do actually deserve some time off."

I roll my eyes. "You're ridiculous."

He winks at me over his shoulder, and now I'm staring at his ass. "Yeah, but your parents love me, so I think it's best you keep me."

Hendrix is always a good-mood type of guy. Never

one to sulk or bring down the temperature in the room, but lately he's just been extra.

*Extra happy.*

*Extra funny.*

*Extra horny.*

Just when I thought our sex life couldn't get any hotter, he's finding ways to prove me wrong. Like last night, when he snuck into my clinic before the show, flipped the lock, and then fucked me hard and fast against the door. Or this morning, when he decided to play a game of let's see how many orgasms we can give Zara before she passes out.

We got to five before I tapped out, and that is why I'm currently lying on the bed while he happily whistles to himself and struts around naked.

"Are you planning on getting dressed anytime today?"

"Says the woman still sprawled out on the bed."

"Hey." I point a finger at him. "I'm getting up. Eventually."

"If you want to lie naked all day long, I'm okay with that. In fact, maybe I'll join you. We could just call this Naked Wednesday. We'll order room service, watch a movie, have some more sex. Then, rinse and repeat."

"You'd like that, wouldn't you?"

His grin is so wide, it's infectious. "I mean, who wouldn't?"

I sit up, and I don't miss the way his gaze lingers on my breasts. "And this wouldn't have anything to do with the appointment we have with my friend today?"

He raises his eyebrows and pretends to be surprised. "Oh, that's today?"

I tilt my head, looking unimpressed. His acting skills are subpar at best. "You know it is. You were there when he called and everything. Blasted me with at least a dozen questions afterward on the exact type of relationship we had in med school. Jealous much?"

"Lost time, Cupid," he says, the playful tone of his voice fading. "Lost time."

"We're making up for it now," I remind him with a tender gaze. "And that means I'm going to take care of you. Even when you don't want me to."

"I just feel like we're making a fuss over nothing, you know? My hand doesn't even hurt. And it only ever happens when I play, so I doubt it's serious."

That's what I'm worried about. But I don't say anything for at least a heartbeat or two. I just smile and nod and try to project a positive attitude. "It's still good to get it looked at. You never can be too careful."

It must work, because his next words are, "Okay, but then Naked Wednesday?"

I smile. "Whatever you want."

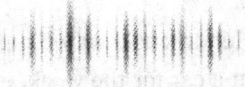

Clearly, luck was on Hendrix's side that day because just as we were about to head to the clinic to meet Eric, my phone rang, and it was his office calling to reschedule.

He had an emergency appointment that morning and couldn't meet us during his lunch hour as planned. Because of the discretion required for Hendrix's appointment, we had to wait until Saturday to find another time when the office would be empty enough to sneak him in.

I feel bad that Eric has to come in during the weekend, but I guess he's used to it. He does run a concierge-style clinic that caters to high-end clients who pay in full for his services, and I bet they are needy as fuck.

I suppose Hendrix is now one of them.

While we waited for Saturday to arrive, we spent our days being tourists in Seattle. We visited Pike Place Market and the Space Needle. We got caught in the rain and sought refuge in bookstores and quaint little coffee shops. He drank coffee, of course, while I sipped on chai. We took a ferry to Bainbridge Island and walked hand in hand along the beach.

It was perfect.

And the whole time, I tried not to think about this day.

But now that it's here, my stomach is in my throat, and I'm trying to remind myself that it's totally normal for musicians to experience pain in their hands.

Even my mom had to visit an orthopedist after a while.

*Totally normal.*

"You okay?" Hendrix asks as we pull up to the clinic. We decided to rent a car for the week, even though we've left it in the hotel parking lot for the majority of the time. But it has its advantages.

And this is definitely one of those.

Hendrix doesn't get recognized often. If he does, it's usually more of a double-take, like people are trying to figure out where to place him. It's not until we're in places like restaurants or in a crowd that they really start to make the connection.

An Uber is a risk neither of us wants to take right now.

With the long list of bands waiting for a decision, he

doesn't want it getting out that there might be an issue with his ability to perform.

"What? Yeah." I nod, probably with a bit too much enthusiasm.

Seattle is dreary today. Kind of like my mood. The clouds are gray, and the temperature is unseasonably cool. I pull my cardigan a little closer as we step out of the car and head to the clinic.

It's an impressive building, sleek and modern, with floor-to-ceiling mirrored windows. Eric meets us at the entrance and quickly lets us in with a wide smile and a handshake for Hendrix. Eric is completely unfazed by his celebrity status, which immediately puts him at ease.

When he turns and pulls me into a full bear hug, even lifting me off the ground, that probably causes his blood pressure to spike a little.

"Valentine!" He finally releases me and steps back. "It's so good to see you."

"You too, Lin." I glance around the lobby and give an approving nod. "This place is pretty fancy. Are you going to offer me a cucumber water or maybe a gold watch while I wait?"

It's more than fancy. If I had walked in here off the street, I wouldn't have guessed this is a doctor's office. There aren't any rows of tacky upholstered chairs or harsh lighting. Instead, it feels more like a spa with a small check-in desk, expensive leather sofas, and fresh flowers and plants decorating the space.

He chuckles, and the sound instantly takes me back to our residency days. Endless shifts, grumpy attending physicians, and bonding over pizza at two in the morning. He gave me the support Tanner should have during those stressful years. "Gold watches come later. I can offer you an overpriced bottle of water and my charming personality, though."

I shrug. "I guess that'll have to do."

He gives us a quick tour of the facility. It has everything from physical therapy to a full lab that includes X-rays, a CT scanner, and more.

"This is amazing, Eric."

"You don't think I'm a sellout?" he asks, a crease forming between his brows.

"What? Why?"

"I remember you and Tanner arguing about what kind of practice you wanted to open. He wanted something like this, and you wanted—"

"A clinic that would be accessible to low-income families. I remember. We settled for something in the middle." Or rather, his parents did. *Good for optics*, I remember his father saying. Just like me, apparently. "But that has nothing to do with your career. And whether or not I would choose this path doesn't diminish its success, Eric. This is incredible. I bet you get a ton of professional athletes coming through here."

He grins, shoving his hands in his pockets as Hendrix watches our exchange. "Best part of my job."

"You're only saying that because you've never worked with a rock star," I tease as he shows us into an exam room. It's just as nice as the lobby, with soft lighting and upscale furniture designed to put patients at ease.

"Can't say that I have." He winks over his shoulder. "Why don't you both take a seat, and we can get started."

Hendrix looks a little nervous until I take his hand and settle beside him on the leather sofa.

Eric fits his wiry frame into a chair opposite us, an iPad in his lap. He's dressed more casually than I imagine he usually is for the office, in jeans and a zip-up cardigan. He's always balanced the preppy, cool look well.

"For transparency, I do have a nurse here who will be coming in later to draw labs if necessary. All my employees sign an NDA since we work with high-profile clients. Now..." He exhales and smiles. "Let's start from the beginning."

And he does. Hendrix explains when he first noticed it, the subtle change in how his right hand behaved when he played, how it started to happen more often, and how it's worsened since he began traveling with the band.

With each question Eric asks and Hendrix's response, I feel a tight band forming around my chest.

When I look at Eric, however, he's the epitome of calm. Nothing but tranquil waters painted across his serene face. I try to emulate his facade and not jump to conclusions.

Because I am. Jumping. Skipping. Fucking leap-frogging to conclusions.

And I need to chill, because this is so not like me.

I've had hunches before when it comes to patients. All doctors have. But I don't let them overrule my critical thinking skills. I'm a data girl. A numbers girl. I'm the person who overanalyzes every detail until I reach a conclusion. I never jump. And I certainly don't leap.

This might be nothing.

*Please be nothing.*

After he gets caught up on Hendrix's pain history, he switches places with me and performs a physical exam. It's similar to what I did that day I witnessed him playing in our hotel room, but more comprehensive. He tests his range of motion, grip strength, and conducts several specific tests to rule out carpal tunnel, which he passes with flying colors.

*That's fine*, I tell myself. I didn't think it was carpal tunnel anyway.

"Okay," Eric says after the physical part of the exam is done. I already know what he's going to say, and I try to keep my face neutral. Positive. "I think it's best that we go ahead and draw some labs, get an MRI to check for any tendon issues, and just to be safe, we should run a nerve conduction study and order an EMG." When his suggestion is met with silence, he adds cheerfully, "Might as well get it all out of the way while you're here, right?"

Hendrix looks over at me, and I give a slight nod. "Okay," he says. "Sounds good."

But none of it sounds good. Not really.

And as we leave the clinic thirty minutes later, after getting his blood drawn, he asks, "Should I be worried?"

"No," I say, downplaying the situation, instead of doing what I should be doing, explaining what each test means and what will happen if one is positive or negative. You know...my damn job. "Like he said, it's just more convenient to get it all done at once."

"Promise?"

I swallow the guilt building in my gut and nod. "Promise."

**VIOLET**

Can you send me your schedule for the int. leg of the tour?

**ME**

Sure, why?

**VIOLET**

I'm your sister. Do I have to give you a reason?

**ME**

No, but you could also just Google it.

**VIOLET**

Yes, but then I would get to have this titillating conversation.

**ME**

Did you just say titillating?

**VIOLET**

I know words!

ME

LOL. Anyway, why do you need tour dates?

VIOLET

I'm going to be in Europe, and I want to see if any of the dates overlap.

ME

Oh, fun! Girls' trip! If only we could get Mom to join us.

VIOLE

I still can't believe you got her to that concert.

ME

She had the BEST time. Seriously, I don't think she ever stopped smiling.

VIOLET

I know. I have the hundred or so blurry photos she sent to prove it.

ME

We should make her a blurry photo album for Christmas.

VIOLET

She would love that.

ME

Oh shit. Gotta go. Someone just came into the clinic. LOVE YOU!

I pocket my phone and look up to find not just someone.

But two someones.

Elena and Zander, who are covered in...blood? His black Metallica tee is sticky with sweat, but there also seems to be blood dripping from his nose, and his lip is split.

And that's just what I notice at first glance.

"What the hell?" I start moving quickly, slapping on a pair of gloves and pointing to the portable exam table. "Get him up here."

"It looks worse than it is," he says, even as Elena mutters, "He's an idiot."

"Why do I feel like you're not the only one I'm going to be patching up tonight?" I raise a questioning eyebrow.

"I better be," Zander growls.

Elena pats him on the shoulder. "Don't worry," she tells me. "The other guy was sent packing. I'm sure he'll seek medical treatment elsewhere."

"Fucking better." Another growl. Or maybe it was more like a grunt.

"Am I missing something?"

Elena licks her lips and takes a calming breath. "I'd explain, but I fear that would just rile him up all over again. Let's just say that a crew member was overheard saying some inappropriate thing about—"

"Inappropriate?" He fumes. "What he said wasn't just inappropriate, Elena. It was inexcusable. No one talks about my wife like that. *Ever.*"

Her gaze softens, and she runs her hand through his tangled hair. I turn away to gather supplies, giving them a moment.

As I unlock the rolling carts, I think about his words, and it reminds me of that night at the gala when I stood there clutching my shoulder as the man glared at me, waiting for an apology.

It's not even that Tanner didn't stand up for me that bothers me the most. It's that he'd worn down my self-confidence so much that I thought I didn't deserve it in the first place. Regardless of who caused the encounter, I embarrassed him, and that was unacceptable.

That's why I apologized.

Elena doesn't need Zander to fight her battles, but she knows he would—without question—if she asked him to.

That is love.

That is what I want.

Maybe I already do.

"Come on, killer," I tease. "Let's get you cleaned up."

It turns out that whoever pissed off Zander not only gave him a bloody nose and a split lip, but also managed to give him a nasty gash on his left arm.

"How the hell?" I ask when I see it.

"Ring," he mutters under his breath. "Ugly-ass ring."

"Well, thanks to that ugly-ass ring, you're gonna need a few stitches," I tell him, causing him to groan and then mutter a few expletives. "Now, either I can do them or, if you're worried about scarring, I can see if we can find you a plastic—"

"Just do it," they say in unison.

All righty then. Wish I could say this is my first time giving stitches backstage, but I'd be lying. This group is a rowdy bunch.

"What is the weirdest thing that you've had to deal with on tour? In general, since I know you can't talk specifics." Elena inquires as I start gathering the suture kit and lidocaine. She pulls up a chair and sits next to her husband.

"To be honest, I thought I would be doing a lot of STD testing, but surprisingly, everyone is pretty responsible when it comes to safe sex."

"That's Asher," Zander explains. "Since Mitch, he really started running a tight ship."

"I noticed."

"Asher and the original members all grew up together. Cutting ties with Mitch was tough on them. I think Asher felt responsible because he didn't see the shit Mitch was getting into until it was too late, and he had gone too far."

"That's not his fault."

"It's not," he agrees. "But he still makes it his mission to keep tabs on everyone to make sure it doesn't happen again."

"That's nice. It's like a family."

"We are a family, and you're part of it, you know?"

I hum a noncommittal response because I don't really know how to reply. Do I want to be part of their family? Yes. But Hendrix and I haven't talked about what happens after the tour ends at all. It's exactly what Elena warned me not to do—get swept up in the tour and avoid real life. But here we both are, avoiding the *what happens next* talk like the plague.

"And, uh, to answer your question..." I awkwardly segue. "I'd have to say this takes the cake." Elena snorts as I start to clean the wound. "Sorry, Zander."

We keep talking as I inject the lidocaine, then begin stitching him up once it takes effect. I ask about their time off last week. They say they chose to stay at home and barely left the house, just enjoying the peace and quiet. When I'm nearly finished, Elena asks about our trip to Seattle, and I almost falter.

They don't know about Hendrix's trip to the clinic.

They don't know about the blood tests or the MRI, the ones that came back normal.

They don't know that each time we get a normal result, Hendrix's attitude improves exponentially.

While mine plummets as I wait for the phone to ring again.

"Good," I manage to say. "It was really fun. I've never been to Seattle, so we hit all the touristy places. I saw them toss the fish at Pike Place."

"I've never seen that," Elena says. "They really throw them?"

"They do! It's impressive." I give his arm a gentle tap. "You're all set."

He inspects the stitches. "Nice. Thanks."

"You need to keep it covered, so maybe stick to a T-shirt on stage for the next few days."

"Good idea," Elena says. "The internet would go crazy trying to figure out what happened to you."

"Definitely don't need that kind of attention."

"Is it hard?" I suddenly ask. "The attention. The constant invasion of privacy?"

Elena presses her lips together as she glances over at Zander. They must have some sort of silent conversation about who's gonna field my question. Zander must win. "Yes. It's hard. It can feel isolating not being able to do normal, everyday things like go to the grocery store or take my family on a vacation without a security detail." He sighs, and I feel a bit guilty for asking, but I have to know. After being out with Hendrix last week and experiencing only a fraction of the attention Zander gets, I need to understand what it's like.

Because if we eventually have that *what happens next* talk, and there's a future for us, I want to know I can handle it.

No matter what *it* might end up being.

"But on the other hand, how many people get to live this life? I know musicians who have worked their whole lives and never got a tenth of the success I've been lucky enough to have. I was never one of those guys who wanted the fame and fortune. That was always Hendrix's dream."

I feel my stomach knot, but I know he's right. Since the moment I met him, there is nothing Hendrix has wanted more in this world than to perform.

To play music in front of a massive crowd.

To live out his dreams through his love of music.

My phone buzzes in my pocket.

When I pull it out, my heart stops. Eric's name flashes across the screen.

"I, uh...I've got to take this."

"Sure." Elena nods, a crease forming between her brow as she watches my mood shift. "We'll get out of your way. Thanks for taking care of him."

"No problem," I manage to say.

As I answer, I swallow down the lump in my throat, knowing this may be the call that ruins everything.

## Chapter Thirty-Five

# HENDRIX

"All good?" Asher says into the mic. We've just run through a chorus of a popular Manic song after doing our individual sound checks, and I can tell Asher is ready to wrap this up. He keeps checking his watch and running a hand through his hair.

"We're good. Thanks, guys." I hear the production manager confirm in my earpiece, and a half-second later, Asher is charging offstage.

"Fucking hell. What's with him today?" Darius asks as he steps up beside me.

"No idea."

"Something must be up because he didn't even make us run through 'Drive' again when you were late into the chorus."

My whole body goes rigid. "Shit. Sorry about that."

"Nothing to worry over, yeah?" He glances over at me.

"Right, yeah." I nod, more for myself than anything. Everything is fine. "Just tired."

He gives me a shit-eating grin and slaps me hard on the back. "I bet you are, mate."

"Hey, now," I warn. "Not cool."

"Speaking of...I never got a thank you for that."

"For what?" I hand my guitar to a young blonde crew member that Darius has been eyeing. He gives her a lazy smile. She instantly blushes.

"For helping you two lovebirds work it out."

I give him an incredulous look. "Are you referring to that time when you felt up my girlfriend and then left her in the middle of the dance floor for some other creepy dude to take over?"

His hands raise to his sides. "Right. That. I can see now why this might not have been the best topic to bring up. Sorry about that. Things obviously didn't go as planned." His eyes go round in a clumsy attempt to look innocent.

I shake my head and then smack him on the back of his. "You're an idiot."

He chuckles. "Yeah, I am. But admit it. This idiot"— he points to himself—"is growing on you."

"Never."

My phone starts to ring, and by the time I pull it out of my pocket, Darius's attention has already shifted to the blonde. Just as well since I probably should take this. It's not often that I get a call from my older brother.

"Hey, what's up?" I greet him as I head down the hall toward the hospitality suite.

"Hey, you got a second?" Leave it to Cash to get right to the point.

"Yeah. We just finished sound check, so you caught me on my way to grab some food." As much as I want to go in the opposite direction, where the clinic is set up, I need fuel. If I don't eat now, I won't get the chance until well after the concert.

"Look, what I'm about to tell you needs to stay between us, okay?"

I stop dead in my tracks. "That doesn't sound good."

"I guess it depends on how you look at it. I overheard Dad talking to Ridge on a conference call yesterday."

My hand tightens at my side. Do they know? About the visit to the clinic? Are they doubting my ability to play? All of my tests have come back normal. "Okay…"

"Evans reached out to Asher. He thinks he might be ready to come back."

I'm momentarily speechless because this is not what I expected him to say. At all.

"How soon?" I find a quiet corner and lean against a wall. It's cool against my spine, and I resist the temptation to just sink down and let the floor swallow me up.

"The consensus was to keep you through the end of the US leg and then—"

"Bring him back for the international tour," I finish, feeling everything inside of me wither. That would mean no more late-night jam sessions with the guys. No more joking with Asher. I wouldn't get to see my best friend proudly carry his daughter on his shoulders backstage.

I wouldn't wake up with Zara in my arms every morning.

They'd all go on without me, while I…

"What the fuck do I do?"

"You stop stalling, look through those contracts, and give Saul an answer, Hen," he says in that pragmatic tone of his. "You decide on your next step before it's decided for you. This is something you've always wanted, right? Don't throw it all away now."

"Dude!" Zander smacks the back of my head, and I jolt upright in my seat.

"What the fuck?" I remove my earbuds and glare up at him.

"I said your name like five times. How loud do you keep the volume on those things? You know you can lose your hearing that way?"

"Okay, Grandpa," I mutter. He stares at me, and I realize how rude that sounded. I've been rotting in this leather chair in the corner of the swanky hospitality suite for the last thirty minutes. I need to get the hell up and go get ready, but I just can't seem to move. "Sorry, Z." I blow out a breath. "I'm in a shit mood."

"I can tell. Want to talk about it?" He plops down into the seat next to me, and I notice he's already dressed. Black jeans and an old band tee peek out of a hoodie. His hair is styled. It's not that different from his normal look. Just a bit more polished.

My brother asked me to keep our conversation between us, and I won't violate that trust, but it doesn't mean I can't talk about everything else. "Saul and my dad want an answer regarding the offers I got."

"Seether still at the top of the list?" He regards me carefully. The guys know about me signing with my dad and the offers that came with it. There's nothing about this I'm trying to hide.

Well, nothing aside from the trip to the clinic.

When Asher and Zander looked through the list of

band names, I swear I saw a hint of sadness or maybe even regret in Asher's expression, but they both agreed. Seether was the best option. Even if it did mean I'd have to jump into another seven months of touring.

I nod. "You know I'd be crazy to turn them down."

"So why the hesitancy?"

"I think I'm in love with Zara," I suddenly blurt out. I feel my eyes go comically wide. "Fuck, I didn't mean to say that."

My best friend breaks into a laugh so loud that the catering staff start to stare. "Are you sure?"

"No, I meant it. I just didn't mean..." I let out a sigh. "I haven't told her yet."

"Okay, so this isn't a denial-type thing?"

"No, it's a *how do I make this work* thing," I tell him, my head falling back against the leather cushion. A few crew members wander in and grab a snack or a drink. Zander waits for them to leave before he continues.

"What do you mean? Do you think she won't support your choice? Have you not talked about it?"

"No," I groan, feeling beyond stupid. "There have been a dozen or more times I've wanted to bring it up, but I always stop myself because what if that's the conversation that ruins it? What if I put too much pressure on her, and she decides it's too soon after her divorce and ends things? I can't—" My voice catches in my throat. "I can barely stand the idea of being away from her for a few months, touring with a new band. If she walked away..."

Zander scrubs a hand down his face. "Look," he says, angling his body toward me. "You know I did a lot of stupid shit in those first few weeks after I met Elena. I blamed a lot of it on the NDA I had to sign with the band, but we both know that was total bullshit. If I had wanted to be honest with her, I could have found a way around it or simply spoken to Ridge. But I didn't. I used it as an excuse to hide my feelings, and in the end, it almost cost me everything."

"It was kind of worth seeing you grovel all over the internet, though."

"It's called a grand gesture, asshat. And at least my viral video isn't of my abs."

I laugh. "It's not my fault you let yourself go."

"Oh fuck off." He laughs, then sobers and says, "You need to talk to her."

"I know. It's just things have been off with us this week. It's like..." I try to think of a way to explain it. "She seems stressed, but when I ask her if everything is okay, she perks up like nothing is wrong."

He tilts his head. "Did you ever stop to think she's worrying over the same shit you are?"

"I—" Shit. "No?"

"Seriously, dude. Talk to her."

I check my watch and grimace. "Right, yeah. I should head out then if I want to get to the clinic before the show."

I move to get up, and Zander does the same. "If it eases your mind, Zara asked me the other day if it was all worth it, the fame and loss of privacy."

"What? When?"

"That day in the clinic after I kicked the fucking shit out of..."

"Yeah, I remember," I say, already seeing his hackles starting to rise. I have no idea what the guy said, but it must have been bad. It's been nearly a week, and Zander can still barely mention the incident without going nuclear.

"Yeah, anyway..." He seems to snap out of it, his eyes blinking and returning to me. "The way she asked, it didn't feel random. It felt purposeful, like she was trying to put herself in our shoes and see what it would be like."

"And?" My heart accelerates.

"And we were interrupted before we finished, but I would have told her the same thing I'm gonna tell you."

"Okay."

"That it's only worth it until it's not." He shrugs. "There is only one thing I can't live without in this world, and it's not music anymore. If I ever get to a point where my career is causing more harm to my family than good, I'm out."

"Simple as that?"

He slides his hands into his pockets and gives a nod. "Simple as that."

Three years ago, those words would have shocked me. Zander, who ran away from home at eighteen with an old guitar and his brother's truck. He'd always had one love, and that was music.

Until now.

"If you're worried about your future, maybe you need to ask yourself the same question. What can you live without? Once you have your answer, I'm sure you'll figure it all out."

## Chapter Thirty-Six

# HENDRIX

I am a horrible doctor.

I am an even worse girlfriend.

It's been over a week since I received Hendrix's final test results from Eric, and I haven't said a word. When he asked if I wanted him to be the one to talk to him, I told him I would handle it.

But I haven't.

Like a coward, I keep hoping Hendrix will check his email and see the message telling him to check his patient portal and then bring it up himself. But I saw that man's inbox one time...

That email is dead and buried and will never see the light of day again.

I need to tell him. Every day I don't tell him is not only a breach of trust but also a violation of the oath I swore as a doctor.

I wipe away the tears from my eyes, hoping the heat from the shower will camouflage the red splotches on my face. The band put on an amazing show tonight in Boston, and tomorrow we're heading to New York.

I've never been to New York City.

Two weeks ago, I was looking forward to this show. Hendrix was going to take me to the Empire State Building and Times Square. We were going to eat hot dogs from a street vendor and ride the subway.

But now, everything feels so up in the air. Like I'm walking on thin ice, and it's starting to crack beneath my feet. Any minute now, it'll break, and I'll be swallowed whole.

I dry off and wrap a towel around myself. With a deep breath, I open the bathroom door to the suite and glance around. Hendrix is sitting at the ornate wooden desk with a frown on his face. Papers are scattered in front of him. He lets out a deep sigh.

He's reviewing the contracts again.

My stomach clenches. This is why I haven't told him yet. Because as soon as I do, everything changes.

"Make a decision yet?"

His head swivels around until those soft blue eyes meet mine. They seem to roam and linger over every inch of me, like he just can't help himself.

"No," he answers with a look of defeat. I grab one of the fluffy white robes the hotel provided and swap it for my towel. I take a seat on the edge of the bed.

"What seems to be the holdup?"

He turns the chair around so he's facing me. He stretches out his long legs, wearing a pair of black joggers. No shirt. His hair is messy, as if he's been running frustrated fingers through it.

"I know which offer I should take," he says. "Seether is a huge band. Almost as big as Manic. Their following is loyal, and their music is edgy and complex. The tour schedule they've put together is insane and super ambitious. They're collaborating with a ton of other bands, and it could be really great for my career."

I swallow hard, my heart feeling like it's been put in a vice. "It sounds exactly like what you've always wanted."

"Yeah." His voice trails off.

I watch his expression fall. "You don't sound so sure."

"I…" He pauses, takes a deep breath before his gaze meets mine. "I need to know what happens next, Zara. With you and me," he clarifies. My pulse quickens. I fist the hem of my robe as my throat starts to tighten. "Because I don't think I can sign any of these contracts without knowing you'll be there by my side."

I start to cry.

His eyes go wide, and he mutters a curse. Suddenly, he's off his chair and kneeling at my feet. "I didn't mean literally by my side, Cupid. I don't expect you to give up your career for me. I just want to know I'm not going to lose you, 'cause—"

My tears turn to sobs. He's being too nice. His words are too kind.

"I'm so sorry," I choke out. My chest heaves with every word. "I'm so sorry."

"What?" His eyes are frantic. "Why?"

"Oh god." I wipe away the moisture around my eyes as I try to speak through the tears. "I don't deserve you."

"What are you talking about?" He runs his fingers through my hair. His words are calming, but I can hear a faint tremor in his voice. "Please, Zara, baby. Talk to me."

I meet his gaze. He looks wrecked. Ruined. He misunderstood me. He thinks I'm panicking over what he said, how he wants me by his side, how he can't do this without me.

Could I fuck this up anymore?

I brush away more tears and face him. I've hidden the truth from him for far too long. No matter how he reacts, I can take it.

For him, I can take it.

I suck in a deep breath. "Eric called."

I watch the words register, and then it's like an avalanche. His expression shifts from acknowledgment to disbelief, then falls into outright fear. "When?"

"Last week."

Fear morphs to shock. "Last week?"

A tear slips down my cheek. "Last week," I confirm.

"But I—" He looks away, stands, and then sits beside me on the bed. I notice his hand tighten, like he's already mourning something he doesn't fully understand yet. "Why didn't you say anything? Why didn't Eric?"

"Because I asked him not to," I explain. "I told him I would take care of it."

His throat bobs as he swallows. "Is it bad? Do I have cancer of the hand or something?"

"No." I shake my head with a pained laugh. "No cancer. In fact, everything came back normal."

He lets out a relieved exhale. "That's good, right?"

"Normally, yes. And if it weren't for one specific symptom, I'd probably just say you have early-stage tendonitis or maybe arthritis and give you some exercises to do to keep it from getting worse. But there's one symptom that doesn't fit tendonitis."

He stares at the floor momentarily, and it seems to sink in. "It only happens when I play?"

I nod, feeling the emotions starting to clog in my throat again. "That, and the fact that there isn't much pain associated with it."

"Just a dull ache sometimes," he agrees.

"Eric and I believe you have a condition called focal dystonia. It's a neurological disorder. Rare, but not unheard of among musicians. People in task-specific professions, like writers or athletes, are also susceptible. Your brain essentially misfires during precise movements, causing your hand and fingers to become unresponsive. That's why it only happens when you're playing or mimicking a chord sequence."

His gaze remains fixed on the floor. I want to reach out, pull him into my arms, and hold him, but I can't get a read on him without looking into his eyes.

*Does he hate me yet?*

*Will he ever trust me again?*

"You said you and Eric believe I have this focal... whatever. But you're not sure?"

"No, neither of us can make an official diagnosis. You'll need to see a neurologist for that."

His voice sounds so far away. "But both you and Eric are fairly certain?"

I nod, feeling overwhelmed with guilt at this admission. "I had my suspicions when I suggested we go see Eric in Seattle, but I didn't want to freak you out. When I watched you play in LA, I just knew something wasn't right. I didn't tell Eric because I was worried I might be jumping to conclusions, but when he called me last week with the final test results, he brought it up. He told me he had a patient with similar symptoms about a year ago."

"Why did you wait so long to tell me?"

My lip starts to wobble, and I have to bite down on it to keep from falling apart again. "Because I wasn't thinking like a doctor," I answer. "I once told you how I dreamed of becoming that woman I saw in the mall, who could raise her hand in a crowd and help in an emergency, who could help people. But when it came to protecting someone I—" My voice catches.

"Someone you what?" His gaze finally meets mine. It's intense. His blue eyes are blazing. "Someone you what, Zara?"

"Someone...I love," I finally say. "I love you, Hendrix."

"Fucking hell." His voice is hoarse as he rubs his eyes into the heel of his palm. "I need to get Zander a fruit basket."

"What?"

"Nothing." He shakes his head and...*smiles*. "Just— god. Say it again."

I start to cry again. "You don't hate me?"

"Why would I hate you? I fucking love you, Zara."

"You do?"

"Are you kidding?" He pulls me onto his lap. His body is warm, familiar, and safe. It feels like home. "I think I've been in love with you ever since you turned me down in college."

"But what about the diagnosis and the contracts and—"

He places a single finger on my lips. "Someone very wise recently told me to take a look at my life and figure out the one thing I couldn't live without." I stare into his eyes as he brushes a tear off my cheek. "I'll give you a guess, Cupid. It's not fame or money. It's not even music. It's you. My heart has been waiting ten long years for you, baby. And I'm done waiting. So whatever future lies ahead, we'll tackle it together."

"Are you sure?"

"I've never been more sure about anything in my whole damn life," he assures me. "Now, say it again."

I smile, feeling like I've just been given the greatest gift in the world. "I love you."

*Chapter Thirty-Seven*

# HENDRIX

It's barely four in the fucking morning again, and I'm wide awake. My mind is racing, and I'm trying to resist the urge to reach for my phone and type in the words focal dystonia in the search bar on Google.

Zara offered to tell me whatever I wanted to know last night about the subject, but it was late. And I didn't want to darken the mood after the words we'd just shared.

Because honestly, nothing else really mattered after that.

The moment she told me she loved me, I felt like I could overcome anything. But now, hours later, the fear is starting to set in.

*What does this all mean?*

*Will I still be able to play?*

*What do I tell my family? My agent? The band?*

I finally cave and reach for my phone, finding a string of unanswered texts from the night before that only add to the growing anxiety in my gut.

CASH

Have you decided yet?

SAUL

Not trying to stress you out, but Seether is pushing for an answer.

DAD

Answer Saul.

CASH

Stop ignoring Dad.

I ignore every single one of them.

I turn to reach for Zara but find the bed empty and the sheets cold. I look around the bedroom, but she is nowhere to be found. What the fuck?

Sliding out of bed, I glance toward the bathroom, but the door is open, and the light is off. Zara has an aversion to early mornings and the gym, so I'm usually the only one awake before seven. We rarely make it downstairs for breakfast most mornings and often order room service so she has extra time to sleep in or get ready.

I have no idea how she survived early morning classes and hospital shifts, because that woman hates to wake up.

I walk into the separate living area, and it's empty as well. Finally, I notice a faint glow coming from the balcony. I walk closer, and that's when I see her. In nothing but a fluffy white robe, she's stretched out on one of the loungers with her laptop in front of her. The screen illuminates her pensive expression as she types.

I pull open the door and step outside. It's still dark, but the water glints under the moonlight, and you can see the outline of ships in the distance.

Zara turns her head. "Hi," I say, closing the door behind me.

"Hi," she replies. I notice a forgotten cup of tea on the table next to her. There are at least a dozen tabs open on her browser. She's been up a long time. I wonder if she's slept at all.

"What are you doing out here?"

"I couldn't sleep," she answers as I sit down in the empty lounger beside her. It's summer in Boston, which means the morning air combined with the breeze coming off the bay is damn near perfect. I lean my head back and turn to face her.

"Why didn't you wake me?"

"Because I wanted some time to do some research before we left for New York."

"What kind of research?"

"Well, at first I just wanted to make sure I emailed Eric before I went to bed to ask for recommendations on neurologists who specialize in task-specific focal dystonia," she explains. "But then he responded, and I kind of lost track of time after that."

"What did he say?"

"He called me, actually."

"Seriously?" Even three hours behind, it would have been late considering I was barely running on two hours of sleep.

"Yeah, that man is a night owl, apparently." She clicks her mouse and pulls up a spreadsheet on her computer with a detailed list of doctors' names, along with their locations, years of experience—and that's just what I can pick out at first glance. "Anyway, he gave me a bunch of names, and I did the rest."

"This must have taken you forever."

She doesn't deny it. "I want to make sure you're seen by someone knowledgeable in the field who can give a definitive diagnosis. Because, even though Eric and I believe all the signs point to focal dystonia, I don't want to take you to someone who will just nod in agreement with us. I want someone who will do their due diligence and ignore us completely so they can make their own assessment." Her voice catches in her throat. "I want the best. Only the best will do."

*This fucking woman.*

"Come here."

She doesn't hesitate. She just closes her laptop and climbs over the arm of her lounger into mine. Her legs wrap around my thighs, and she burrows into my chest. I don't know how long we'll stay like that, with her clinging to me, listening to the steady rhythm of my heartbeat.

"The first time I saw you play, it nearly took my breath away," she murmurs. "It was that first night in Miami. I'd never been to a rock concert. Never seen anyone play live, except my mom."

"Not really the same," I interject.

"Not in the least," she agrees, and when I glance down at her, I see the faintest hint of a smile.

"I'm not sure what I expected when I walked to the side of the stage with Elena that night. I knew it would be loud, and the crowd would be huge and chaotic. But I never expected to get so swept up by it all. Seeing you perform was like a work of art. It actually made me mourn all those times you came into our tutoring sessions with your bass locked tight in its case. So many missed opportunities to hear you play."

She glances up at me, her brown eyes wet with unshed tears. "You can't lose that gift, Hen."

"I know, baby. I know." I bend down and gently kiss her lips. "And I won't lie and say I'm not scared. I'm not even sure I would have ever recognized the symptoms as anything serious if you weren't here, and it's scary to think how much worse it could have become."

"I'm going to be honest with you. There is no cure for this. There are treatments and specialists. There are medications, but there is nothing that makes it go away. If this is truly what you have, it's something you'll have forever."

"Will I lose my ability to play?"

Her gaze turns fierce. Resolute. "Not if I have anything to do with it."

I kiss her again, but this time it's anything but gentle or chaste. My fingers grip her hair as I tilt her head. Her lips are soft, and her cheeks are stained with dried tears. I hate that she's cried so much over me, and I want to erase every single one of them.

I reach for the tie on her robe and tug it free. She pulls back. Her eyes are wide and a touch curious. "Here?" She looks around the stone patio. Walls on either side separate us from the other suites, but the iron railing is open to the harbor, and our only cover is the darkness.

"Here," I confirm, kissing a path down the side of her neck. "I need to feel alive right now, Zara. So let me have you out here by the water before the sun comes up."

Her mouth is on mine before I can take my next breath. The robe slips off her shoulder, and I take it as a sign just to tug the whole thing off and toss it to the ground.

I take a long look at her, and damn if she doesn't take

my breath away. Naked under the moonlight, she looks ethereal.

Like a fucking goddess.

My hands are everywhere. Every delicious curve, every inch of smooth skin. I can't get enough of this woman. I don't think I ever will.

I know we're short on time, but I'm not leaving this balcony without a taste of her. Gripping her waist, I lift her and in one quick motion, I have her beneath me. She lets out a little squeal, which immediately turns into a breathy moan the minute my mouth closes over one of her rosy nipples. Her fingers grip my hair as I shift and pay some attention to the other side, swirling my tongue around the hardened peak.

Her back arches. "Please, Hen. I need more."

"I know what you need, Cupid."

It's exactly what I need too.

I kiss a path down her body, watching her breath grow ragged the closer I get to the valley between her thighs.

*Yeah, I definitely know what my girl needs.*

I grab one of her ankles and place her leg over my shoulder, spreading her wide. Even in the dark, she's a sight to behold.

Pink, perfect, and so fucking mine.

I slowly run my hand down her inner thigh. She shivers in anticipation. If we weren't chasing the sun, I'd draw this out, kiss every inch of her skin until she was begging me to make her come. But I don't want to take any more risks than we already are.

Even though I'm down with the idea of fucking her out here where anyone could technically see us, I'm not about to do it in broad daylight.

Like I told her in the tattoo studio, all this is just for me now.

And god help me, I plan to enjoy it every chance I can get.

My first taste of her is divine. I swirl my tongue around her clit and suck hard.

"Oh fuck," she cries.

I do it again, and she pulls on my hair and grinds her hips into my face.

"Fucking love it when you do that," I growl.

"Don't stop!" she protests, making me laugh. Two months ago, she would never have said something like that in the bedroom. Now she's pulling my hair and taking control of her orgasms.

It's sexy as hell.

I do exactly as I'm told and rub my tongue back and forth along her sensitive nub. When I slip two fingers inside her, she lets out a curse, and then she's riding my face.

My cock is so hard, I have to keep myself from fucking the damn cushion so I don't blow my load before I can get inside her.

Thankfully, I don't have to wait long.

I curl my two fingers, and suddenly her back bows, and I feel her whole body go rigid just before she shatters. She moans my name as I carry her through every aftershock, licking her clit until it becomes too much and she's pulling me up on top of her.

This time, when her fingers move through my hair, it's gentle. Sweet. Reverent.

And when I kiss her, it's slow. Purposeful. Loving.

No words are exchanged as she reaches for the waistband of my boxers and pushes them off my hips. When I slip them the rest of the way off and toss them to the ground, she only gazes up at me with a look of complete adoration.

This is what it feels like to make love, I realize. To know your partner so well that no words are needed. To be so deeply connected to another, feelings and emotions can be conveyed through physical touch.

When I slide into her slick entrance seconds later, I feel whole. Her legs wrap around me, and I bend down and kiss her. She moans into my mouth as I grind my hips and set a slow, torturous pace.

I run a hand over her smooth skin. I kiss her everywhere. I tell her how beautiful she is, and when we're both desperate and covered in sweat, I grip her waist and flip us so she's on top, giving her all the control.

"The sun is about to rise, Zara," I say, causing her to look over her shoulder. Tiny streaks of amber and gold are cresting the horizon. "And you know I don't share."

She leans down and places a sweet kiss on my lips, then whispers in my ear. "Neither do I."

Then she lifts her hips and nearly slides all the way off my cock before slamming her hips back down. My eyes nearly roll back in my head as she reaches forward and interlaces her hands with mine. And then begins to move.

It's mesmerizing. The way her hips rock, the steady bounce of her tits, and the look of sheer pleasure on her face while she does it.

But it's the confidence I love most.

She knows she looks good, and it's so hot. I know I'm not going to last much longer.

"Zara," I warn her.

She leans back, which only deepens the angle. She

lets out a throaty moan I recognize well. She's close. I let go of one of her hands and reach between her legs to rub her clit.

That's all it takes.

She detonates above me, writhing and squeezing my cock as she cries out my name.

*"Hendrix."*

It's music to my fucking ears. I grip her hips and thrust hard. Heat races up my spine, and I feel my body tighten, and I come, letting out a guttural groan as I empty myself in her just as the sun breaks through the horizon.

Just in the nick of time.

## Chapter Thirty-Eight

# ZARA

After Hendrix and I celebrated the coming of a new day —literally—we went back inside, and he did what he does best and ordered way too much food for breakfast.

After we were fed and caffeinated, we got to business and started making plans.

I quickly discovered Eric is one of those people who likes to stay up late and wake up early. I was surprised when he called me late last night, and I'm just as surprised when he does it again, five minutes after I send him an early morning email.

"Eric, it's eight o'clock," I say, not even bothering to say hello, placing him on speakerphone.

"Actually, in Seattle, it's five," he states.

"Do you have insomnia or something?"

"Nah, I'm just a thirty-something single guy who works too much. Does your rock star boyfriend have any brothers? Or a single rock star friend, perhaps?"

I laugh. Hendrix's eyebrow raises. Guess I forgot to mention that. It was just too fun to see him get so jealous. "Yes, but I think they're all straight."

"I think Evans is pan," Hendrix interjects with a shrug. "And my brother Myles is bi. But he's only twenty-five and not ready to commit."

"You sort of just described the male version of Violet." I joke.

"Too bad they didn't cross paths at the LA concert. It would have either been a match made in heaven or a total shitshow."

I hum in agreement before I hear Eric clear his throat. "I feel like we're getting off topic," he says. "And nothing about this conversation gets me laid, so..."

We both laugh. I could honestly kiss Eric. Hendrix needed a distraction before we get back into the heavy stuff. During breakfast, we had a very frank discussion. I went over the research I'd done last night, and I told him everything I know about focal dystonia.

After we talked, I suggested he see a doctor in LA since we would both eventually return there after the tour. We could even fly out today. The NYC concert wasn't for a couple of days, and with Eric's connections and Hendrix's ties to the band, I knew we could get him in right away.

But Hendrix didn't want to go to LA yet.

LA meant telling his family, and he wasn't ready for that.

So we were headed to NYC. He'd see a doctor there, and if he was diagnosed, we'd arrange to transfer his care to LA after the tour.

"I'm assuming you're calling to help us out with getting an appointment with a doctor in New York," I ask, steering the conversation back on track.

Unfortunately.

We only have so much time before we need to head downstairs to the airport.

"Nope," he answers. "I'm calling to tell you I already scheduled you an appointment with a doctor in New York."

"What? How?" I check my watch. Yep. Still says eight o'clock. Well, a few minutes past now.

"I'm just that good," he responds very matter-of-factly. "Now, the appointment is tomorrow at eleven. Does that work?"

I turn to Hendrix for an answer. This is his body. His career. His decision.

He nods. "Yes. Thank you so much for this, Eric."

"No problem. And let me just say..." He lets out an audible breath. "I hope we're both wrong."

"Me too, Eric," I say as I slide into Hendrix's embrace. "Me too."

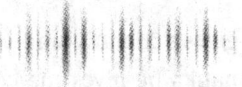

Hendrix is one big ball of nervous energy by the time the doctor's appointment rolls around the next day.

It's been mounting since we left Boston, and now he can hardly sit still without his knee bouncing or that right hand of his plucking out a tune on his thigh. He'll start and suddenly stop, either because his brain forces him to or because he remembers he might not be able to down the road.

It's heartbreaking to witness.

Luckily, we don't have to wait long to see the doctor. After checking in at the front desk, we sit in a small waiting area. The neurologist Eric recommended is located at New York Presbyterian. This place is a maze. I wouldn't ever want to get lost in it.

We asked at check-in if they could avoid calling out Hendrix's name. He already stands out with the guitar case strapped on his back. He doesn't need someone pulling out a phone to sneak a pic when they recognize his name.

So when the nurse comes out, she simply signals for us. Hendrix takes a deep breath and grabs my hand, and we follow her through the double doors to an exam room.

Shaunda, that's the nurse, follows us in and waits for Hendrix to set down his bass before asking him to take a seat on the exam table.

He glances at it and hesitates. He's visibly nervous.

"Is it okay if he sits next to me for vitals?" I ask. I don't usually like to interfere or pull rank, but for him, I will.

She nods and gives a friendly smile. "Not a problem."

The look of thanks he gives me could melt a damn iceberg. He takes my hand as he sits down in the open seat, and I stay quiet while he answers all the nurse's questions.

Finally, after she types a few notes into the laptop, she says, "Dr. Lin sent over all your records yesterday, so we have all your test results and his notes from your visit, but don't be surprised if Dr. Deshmukh asks questions you've already answered. She's very thorough."

"Thank you."

She leaves, and we're left alone. Suddenly, the room feels five times smaller. I want to crawl into his lap, wrap my arms around him, and...

I let out a snort. "You were so right."

His head turns. An amused smile tugs at the corner of his mouth. "I'm right about a lot of things. Care to elaborate?"

I roll my eyes but take a moment to memorize that tiny smile. I think it's the first genuine one I've seen all day. "I was just mentally scolding myself for causing so much turmoil in your life. And all I wanted to do was turn to you and apologize. For all of it."

"Even though it's a disorder you have no control over?"

"Yeah."

"Crazy how that works, huh?"

"It really is." I lean back in the uncomfortable metal chair, wondering how many times in my life I've apologized for things that weren't my fault. Things I felt responsible for simply because I existed. "I'm trying to remind myself that I can be sorry that you are experiencing anxiety or pain but not feel responsible for it."

He takes our joined hands and kisses mine, saying, "That's my girl."

Just then, there's a knock on the door, and a few seconds later, a middle-aged Indian woman I recognize from my research walks in. Her dark hair is peppered with gray, and she's wearing plain scrubs and glasses.

"Hi." She offers her hand to Hendrix, then to me. "I'm Dr. Priya Deshmukh."

"I'm Hendrix, and this is my girlfriend, Zara."

"It's nice to meet you. Eric spoke highly of both of you." She sets her laptop down on the laminate counter and sits on the small stool in front of it. "Now, I'm sure you're both anxious. So how about we get to it?"

We both nod.

She begins by reviewing his family history. Focal

dystonia can be hereditary, but given how difficult it is to diagnose, there would likely be no record of it.

"There is, however, a slight chance it could be passed down to your children," she states after explaining some of the genetic elements.

My stomach does a full somersault when I see the way Hendrix smirks.

After the baby bomb, she begins to ask when he started noticing the symptoms. Like the nurse warned us, many of these questions are redundant, but neither of us minds. I appreciate her being thorough.

"Does it ever happen when you're not playing?" she asks.

"Only when I'm plucking out a rhythm," he says before explaining, "It's something I do when I'm bored or nervous." His fingers twitch on his thigh. "Kind of like now."

She smiles and nods. "My son plays the cello, and he does the same thing."

She asks a couple more questions. Does he experience any pain? What makes it worse? What does it feel like when it happens?

Then she moves on to the neurological part of the exam. She tests his reflexes and strength. She has him touch the tip of each finger to the tip of his nose. He passes it all with flying colors.

None of us expected anything otherwise.

"Now, for the part of the exam that is slightly out of the ordinary," she says after typing a few notes.

"I'm guessing this is why I brought my bass?"

"Yes," she confirms with a warm smile. "I'd like you to play something, preferably a piece you've played in the past when you've experienced these symptoms. We'll have you run through it several times since repetition seems to trigger it. This will let me observe what the two of you have already seen."

And allow her to make her final diagnosis.

"Okay," Hendrix agrees. He reaches over and grabs the case while I stand to give him space to play. He's methodical as he places the large black case on the exam table and lifts each latch. When he pulls out the acoustic bass, he handles it as if it's precious, like it's part of him.

I want to scream.

This isn't fair.

*You could be wrong*, a tiny voice inside me whispers. It's my final sliver of hope, and I hold on to it as he slides the strap over his shoulder and takes his seat to perform what could be the most important show of his life.

He takes a deep breath, closes his eyes, and starts to play.

I recognize the song almost immediately. It's quickly become one of my favorite Manic at Midnight songs. It's called "Someday," and it's a song Asher wrote for their latest album. It's as beautiful as it is tragic, talking about how he's so alone, but maybe someday it will all be worth it.

Hendrix plays the chorus perfectly on the first and second tries.

But it's the third that his fingers stick, and the music comes to an abrupt halt. He stares at his hand and the way his fingers curl, as if they just betrayed him.

Dr. Deshmukh nods and jots down a few notes. She doesn't say anything but asks him to play it again. He does, five more times. He's only successful on two of the attempts.

"It's not usually this bad," he tells her. "I can get

through a whole concert with maybe one mistake, if any."

"You're stressed," she explains. "That, combined with the repetitions, is causing your symptoms to worsen."

"So I'm guessing I failed that test?" he says after she tells him she's seen enough, and he places it back in the case.

"It wasn't a test, Hendrix, and you are a very talented musician," she says.

"But for how much longer?"

She folds her hands in her lap and tilts her head in a way that's all too familiar, because it's the same expression I have just before I deliver bad news to one of my patients.

My heart plummets.

"Based on your test results and what I've observed, I think it's safe to say you have all the signs of task-specific focal dystonia."

That last flicker of hope that I might be wrong fades as I feel Hendrix's whole body go rigid next to me. Dr. Deshmukh notices it too and looks to me for guidance.

"Could you give us a minute?" I ask.

"Absolutely. Take all the time you need." She grabs her laptop and stands. "Just crack the door when you're ready."

"Thank you," I say, truly meaning it. I know she has other patients waiting, and considering we're a work-in, this is more than generous. The door softly clicks behind her.

The room is blanketed in silence before I hear Hendrix suck in a long, ragged breath. It's full of pain and sorrow. It breaks my fucking heart.

I get up from my chair and crouch down in front of it. His eyes are red and brimming with tears.

"It's such a stupid thing to be upset about." He lets out a hollow laugh, wiping his eyes. "It's not like I'm dying. Hell, I'm not even in pain."

I reach for him. He covers his hands with mine, holding onto them like a lifeline. I wait until his gaze finds mine, then I say, "Story Time." My voice is a little hoarse and tinged with emotion, but this is our thing. If I can get through to him, this will be how. "I read about this musician last night—a guitar player. He was diagnosed with focal dystonia in the late nineties, and the process took years. Before his diagnosis, he sank into a deep depression and stopped performing altogether. He couldn't trust his own body to do what he'd trained it to do. What he loved to do."

A single tear falls down Hendrix's cheek. I know this is the future he is envisioning for himself. I know the reality of the diagnosis is probably causing him to catastrophize and see only the worst possible future.

I need him to know there is hope, even when it feels utterly hopeless.

Maybe I need it too.

After his diagnosis, everything changed. He finally had doctors willing to treat him. He was able to stop focusing on what didn't work and focus on what did. And that's when he realized...he had a perfectly good left hand. So he started teaching himself how to play the instrument he loved, all over again, with his other hand.

I see a tiny flash of emotion in Hendrix's eyes, and I feel my chest tighten and my eyes sting.

"It's okay to be upset, Hen. It's okay to feel sad or angry. This is something you love, something you're passionate about, and it's not fair that this is happening to you. And it's not because some musician or band is fucking you over. It's not due to a lack of opportunity or talent. It's your own damn body that's betraying you. So no, you're not dying, but that doesn't invalidate your feelings. You're allowed every one of your emotions."

It's as if those words shatter the last of his defenses. His face crumbles, and the tears begin to fall. I climb onto his lap, and he wraps his arms around me. He holds me tight, and I listen as he mourns the life he could have had.

And tries to make peace with his new reality.

"Fuck, Zara. I don't—" His voice cracks as he buries his face into my neck. "I don't know who I am without music. When you said people have layers? I don't. Music is all I've ever have. It's the only thing I've ever been good at."

"That's not true."

"It is." He's adamant. "I was never good at sports like Myles. I couldn't play the piano like Cash or sing like Presley. I was decent at school, but not a brainiac like Mercury. That bass"—his crestfallen gaze lands on his black guitar case—"is all I had."

I lift my head. "You have me. And I don't know much about sports, but I know you're pretty damn good at loving me."

Those denim blue eyes burn with intensity as his mouth curves into a warm smile. "Fuck yeah, I am."

My forehead touches his, and I run my thumb along his cheek, wiping away the last of his tears. "You ready to kick some ass?"

He nods. "Yeah. Let's do this."

"Love you too, Mom," I say for the fourth time. My mom's cheeks are wet from crying, and my dad has an arm wrapped around her. They're both sitting in the family room where we gather for Christmas morning and lazy Sunday dinners.

I can't wait for Zara to be part of those memories.

Right as I'm about to end the video call, she waves her hand and practically shouts, "Oh, and tell Zara we love her too!"

My mom always gets extra emotional when there's bad news...or she's tipsy. Unfortunately for me, it's the former. After I visited with Dr. Deshmukh yesterday, I didn't feel right about keeping the news from my family, especially my parents. So I decided to call and tell them today. My dad was pragmatic as usual, asking the logical questions while also making plans for my future as a musician.

My mom, however, was a basket of emotions. She burst into tears and told me how devastated she felt for me. That's when Zara stepped in and tried to smooth things over, explaining the kind of treatment I would be undergoing and how it might help. That improved things, but I can still tell she's upset.

I don't blame her, though. It's not like I exactly took the news well either.

I don't know how long Zara held me in that exam room while I cried. No, not just cried. Fucking sobbed.

Pretty sure it won't be the last time, either.

"No need to shout," I laugh. "She's just in the other room."

"Okay. Well, I just wanted to make sure she knew. I'm so glad you two found each other, and I'm so grateful to her for everything."

"I know, Mom," I say as I turn toward the desk where Zara's laptop rests. She's been on it doing nonstop research. I practically had to drag her off it to go get ready for tonight's concert. "Me too."

Dr. Deshmukh gave us a treatment plan that included a recommendation for a movement specialist. Most people would just pick the one closest to their home, right? Not my girlfriend. She's currently in the process of making another spreadsheet to compare and contrast all the movement specialists that were recommended to determine the best one, location be damned.

A small smile crosses my lips. "I've got to go," I tell my parents. "I'll call you soon."

"Okay." It's my dad who responds this time. "I'll have Saul reach out to Seether and inform them of your decision. He'll also send replies to the rest of the bands."

"Thanks, Dad," I say, knowing I'm doing the right thing. I was hesitant to accept the offer even before I knew about the diagnosis. Now, I'm even more sure.

With my future so uncertain, I know now is not the time to make any major life changes with my career.

I finally end the call and let out an exhausted sigh. It was a long, emotional conversation.

"You okay?" Zara asks as she emerges from the bedroom, looking hot as fuck. She's fully embraced the rocker look since that night in LA when Elena helped her dress up. For tonight's concert, she's wearing a tight leather skirt and a cropped NYC shirt I bought her today when we went to Times Square.

"I am now," I say, eyeing her up and down. "You look incredible."

She grins. "Not sure this is appropriate attire for a doctor, but I decided I don't care. I'm a rock doc. I can dress however I want."

"That's the spirit," I say, then fall silent.

She notices the change in tone almost immediately. "What?" she says, crossing the room in seconds. "What is it? Did your parents say something? Are you worried about playing tonight?"

I hold her waist to steady her. "No." I shake my head. "Nothing like that."

"Then what—"

"Evans is coming back." I watch her eyes go wide. She knows what this means. "I wasn't supposed to say anything. Cash gave me a heads-up."

"What did your dad say?"

I just shake my head. "Not a damn word. That's what's bothering me. Saul hasn't said anything either. I thought that after I told my dad about my diagnosis, he'd finally mention it. Not as big of a blow when they'll probably just ask me to leave the second I tell them anyway, you know?"

"You think Asher would really do that?"

"I don't know," I answer honestly. "I don't think so, but it puts them in a tricky spot. I'm unreliable and Evans—"

"Is just coming back from extended time off."

"This whole thing is confusing as fuck."

She wraps her arms around my neck and kisses my cheek. "Well, there's only one way to solve it."

I slide my hand up her bare thigh. "Stay here and see what kind of panties are hiding under that skirt?"

She grins and playfully smacks my hand. "Nope, sorry. But I might show you later, after you go talk to Asher."

Before I can decide when to ambush Asher with the news, I get a text from him instead.

ASHER

Can you meet me in the green room
before sound check today?

Well, I guess I can stop wondering how soon I'll be leaving the tour.

*Fuck.* I don't want to say goodbye to Zara.

Not so soon after my diagnosis.

It's too new. Too raw.

*I'm still too raw.*

Maybe I can just tag along with them until the end of the US tour, then head home. We'll still be apart for two months, but at least it won't be right away.

Two months.

I try not to think about it as I type out my reply.

ME

Sure.

The treatment plan Dr. Deshmukh put together is thorough and aggressive. She wants me to see a movement specialist right away. They'll try to rewire my brain's fine motor patterns using different techniques like mirror therapy. Depending on what goes on, we'll discuss further treatments such as medications or even Botox injections.

Zara's story about the guitar player who taught himself how to play with his left hand gives me hope. I guess if someone can do that, anything is possible.

But the only goal on my mind right now is to finish this tour and stay with the group of people I've come to consider family, but as our car pulls up to Madison Square Garden, I start to think this all might be coming to an end.

As we go inside, Zara takes my hand and asks, "Do you want me to come with you?"

I give a solemn nod.

We pass by crew members, and we both say hello as we follow the signs to the green room. When we finally arrive, I stop and take a deep breath.

Zara gives my hand an encouraging squeeze.

I push open the door and freeze.

Standing front and center in the middle of the room is Asher. Flanked on either side of him are Darius and Zander. And next to Zander is Evans Sterling, the original bass player for Manic at Midnight.

Fuck.

*Is this an ambush?*

*Am I being fired?*

It takes me a moment to notice Elena sitting toward the back, holding a sleeping Marisa in her arms. Next to her, Ridge sits in a tan suit and blue tie, typing furiously on his phone.

I turn to Zara for guidance, but she appears just as clueless. What's going on here?

Zander gestures to the table nearby, filled with bottled water and snacks. Who the hell wants to munch on a bag of chips right now?

"Hey, Hen. Wanna take a seat?"

"You first," I reply coolly.

He chuckles. "Okay, I guess we deserve that. This does look kinda sus."

I refrain from commenting on how he's too fucking old to be using a word like sus.

Instead, Zara and I take seats across from him and Asher. Darius picks the seat next to Zara, giving her a flirty wink I don't appreciate. And Evans? Evans looks like a fish out of water, his eyes flicking from me to Zara to Zander before finally sitting next to Asher.

"This is all starting to feel a touch hostile," Asher begins, his attention focused on me. "So I'm going to get right to the point. Hendrix, you've put us in a bit of a bind."

My heart begins to race, and my eyes dart around the room.

Who told them?

*My dad would never...*

"When we brought you on, we knew we'd like you. Zander spoke highly of you. What we didn't expect...was how quickly you'd become someone we couldn't afford to lose."

"What the fuck?" I mutter under my breath, causing Zander and Darius to chuckle.

"But a band can't have two bass players," he says, turning his gaze from Evans back to me. Then he shrugs. "Or can it?"

"I don't understand."

"He's asking you to join the band, dipshit." Zander grins from across the table.

I turn my attention to Evans because surely he can't be on board with this idea. He's the bass player, after all.

"Hey, Hendrix. It's been a while," he says softly. That's when I realize how different he is. The Evans I remember was loud and boisterous, always up for a good time.

This version of Evans seems to have gained some much-needed weight on his gangly frame. His cheeks are flushed, and his once-long brown hair is cut short and close to his scalp.

"Good to see you, man. This is Zara Valentine." I introduce him. "She's the in-house doctor. And my girlfriend."

They exchange pleasantries, followed by a brief, awkward silence as Evans rubs his face and exhales. "Right, so Asher's been covering for me, yeah? Telling everyone I just needed some time to myself, but the truth is, I just got out of rehab a couple of months ago. I'm an alcoholic."

"E—" Darius rises from his chair, walks over to his friend, and pulls him into a tight hug. After a few hushed words and a pat on the back, Darius doesn't return to his seat and instead takes the one next to Evans. "Why didn't you tell us? We would have been there for you."

"I was ashamed," he admits. "After everything that happened with Mitch, I couldn't believe I let things get that far. I should have known better, you know? I should have learned my lesson."

"Addiction doesn't follow the rules," Zara chimes in, her voice gentle and encouraging. She might think she let her emotions override her judgment regarding my diagnosis, but I believe it's those same emotions that make her an incredible doctor—a compassionate one. "It's not logical. It's a disease, and it doesn't care about what's right or wrong."

He nods. "I know that now. I do. But at the time, I felt like I let everyone down."

"You did the opposite," Asher says. "You made us proud. You recognized that you needed help, and you went and got it. But now that the truth is out, you need to know we're here for you. So tell them what you told me when you rang me up and said you were ready to come back."

His throat bobs. "I want to play again. I want to be here with you guys. You're my family, and not being here feels wrong. But I'm not sure I can handle the pressure of playing full time. I'm afraid—" His voice cracks. "I'm afraid the stress will get to me, and I'll relapse."

"And we would never want to put you in that position, Evans. Which is where you come in," Asher says, pointing at me. "We know it's unorthodox to have two bass players, and I know it's asking a lot of you when you have better offers out there."

"I don't." I cut him off, knowing now is the time to speak my truth before they get their hopes up. "I turned them all down."

"What?" I hear everyone say at once. Even Elena, in

the far back, yells something in surprise at my declaration.

"Why would you do that?" Darius is the one who asks the obvious question.

I turn to look at Zara, and she gives me an encouraging smile. "Well, as it turns out, I also have something to tell you, and once I do, you might want to think twice about bringing me on as a band member."

Asher's brows furrow. "What could change our minds?"

"I recently found out that I have a condition called task-specific focal dystonia. It's a neurological disorder that basically causes a disconnect between my brain and my nerves."

"Like ALS?" Zander's face pales.

"No." I shake my head. "Nothing that severe. This only affects my ability to play the bass. It only affects my right hand."

"Are you serious?" Darius looks wrecked. I've never seen him so serious and solemn. It's weird as fuck.

"I wish I weren't," I reply. "Zara and I met with a neurologist yesterday, who confirmed it. I'm starting treatment, but I can't guarantee how long I'll be able to play at my current level, if at all. You'd be safer going with someone else as Evans's backup. I'm too risky."

The whole table falls silent, and I wait for it.

*The apologies. The sympathetic glances. The relief that it's not them...*

I wouldn't blame them for any of it.

"Our offer still stands," Asher says, and I hear Zara gasp.

I look up at him in surprise. "Are you all crazy? Did you not just hear what I said?"

"We did." Darius nods. "We just don't care."

"We care," Evans interjects, waving his hands and giving Darius a sharp glare. "What this tosser is trying to say is that it doesn't matter to us."

"You're family," Asher states. "We take care of our family."

"Yeah, man," Zander agrees. "You're stuck with us."

I hear Zara sniffle, and I turn to see a tear trickling down her cheek. I catch it, and she smiles happily up at me.

"Fucking hell," I mutter. "The woman I love is here. I wasn't going anywhere anyway. Might as well play some music while I'm here."

"That's the spirit!" Darius cheers.

"I'll take it." Asher shrugs.

Everyone congratulates me, and hugs are exchanged. Elena and Zara both cry. The guys dump water bottles on Evans's head as a welcome-home tribute. Darius eats five bags of chips. Ridge finally puts down his phone, but only to come over and tell me my contract will be coming soon.

All business, that guy.

I wrap an arm around Zara's shoulder, feeling lighter than I have in months, despite having one of the hardest weeks in my life.

And it's all due to the people in this room.

A techie sticks his head in the room and says, "Sound check in twenty, guys."

Evans and I turn to one another.

"How do you want to do this?" I ask, wrapping an arm around Zara's shoulder. "You wanna rotate? Or work out a schedule?"

He shrugs, stuffing his hands in his pockets. "Rock, paper, scissors?"

"Tonight, you're both playing," Asher announces, much to our surprise. "We'll figure out the logistics during sound check, but this is one announcement we are not delaying."

"Amen to that," Zander mutters.

Asher heads out, and the rest of the guys follow close behind, patting me on the back and congratulating me again.

Soon, it's just Zara and me.

I pull her into my arms, feeling like the luckiest damn person on the planet. I know the road ahead will be scary and uncertain, but if there's one thing I'm sure of, it's her.

"Story Time," I say, as my lips curve into a smile. "Once there was a rock star who fell for a ridiculously hot doctor...and she set his world on *fire*."

# EPILOGUE

## Zara

**THREE MONTHS LATER...**

"Zara! We're going to be late!" Hendrix hollers from the kitchen.

I let out an amused laugh. "It's a Halloween party at your family's bar. I don't think it's possible for us to be late."

I check myself out one last time in the floor-length mirror and grin. He's going to lose his shit when he sees the costume I picked out. Turning on my heels, I flick off the lights and exit our master bedroom and head toward the kitchen.

We've been back from tour for about a month, and we've been officially living together just as long. As soon as our plane touched down in LA, I was already packing my stuff at my sister's place and hauling it over to Hendrix's.

I'd like to say my sister was sad over me leaving, but she wasn't. She values her freedom and her apartment.

Plus, she's just so damn happy I'm not with Tanner anymore.

That makes two of us.

I look at the photos we've added to the hallway since we got home: pictures of the guys on stage and playing together in Asher's hotel suite, a candid shot of Hen's sisters and me, and one of the two of us with my parents.

I'm amazed at how quickly we turned Hendrix's house into a home for the two of us in such a short time. I spent years with Tanner in that cold, sterile house his parents bought us, and it never once felt like home to me.

I've quickly come to realize it's not the duration, but the quality of time spent together that makes a relationship last.

"Hey, I'm ready—" My voice gets caught in my throat the second I round the corner and see him standing in the kitchen in... "Oh my god. Where did you get that?"

When he turns around, my jaw drops to the floor.

He's not only wearing a white lab coat, but he's also dressed from head to toe in scrubs, complete with a stethoscope and a fake badge. I thought that after marrying and divorcing a doctor, I'd be totally over them. But it turns out, seeing my incredibly hot boyfriend in scrubs really does it for me.

"Eric got them for me. They're the real fucking deal. Well, except for the badge." He waves it in the air next to his face, and that's when he finally looks up and notices my shoes. Then his eyes lift upward...

"Jesus Christ. Please tell me you're not dressing up as—"

"A bass player?" I press my lips together, trying to hold back my smile. "Okay, I won't."

He scrubs a hand down his face as he takes it all in:

the shiny Doc Martens, the fishnet stockings, and the tight black miniskirt. There's also a shredded white band tee over the black leather bra. That's my favorite part. I look like a rock star's wet dream.

"All I need is a bass to hang around my shoulders."

"Cupid, I love you, but there's no way you're taking one of my bass babies to a crowded bar." *Bass babies.* This man.

"I know. I'm just messing with you. I wouldn't want to lug that giant thing around all night anyway. But I wouldn't mind doing a private photo shoot later."

"Fuck me. How about we just not go?" he suggests, his voice dropping low. "We could just stay in, maybe play a nice game of doctor. I think you're in need of a checkup."

I laugh and then squeal as he reaches for me. I dash toward the door. He quickly catches up and, within seconds, has me pressed against it, caged between his large hands. "I cannot believe you just said that."

He shrugs with an amused grin. "Seems only fair since I've been to the doctor so much lately." My heart skips a beat at how at ease he is with his diagnosis now. His acceptance has not been a straight line. These things never are. It's been a roller coaster of emotions, filled with grief, regret, and sometimes even anger.

There were days when I could see him drowning in doubt, especially after he messed up during a show. Once, after a particularly bad performance, he even tried to convince Asher to let him go, but the guys are firm in their decision.

Family is family, and they will support both their bass players through whatever life throws at them.

To say the internet went wild with that announcement is an understatement. Two bass players? It was unheard of. But when they discovered the reason, they rallied.

I knew Manic fans were passionate, but I didn't realize just how intense their support is. The love and encouragement Evans and Hendrix have received have been overwhelmingly positive, and because of this, Evans has been able to stay clean, and Hendrix has been able to continue his treatment.

It's been an amazing partnership.

But now we're finished with the tour for a while, and this man has earned his damn rest.

"Movement therapy isn't the same as a doctor appointment, and you know it."

"It is, if you do it right." He waggles his eyebrow suggestively.

I burst out laughing. "You're insane."

"About you? Always."

I paint his cheek with a kiss, thanks to my blood red lipstick, and squeeze his ass. "Come on, *Doc.* Halloween awaits. And although I doubt we can actually be late, your sister texted me and said she had a surprise."

"Which one?"

"Which one do you think?"

"Presley," he mutters. "It's always Presley."

## HENDRIX

Walking into Creeds feels like coming home, if home were covered in neon lights, and smelled kind of like cheap perfume, beer, and sweat.

But home, nonetheless.

The walls are covered with photos of famous bands that performed here and celebrities who visited. I'll never forget how Zander used to stare at them when he worked here. I remember asking him if that's what he wanted to be someday—famous.

*I just want the money and freedom to do whatever I want*, he said.

Zander didn't have a lot of either growing up.

My dad used to play a larger role in the bar, but in recent years, he's stepped back. Now it's Presley's baby, and despite Cash's doubts about the arrangement, my sister is doing a damn good job.

The Halloween bash is one of her best ideas yet. We used to host a big party on St. Patrick's Day, but the rest of the year, it was business as usual. Presley saw this as an opportunity and has been trying to gradually add events whenever possible.

*Creeds' Creepy Halloween Bash* is the most popular of them all, probably because it involves a boatload of alcohol and skimpy costumes. Always a winning combination.

When Zara and I step into the bar, it's like walking into a brick wall of people. There are bodies everywhere.

And everyone is dressed up as something.

There's Homer Simpson kissing Poison Ivy in the corner. Captain Marvel and a sexy maid are grinding to the music pumping through the sound system. It's a total mindfuck, and before I get too caught up in people watching, I hear my name being shouted over the crowd.

"Hendrix!" I turn to see my sister behind the bar, waving. She's dressed as a witch—I'm sure it's the sexy kind, but like hell I'm saying that—and is bopping her head to the music. We usually have a live band, but it's too crowded and loud tonight.

I hold tight to Zara's hand, and we make our way to the bar. It's a short distance, but it seems to take forever. When we finally make it, my sister waves to a few customers. "Make some room. We've got a celebrity here!"

"You're a fucking menace."

"Love you too," she says, her blue eyes scanning my costume. She smiles. "Cute. What can I get you?"

"Beer," I tell her. "Whatever is on tap."

"You got it. And for you, Zara?" she says, motioning to her. "You look so hot. I love the leather and the makeup."

"Thank you! Not sure I could have pulled off the winged liner without your help."

She tips her pointy black hat. She's in an unusually good mood. When I talked to her during the tour—the times I was able to get a hold of her, that is—whenever I asked why, she'd change the subject and ask what we were doing or what city we were headed to next. I'm glad to see she's doing better, or at least better tonight. "Always happy to help."

"I'll have the Pinot Noir. I had that last time we were here, and it was amazing."

"I picked that out myself. It's from a winery in Paso Robles. It's beautiful up there. You two should spend a weekend up there sometime."

"Maybe in the spring, but right now, I think we just want to stay home for a while. Zara is taking some time off, and I just want to sleep for like a year straight."

"Right." She rolls her eyes. "It must be so hard to travel all over Europe. How did you ever survive?"

I let out an exaggerated sigh. "It was a hardship, I tell ya."

It was actually a fucking dream, but I don't tell her that.

Zara and I walked the streets of Rome and London. We toured castles and kissed at the top of the Eiffel Tower. It was magical.

She's magical.

"Jerk." She laughs before walking away for a moment to grab a wine glass and the Pinot Zara requested. She pours it and then slides the glass over.

"This is great, Pres," I tell her, leaning against the bar as I look out onto the crowd. "You've done a really good job with the place."

She smiles proudly. "I know. Hey, how's treatment going?"

"Good," Zara and I say in unison. I can't help but smile. She's been so supportive through all this.

When I wanted to give up and quit, she talked me off the ledge.

When I got angry and asked, *Why me?*, she was my voice of reason.

When I just needed to be held, she never let go.

"Now that the tour is over and my schedule is less intense, I'm going to increase my sessions with my movement specialist."

"And he's even started teaching himself how to pluck

with his left hand." Zara beams a proud smile at me. God, I fucking love her.

"Yeah." I grin. "But it sounds like absolute shit."

"Clearly, you don't remember the early days when you started playing," Pres says. "Sounded like shit back then too."

"Yeah, I guess it did." I chuckle. "Are we the only ones here?"

She grabs a pint glass and starts filling it up. "Yeah. Myles is...somewhere. Atlanta, maybe?" She waves a hand. "Anyway, he got a small part in a show. Two lines, but he's convinced it's going to take him somewhere."

Zara takes a sip of her wine and lets out a happy sigh. It's the same contented sound she makes after she comes, and it leaves me momentarily distracted. I double-blink before turning back to my sister. "Maybe it will."

It takes all my willpower not to turn back and fixate on Zara's red lips. Her long neck. That sexy black bra.

How long is long enough before we can go?

"I hope so, 'cause that boy has way too much talent to be wasting it on two lines."

I clear my throat. "Agreed."

"What about Mercury?" Zara asks, taking another sip of her wine.

"This isn't her type of thing," I answer, as the mention of my baby sister almost instantly douses all my inappropriate thoughts about my girlfriend. "Too loud. Too crowded. She'd rather spend Halloween handing out candy and watching scary movies."

"And Cash?"

"Cash doesn't like fun," Presley says, while I say, "It's not his thing either."

She finishes filling my glass, and as she lifts it over the bar, something winks under the glow of the lights.

It catches my eye, and I realize it's a ring...on my sister's finger.

It's not just any ring, though.

It's a diamond ring on my sister's left hand.

And right next to it is a slim gold band.

"Presley." I stare at it like it's a rattlesnake about to strike. "What the fuck is that?"

She glances down, and I see her expression falter as she sets down my beer. "Oh!" She licks her lips before plastering on a smile. "That's the surprise I wanted to tell you about. I got married!"

I look to Zara and see the same confused expression on her face. "To who? If you say Jace, I swear to God—"

"Hey, Hendrix." I hear a deep voice say behind me.

It's a voice I haven't heard in years.

Presley swallows nervously and then says, "You remember Hollis, right?"

I turn and yep, there he is. My former best friend.

And he's wearing a matching gold wedding ring.

# A LOOK AT BOOK TWO

## Trouble

**A steamy, slow-burn marriage romance with fake vows, real feelings, and one very inconvenient Vegas wedding.**

Presley Creed is doing everything she can to keep her life together—running the family bar, fixing her past mistakes, and proving she's not the Creed sibling destined to fall apart. But a blurry night in Vegas lands her with a surprise husband: Hollis Beck. Her brother's ex-best friend. The one who disappeared without a goodbye.

Now he's back—with a nightclub empire, a calm smile, and a wild proposal: stay married, save her bar, and prove to everyone—including herself—that she's not a lost cause.

It's supposed to be temporary. Clean lines, clear terms. But the longer Hollis sticks around, the more those lines start to blur.

For Hollis, it's a chance to finally find a home. For Presley, it's a risky gamble she never planned to take.

*AVAILABLE FEBRUARY 2026*

# ACKNOWLEDGMENTS

I knew from the first chapter of *The Bridges I've Burned* that Hendrix had main character energy. He and his crazy siblings were the perfect segue into a new series, and I couldn't wait to get started.

Guys, I can't tell you the number of times I've tried to start this book. I knew the story I wanted to tell, and I knew all the characters and their backstories. I just couldn't get it out of my brain and onto the computer.

So I walked away and wrote another book, and I'm so grateful I did.

Because I don't think this book would be half as good if I had forced it, and I hope you agree it was worth the wait.

This book—and the twenty others before it—would never have been possible without the support of my family. Romance authors are all about the grand gestures, but it's truly the little things that make the difference.

Chris, Ollie, Ember, and Parrish—thank you for making sure I was fed, caffeinated, and loved, especially during those final grueling weeks. I love you all.

I'm beyond grateful to Ellie, Kayla, and everyone at Love N. Books Press for their trust in me and this series. I can't wait to see where it leads us!

To my beta readers—thank you for being my guinea pigs and enduring my rough draft. You are the best!

Finally, a huge thank you to all my readers who loved the By the Bay series and kept it alive. Without you, this series wouldn't have come into being, and I'm always grateful for your encouragement and support!

J.L. Berg is the USA Today bestselling author of the Ready Series and has written over a dozen other novels in the past decade. She is a California native but currently calls Virginia home.

When she's not writing, you will likely find her spending time with her family or watching Doctor Who. J.L. Berg is represented by Jill Marsal of Marsal Lyon Literary Agency, LLC

www.jlberg.com
J.L. Berg's Readers Group